An Angel to Die For

An Angel to Die For

MIGNON F. BALLARD

ST. MARTIN'S MINOTAUR
NEW YORK

W

www.minotaurbooks.com

Library of Congress Cataloging-in-Publication Data

Ballard, Mignon Franklin.
    An angel to die for / Mignon F. Ballard.—1st ed.
       p. cm.
    ISBN 0-312-24174-7
    1. Guardian angels—Fiction.   2. Sisters—Death—Fiction.
I. Title.

PS3552.A466 A86 2000
813'.54—dc21

                                              00-040530

First Edition: October 2000

10 9 8 7 6 5 4 3 2 1

For Gene, my "happily-ever-after"

Acknowledgments

Special thanks to my agent, Laura Langlie, and editor, Hope Dellon, for their skill and patience and for keeping me on course; to fellow writer Ruth Moose for her friendship and advice; and to my sister, Sue Marie Lewis, for her valuable help in so many ways. Thanks also to John Turner for sharing his pharmaceutical knowledge, and to Spratt White and Bob Collins for their legal expertise.

An
Angel to
Die For

CHAPTER ONE

Uncle Faris wasn't where he was supposed to be. Dead men don't just get up and walk away, and according to his overturned stone, Faris Haskell had been dead twenty-five years, a couple of years after I was born.

An icy numbness worked its way from my toes to the top of my head. How long had I been standing there with an empty grave yawning from the lower part of the family cemetery, a pile of rocks and gooey earth mounded beside it? The chasm-deep pit was dark and full of water the color of blood and the name on the marker was just about obliterated by terra-cotta splatters. I almost slipped in the mud as I turned to go.

I had come here to make peace with my sister, whose grave was marked by a serene stone angel with a rather insipid face. Maggie would have hated it. But it was as close as our mother would come to having angelic off-spring, and what did it matter now?

Graveyards are meant to be lonely, and today this one was. Bare oaks clawed at a somber February sky. Brown leaves whispered beneath my feet. Our nearest neighbor was over a half mile away, yet until my father died last year, I had never felt afraid here, or even sad.

This was family land and all the grands and great-grands were buried here—as they should be. It was comforting to know they were there. Maggie and I played hide-and-seek among the grave markers, follow-the-leader along the crumbling stone wall. If I closed my eyes I could see her dark hair blowing in the wind, hear her laughter as she ran ahead chasing butterflies.

"Look out for your baby sister," our mother used to tell me, and I did—or tried to. Once when she stepped on a bee I carried Maggie piggyback all the way to the house with her screaming all the way.

We knew the names on these stones as well as our own: Sarah, Minerva, William, James. All Dobsons, Scotts, or McCaffertys. Still, it always made me feel a little weird to look at my grandmother Dobson's marker because we had the same name. Prentice. Prentice Scott Dobson. My little sister Maggie used to say when my time came they could just toss me in on top of her and save the price of a stone. Who would have thought Maggie would be here first?

Loneliness spread through me like a cold pain, and I ached from the inside out. A squirrel scurried over a limb above me. I took a few steps back and looked about. Anyone could be watching from the bleak winter woods. The pine sapling on the hillside seemed to tremble. I stood in one spot so long I felt I had grown roots there. If I could find someone to blame, maybe I wouldn't be so afraid. Who would do such a thing? And why? My fingers knotted into fists in the pockets of Dad's old khaki jacket, scorching words ready on my lips, but whoever had done this was gone. Long gone, I hoped.

I had to get away from that obscene hole in the red Georgia clay where Uncle Faris had been. Ahead, in the curve of the hill, gray in the gloom of late afternoon, I glimpsed the first sprinkling of daffodils where my great-grandmother's dooryard had been. I came here meaning to pick an armful for Maggie and for Dad. The two, who hadn't shared a spoken word in the last three years of their lives, could at least share this flower they both loved, a symbol of new beginnings.

"Forgive me for resenting you," I was going to tell them. "For all the rotten things I thought and said." I had a speech all prepared, but I wasn't going to deliver it looking over my shoulder on this forsaken, windswept hill.

Six weeks ago Maggie had been alive. A month ago I worked at a job I loved as assistant editor of *Martha's Journal*, an Atlanta-based magazine for women. Now both were gone.

Sticking to open spaces, I skirted the hill, shivering in the brisk wind as I tramped across fallow fields past the tumbled foundations of the old Dobson place. My granddaddy had been born here, and his granddaddy before him. My own dad remembered Christmases here with seven kinds of cake and syllabub made in a churn. Now a clump of cedars guarded a hearthstone, gray with moss, in what once had been the parlor. I watched a cardinal flit from limb to limb of the blackjack oak that long ago shaded the porch. There were too many shadows here.

Did Aunt Zorah know that someone had made off with her husband's remains? Would she even care? I doubted it. Uncle Faris had been the black sheep of the family. It was whispered that he drove his car off that nasty curve on Poindexter Point after being incriminated in some kind of shady deal. Of course, our dad often reminded us, he wasn't really a member of the family, he only married into it. Maybe that's one reason Aunt Zorah had him buried so far from the rest. I must've been five years old before I realized his first two names weren't *That Fool*. That fool Faris, my aunt always called him. She buried him at the foot of the hill, she said, so he wouldn't have so far to go. Mama said it just about did in my straight-arrow aunt to have her husband go against the law and tarnish our good name. Aunt Zorah never did get over it.

Water gushed with a clamor in the creek bed that zigzagged through the pasture. Maggie and I made daisy chains there, waded and splashed in the cool, shallow water. *Oh, Maggie! How am I going to get through this alone?*

Home, the house where I grew up, waited on the

other side of the next hill. We called it Smokerise. If I could just reach Smokerise I would be safe. Maybe. But I would be alone. My mother had taken her clothing, her piano, and that expensive set of cookware she ordered from a catalog and moved in with an old college friend in Savannah. "I just can't stay here, Prentice," she said. "The memories hurt too much." Now there was just me—unless you count Noodles. Only I call her Silly Cat, and she wasn't speaking.

I plodded through the stubble of awakening woods, eyes straight ahead. To anyone who might be watching, I was a solitary stroller on an afternoon jaunt. But how did one pretend not to notice the jolting gash of an empty grave?

Breathless, I tromped through the crust of the cornfield Dad had plowed under in late September, only a few weeks before he died of a heart attack soon after his sixtieth birthday.

"Maybe it's just as well your father didn't live to learn about Maggie," my mom had said. And for once I agreed. Maggie had split with our parents more than three years before when she roared away on the back of a big gleaming motorcycle to live with a beer-swilling lump of oozing testosterone named Moose or Sledge or something. In spite of Mom's efforts and mine, our father refused to forgive her, to even mention her name.

I remembered when Dad laughed freely, played rollicking tunes on his fiddle, and called me Jemima Puddleduck because of my waddling steps when I learned to walk, but my sister's rebellion had turned him into a sad, stony-faced man. I missed the loving daddy I used to know, and now it was too late.

At last I could see the slate-gray roof of Smokerise, twin chimneys russet against the pines. Just a little farther and I would bolt the heavy oak door behind me and—what? Call the sheriff? Aunt Zorah? I had never felt so alone.

I didn't stop to look back until I reached the gate that led to the barnyard. Even then, I didn't expect to see anyone watching me. Why would they? Everyone knew where I lived. Out of habit, I took the time to latch the gate behind me—a waste of time since there weren't any animals here, and hadn't been since Dad sold Maggie's mare Cindy the day after she left home. Only the calico, Noodles, remained bathing primly on the back porch. Maggie had adopted her as a kitten while I was away at college, and from Noodles's point of view, I was an intrusive stranger who sometimes invaded her house. Whenever I approached, she usually ran. Today I expected the same.

"Silly Cat, I'd welcome the company—even yours—if you'd care to join me," I said, pretending not to watch her as I pulled off my shoes and opened the door. So far she had avoided the house for the few days I'd been home.

I was surprised when she streaked in front of me and bolted into the kitchen. In the dark sitting room, Dad's old leather chair waited by a cold hearth. A novel

Mom had set aside gathered dust on the end table along with a folded newspaper two weeks old.

I felt a dark heaviness rising, spreading inside me, making me a prisoner within myself. I should turn on a lamp, light a fire, make tea. Anything to bring myself out of this dungeon, but I couldn't. I couldn't.

What had happened to my life? My family?

"Prentice, I'm scared. Can I sleep with you?" During thunderstorms, Maggie would crawl into bed beside me and I'd tell her silly "knock-knock" jokes to calm her fears. But I couldn't protect my little sister from the worst fear of all.

And Rob, the man I had thought I loved, had vanished from my life to the other side of the ocean. I sank into my father's worn chair and hugged myself because there was nobody else to hug. I cried. And finally I slept.

The smell of chocolate woke me, the sweet, dark, milky kind like Mom made for us when it snowed, and for a minute I thought she had come home. According to the clock on the mantel, I had slept almost two hours. My foot was numb and a pile of soggy tissues filled my lap. Behind me in the kitchen I heard the clatter of a spoon against metal and the sound of someone lightly humming. It was a tune I'd never heard, and it wasn't my mother's voice.

Earlier when I carefully locked the door behind me, it hadn't occurred to me that somebody may have already been inside, that I had locked us both in. Was this the same person who dug up the grave? Why hadn't I checked? Quietly I rose from the chair.

A light shone from the kitchen and I heard the homey rattle of china, only it wasn't comforting today. Whoever was in there mustn't know I was here. I took a silent step toward the wall phone. Another. And another, my hand reaching out.

But I had forgotten about the loose floorboard. It squalled like a cat in heat, and I felt vibrations all the way through my teeth!

"Oh, good, you're awake," she said. "The chocolate's almost ready, and I hope you like cinnamon toast."

She looked like one of those women from an old cowboy movie. The one who always gets her man, but never gets kissed. A Dale Evans look-alike stood in the doorway with the light from the kitchen behind her. But this person was taller than Dale Evans, younger—surely not much older than thirty. And she had longer hair. Her hair, worn in soft waves about her face, trailed in a thick, bright braid over her shoulder. I had never seen hair like that outside of a painting and I'm sure I must have stared. Except for the outfit she wore, she might have stepped from an early canvas. Her blue and white Western blouse was stitched in something that gleamed like gold, and around her neck a strand of stones glimmered like crystallized sunlight. A gored skirt in blue denim and calf-high boots with brass studs completed her attire.

"The rodeo left in October," I said, sidling toward the door.

I think I hurt her feelings because she lowered her eyes and gave her skirt a little flounce. "Sarcasm doesn't become you, Prentice. I wear this for line dancing," she explained. "Helps to stay in practice, or one tends to forget the steps." She fingered the fabric for a minute and sighed. "Though I am ready for something a little softer, a bit more buoyant, I think. Don't you just love the way a skirt twirls when you dance?"

I was about to demand that she dance herself right out the door when it occurred to me that Aunt Zorah might have sent her. After all, she knew my name. "Are you from some kind of agency?"

She smiled. "You might say that. I'm here to help you." Silly Cat curled about her legs and the stranger scooped her up in her arms. "I hope you'll let me."

The kitchen could use a good cleaning, and dust was deep enough to plow, but I didn't think that was what she intended.

"How do you mean?" I looked past her into the kitchen where chocolate steamed on the stove and my stomach rumbled.

"There'll be time enough for that." She stepped aside, then followed me into the kitchen and pulled out a chair, indicating where I was to sit. I sat. It was the chair near the window that had always been my place, and I wouldn't have been surprised if she had tucked a bib around me. Cinnamon toast, arranged in dainty triangles, looked tempting on Mom's violet-painted cake plate. The stranger sat across from me and poured chocolate into cups.

"You knew my name," I said. "How?" I might as well taste the toast and chocolate—just to be polite. Meanwhile, I had to think of a way to get rid of her.

The sparkling necklace shifted through her fingers, the colors winking from turquoise to violet to deepwater green. I'd never seen anything like them. "It's my business to know these things. Now, drink up before your chocolate skims, it'll warm you up a bit. It's most unpleasant out today."

I didn't argue. The chocolate was perfect. Warm and smooth, sweet and bitter. I licked cinnamon from my thumb.

"More toast?" The woman offered the plate. "Such lovely china. Your grandmother painted it, didn't she? I don't suppose you—"

"Who told you that? Does my mother know you're here?" But the strange visitor only smiled in answer. Mom was particular about her hand-painted platter, bringing it out only for special occasions. She wouldn't like this woman making herself at home with her treasures, and I started to say so, but I didn't want to annoy her. Who knew what she might do?

"How did you get inside?" I asked after gobbling most of the toast and downing two large cups of chocolate. "Did Aunt Zorah give you a key?"

She looked at me over the rim of her cup with eyes the color of the sea: gray and green with a hint of blue. Gentle ocean eyes. I let their calmness wash over me.

"Let's move into the sitting room," she said, scooping

up Noodles and nuzzling her against her cheek. "We can warm ourselves by the fire."

Silently I followed her, the denim skirt flowing like satin, although it wasn't. This peculiar woman didn't know my aunt Zorah, had offered no acceptable excuse for being here, and for all I knew, *she* might be the one who dug up Uncle Faris. But for some reason I didn't care.

A fire leapt and danced in an orange frenzy in the sitting-room fireplace that had been cold thirty minutes before. When on earth did she light it? And why wasn't I surprised?

Again I sat in my father's chair and held my feet to the warmth. The woman in the cowgirl clothes perched on the braided rug in front of me with the cat in her lap. Night had come down like a dark shade and rain sliced across the back porch. A rocking chair bump-bumped out there in the wind.

She looked at me like she knew what I was thinking. I was thinking I didn't want her to be a grave robber or someone who poisoned her victims with kindness and cinnamon toast. And I didn't want her to leave.

"You said you came to help," I began. "You could start by telling me who you are. What are you really doing here?"

She traced the cat's white muzzle with a slender finger. "I'm Augusta Goodnight, your guardian angel—for now, and from what I've observed so far, we're going to have a tough row to plow—as you say down here on earth."

"I've never said that."

"Said what?" The faintest suggestion of a crease marred her brow.

"I've never in my life said I had 'a tough row to plow.' I think you must mean—"

She tossed her head. "I probably picked that up before your time. It means the same thing as 'a hard nut to break.' "

I tried to keep a straight face. "And you're going to help me plow it, break it, whatever?"

She stood and gave the fire a little poke. "That's why I'm here. We can start in the morning."

"And you're really my guardian angel?"

"That's right." She twirled lightly, settled on an ottoman, and crossed her booted feet, tassels swinging.

"But only *for now,* you said?"

"Right again. I'm a temp. I'll be filling in for Lillian until they find a permanent replacement. Lillian's been promoted." Augusta's face fairly glowed. *"She's singing in the choir!"*

"The heavenly choir, I suppose?"

"The very same. I'll be around until they decide on the right one to take her place. Usually I'm assigned to the strawberry fields," she said.

"Weeding them?"

"Oh, no! Weeds don't grow in heaven. Picking them mostly. And I sometimes work with flowers as well."

"Uh-huh," I said, although I did detect a sweet berry scent. "Then maybe you can tell me who moved Uncle Faris."

From the look on her face, I could see she hadn't made his acquaintance. I wasn't surprised. Aunt Zorah always said he'd gone the other direction.

I told her what I'd found in the family burying ground.

She fished a dog-eared notepad from a huge tapestry bag I hadn't noticed before and scribbled something on it. *"Uncle Faris.* We'll get to him in time. But aren't there more urgent concerns?"

I took a deep breath as she leaned closer, and the room smelled of lavender and something else, something clean and fresh and new like the first day of spring.

I nodded. "My sister. Where is Maggie? Why did she have to die? And my dad . . . I hope they're speaking now."

Augusta reached out and touched my hand. "I'm sure they are. I rarely see the newcomers, Prentice, but everything's *right* up there. It's down here that concerns me."

It concerned me too, but not enough to keep me awake. After weeks of restless nights, I felt as though I could sleep forever. I didn't even bother to go upstairs, but curled on the couch wrapped in my grandmother's faded afghan. Just before I closed my eyes I remembered I hadn't phoned Aunt Zorah or the sheriff. The wind slammed shutters against the house, and surges of dark rain pounded the windows. Tomorrow would have to do. It seemed a shame to bring anyone out on a night like this for somebody who had been dead for more than twenty-five years.

As I drifted off, I heard Augusta singing that same song in the kitchen as she tidied up after our unusual supper. It was the tune she'd been humming earlier. Then, except for Noodles purring at my feet, the house grew still.

Augusta Goodnight, guardian angel. Surely I had dreamed her; when I woke in the morning, she would be gone. Yet embers still glowed red in the grate, and the taste of chocolate lingered on my tongue.

CHAPTER TWO

"You'll never guess what I dreamed last night," I would tell my friend Dottie when I called. And she would burst forth with her froggy laugh and say something silly like, "How about dreaming me up an angel with money? We'll need big bucks to get *Martha* up and running again."

I missed Dottie Ives. She always made me laugh, and I knew I'd find her at home because as editor of the "late" *Martha's Journal*, she didn't have a job either. I pulled the soft old afghan a little closer, stuck a tentative foot from under the cover, and opened one eye. Sun glinted off the brass fender in front of the fireplace and made a yellow path across the floor. I hadn't seen that fender looking as bright since Dad made me polish it every week for staying out too late back in junior high. The rich wake-up aroma of coffee wrapped itself around me and I sat up and sniffed. A wholesome, start-the-day-off-right smell came from the kitchen, and I knew the cowgirl with angelic delusions wasn't a figment of my imagination after all. I wasn't sure if I should be glad or disappointed. I *was* sure I was hungry.

The muffins were bran with walnuts, dates, and a slight tang of oranges. They were sweetened with honey, Augusta said, and she served them with a bowl of fresh peaches, cantaloupe, and strawberries that must have come from heaven. I didn't ask.

Today Augusta wore an emerald skirt with a liquid green sheen that might have been fashioned from lake water. Her blouse was a soft, shimmering yellow, and the necklace, an iridescent rainbow, glinted in the morning light. Its brilliance fascinated me, and I had to force myself to look away. The ensemble was tied at the waist with a filmy, chiffonlike scarf that trailed behind her when she walked. Her boots, I noticed, had been replaced with something that looked like silvery ballet slippers.

"Aren't you afraid you'll trip on that?" I asked, letting her scarf trail over my hand. It felt like air. "What happened to Dale Evans?"

She twirled about, and I was reminded of the Sugar Plum Fairy—but only briefly. Augusta's not nearly as dainty. "I've had my fill of tailored clothing," she said. "There was a shortage of nearly everything—including fabric—during my stay here in the forties, and on my last assignment, I hardly had time to dwell on secular things."

She smoothed her secular skirt, rose on her secular toes, and sighed happily. "It's time for a change, and this suits me, don't you think? Makes me feel like floating."

"I thought angels flew," I said, dodging as the skirt whirled past.

"Only when it's necessary." She smiled at me over the coffeepot. "Drink up now. Morning's half gone."

I groaned. It was barely eight o'clock. The first thing I needed to do, I decided, as Augusta joined me in a second cup of coffee, was phone Aunt Zorah about Uncle Faris's sudden disappearance. Maybe she would know what had happened.

"I imagine you'll be speaking with your aunt this morning," Augusta said brightly. "About your uncle's grave?" She raised an elegant eyebrow as if she expected an answer. I grunted. I'd be darned if I'd give her one. I ate another muffin oozing with strawberry jam.

After breakfast I phoned Aunt Zorah at the library in Liberty Bend where she has reigned for the last forty years and told her about Uncle Faris. For a moment there was only silence at her end. I was afraid I'd upset her.

"He's *what?*" Was Aunt Zorah *laughing?* "Prentice, are you sure?"

It would have been hard to pass over something as

big and unsettling as an empty grave, but I tried to be tactful. "At first I thought you might have had him moved," I said. "But I'm sure Mom would've told me—and the stone—well, it was still there." I couldn't bring myself to describe the ghastly reality of the scene, even if the two hadn't been especially cozy when Uncle Faris took the dive off Poindexter's Point.

Aunt Zorah muttered something about That Fool still giving her trouble. "I'd check with Simmons and Griggs at the funeral home before calling the police, Prentice. Your mother and I have discussed having Faris moved to the upper part of the cemetery, but we hadn't—excuse me—*No, no Hollis, we don't climb on the library shelves. Get down this minute!* As I was saying, we hadn't made definite plans. They're building a road through there, you know, and I'm not sure about the property line." Her voice softened. "I wouldn't mention this just yet to your mother. Virginia's been through enough lately."

I knew my mother had already sold her share of the estate to a developer, and the back part of the property would be divided into one-acre lots. Dad's life insurance policy had been a modest one, and this was about the only way she could get by, she said. Besides, Mom always disliked the loneliness of living "so far from town," although it was only a little over six miles to Liberty Bend. The other part of the farm, including the house, I was to share with Maggie. I only wish my sister could have known before she died that our father still claimed her as an heir.

As a small child, Maggie was always about three steps behind Dad wherever he went, followed by a menagerie of animals, since she collected every stray that came around. When she asked for a pony for her fifth birthday, Dad bought her a Shetland and taught her to ride. "How come I never got a pony?" I asked, wishing at that moment my little sister would ride off into the sunset and stay until she was at least thirty.

"Why, Jemima Puddleduck!" my dad said, laughing, "you never asked for one." But Maggie never cared for the rough elements of farming as I did. Digging potatoes was like a treasure hunt for me, and I liked keeping weeds from the neat rows of vegetables in our family garden while my sister rescued baby rabbits and dressed kittens in doll clothes.

Clyde Simmons of Simmons and Griggs momentarily lost his staid undertaker's demeanor when I called and told him about the grave. "You mean it's *gone*? They haven't already moved it, have they? I didn't think your aunt had decided about that for sure."

I told him if they'd moved Uncle Faris, I didn't know where they'd put him.

"Dear God in heaven! Don't tell me this is happening again. Had a wave of freakish incidents like that about seven or eight years ago—high school kids into some kind of cult silliness—but the sheriff put an end to that. Sounds like a new crop of meanness brewing.

"Your mom did come to see me a few weeks ago about the possibility of having that grave moved when they put a road through there," he added. "Not a bad thing, really. I've noticed that lower part of your lot's been eroding. Too much wash comes down. I told Virginia we'd do it whenever Zorah gave the word; your mother said she'd let us know." His voice became soothing, more in-charge. "I hope you've notified the sheriff about this, Prentice. Somebody's up to something worse than mischief here." He hesitated. "And don't you be going back over there alone."

I sat at the oak trestle table in a spot of winter sun and turned my coffee mug in my hands while Noodles washed her paws on the hearth. What if whoever was doing this came back again? Maybe next time for Dad or Maggie. Or me. I felt sick as I phoned the sheriff.

"Mighty good coffee," Deputy Weber said, shoving his cup aside. Again I sat at the kitchen table, this time with the policeman across from me in the place my sister used to sit. "Now, when was the last time you were in that area where we saw the grave?"

"The last of December when we buried my sister," I said. "The twenty-ninth."

"I'm sorry." He sounded like he meant it. Donald Weber had been in the class several years ahead of ours and had married a friend of mine soon after high school. I thought him good-looking then, and he was still attractive although he was beginning to lose his hair.

"And you haven't been back since then?"

I shook my head. I couldn't bear to go there. "I've only been home a few days," I said, explaining that I'd been living in Atlanta. "But my mother was here until about two weeks ago when they got my sister's stone in place. I'm sure she would've seen something as obvious as that."

"Hard to tell because of yesterday's rain, and we had that hard freeze last week. Any footprints would've been washed away, but I believe this happened within the last couple of days." He flicked a look at me. "You might've interrupted something, you know."

I nodded. I didn't need reminding.

He frowned. "And there's nobody here but you?"

I could hear Augusta rocking in my mother's old cane-bottomed chair in the parlor, but the deputy must not have noticed. "My mother's staying in Savannah for a while," I told him, "and the house has been closed for a couple of weeks."

"You haven't noticed anyone around who shouldn't be?"

I started to tell him about Augusta, but I didn't want to share her. Not yet. Maybe it was for the same reason I hadn't mentioned her to Aunt Zorah. If Augusta Goodnight had sinister motives, I wasn't ready to deal with it.

"When I first got here I found that sorry Jasper Totherow making himself at home in our barn," I told him.

"Claimed my mother asked him to keep an eye on the house, but I know better." I picked up the saltshaker—the one shaped like a rabbit I had bought at the dime store when I was eight—and brought it down hard on the table. "I told him to take a hike!"

"Have you told your mother about this?" He glanced about the room.

"In a roundabout way. Didn't want to alarm her. I did check to see if she'd asked anybody to keep an eye on the place, and she said Suzie Wright promised to have a look around when she came by to feed the cat.

"Suzie delivers our mail," I explained. "Lives about a mile down the road."

"Jasper Totherow. He *is* bad news," the deputy said. "Wife finally filed a complaint against him, learned the hard way, I reckon. Wish I had a dollar for every time we've been called out to their place."

Ralphine Totherow rented a small house a few miles away and supported the couple's two children by cleaning other people's houses, including ours from time to time. I remembered Mom telling me she had her out to Smokerise just before Christmas. After Dad died, she didn't have the heart for the usual holiday flurry, she said. And that was probably the last time the house had been cleaned, I thought. Until Augusta came. From what my mother told me, Ralphine Totherow didn't receive any financial help from her husband. Didn't want it, she said. All she wanted was to be rid of him.

"That man's trouble. I'd be mighty careful around

him." The deputy went to the window, zipping his jacket as he stood looking down the long, curving drive. After returning from the grave site earlier, he'd called for another policeman, his radio crackling. "If we can't get prints, we can at least get pictures," he said, explaining that Sergeant Sloan would be bringing a camera.

"Do you think Jasper had anything to do with what happened to Uncle Faris?" I asked.

He shook his head. "Who knows what Jasper might do?"

"But why?"

"To get even maybe. Or for just plain meanness. We'll be having words with that one—as soon as we can chase him down."

But mean and shiftless as he was, I couldn't imagine Jasper Totherow exerting enough energy to dig up a grave—unless, of course, he was being paid for his efforts.

Behind us in the dining room I heard Augusta humming, and from the doorway I could see her, stretching on tiptoe to reach into far corners with a feather duster.

"Before your sergeant comes, would you mind looking around?" I asked. "I'd feel a lot safer knowing no one else is here."

Hat in hand, he followed me into the dining room where Augusta stood with the light of the window behind her.

Deputy Weber took a couple of steps into the room, then stopped and inhaled deeply. "Ahh . . . somebody's been making strawberry jam . . . but isn't that out of season?"

"Room deodorizer," I explained. Augusta, sparkling beads swinging, did a little dance step as she quickly hid the duster behind her.

"I don't see how anyone could be hiding down here," the policeman said after completing his circuit of the first floor. "Why don't you wait while I take a look upstairs?"

Augusta had decided the brass candlesticks on the hall console needed a vigorous rubbing. Her sunshiny locks, I noticed, were now confined in a flower-dotted kerchief. "Seems competent," she said, buffing briskly, "but I doubt he'll find anyone here."

"He didn't *see you*." I sat on the bottom step and stared at her. She looked solid enough to me in her buttercup-yellow blouse and daisy-sprinkled headgear.

"Did you really think he would? Isn't that why you wanted him to look around?"

"What did you expect?" I shrugged. "I had to know. Do you blame me?"

Augusta moved to the grandfather clock that hadn't run in twenty years. "I'm not in the business of blame." She opened the door of the clock and touched something inside. It whirred and struck eleven times. The correct hour. Naturally.

I looked up as the deputy started downstairs. "Everything seems okay up there," he said. "I think I just heard Sergeant Sloan drive up; we'll go out to the grave site and get some photographs, and then I want to have a look around your barn."

"What do you think you might find?"

"That grave looks like it was excavated by hand. Maybe they left behind some digging implements, like a shovel with fresh prints on it."

I just hoped they hadn't left behind Uncle Faris.

Even with Augusta there, it was quiet in the house after the two men left for the cemetery. Augusta wandered quietly from room to room, absorbing my history, I suppose, so she would be better equipped to do whatever it was she was supposed to do. And I hoped she would hurry and think of something because I didn't know where to begin. Smokerise, the home that had nurtured me, offered no comfort. I knew why my mother had left, but I couldn't help but feel abandoned. Friends who had flocked to comfort me when Maggie died had dropped out of sight one by one as if they were uncomfortable in my presence, and it was partly my fault, I know, for not being very receptive to them. Even my annoying cousin Beatrice (only she pronounced it Be-trice), who lived nearer than I'd like, had left me alone. I suppose I should be thankful for small favors.

The pendulum of the clock in the hall measured heavy minutes as I moved from the stiff-backed Victorian love seat in the living room to the mantel where my mother's favorite figurines—a colonial couple—stood. The porcelain lady had a chipped elbow I had broken playing ball in the house. Sepia photographs from a long-ago family reunion hung on the wall near where Mom's piano used to be. I missed my mother, missed her music, her voice, yet a part of me resented her. It wasn't a part I was proud of. My mother had deserted me for Savannah and a gig playing piano in classy restaurants. *To save her sanity*, my reasonable self chided. Yet hadn't I given up a chance to live happily ever after just to stay behind and soothe her grief?

I picked up the porcelain gentleman. If I bashed his dainty arm against the wall, the two would be a matched pair. "Oh, the hell with it!" I set him down again.

"Does that really help?" Augusta sat in the rocking chair with Noodles on her lap.

I looked up and glared at her. "What?"

"The use of . . . well, unnecessary language."

"You mean, *hell*? Damn right it does!" I dropped into the chintz-covered wingback chair and threw my legs over its rose-splashed arm.

"You can tell me about it if you like." Augusta stroked Noodles's pied back until I could have sworn that silly cat smiled.

"About what?"

"Whatever's poisoning your heart."

"You mean other than the fact that my sister and father lie buried out there in the graveyard, Mom's now living in Savannah, and Uncle Faris has taken off for parts unknown?"

26

She didn't miss a stroke. "Yes. Other than that. It has something to do with a man, doesn't it?"

"My life doesn't revolve around a man. Why would you say that?"

"Look in the mirror," she said. "What do you see?"

I glanced at my reflection in the gilded oval behind her and made a face. "I see somebody who needs a haircut." My hair, although light like my father's and not a bad color, was long, thick, and curly, and if not controlled properly, took on a life of its own.

"I see someone young and attractive—although one's physical attributes aren't at all important in the overall scheme of things, mind you . . ." Augusta turned to sneak a glimpse at her own reflection and looked rather smug I thought. "It's only natural you would be keeping company with someone you care about, someone you might hope to spend your life with."

I didn't answer. Again I saw Rob's face, heard his voice. *Come to London with me, Prentice. It's lonely over there without you. I want us to be together.*

I swallowed, looked away, but there was no way to hide my tears. "Rob McCullough," I said. "His name is Rob McCullough."

I had met him in Atlanta a couple of years before when he did a story on *Martha's Journal* for the local newspaper. A few weeks later, he invited me to a party with some of his friends, and I think if he had proposed that very first night, I would have said, "Say when!" He was rangy and tall with a nose broken from high school football, a chin he could use as a weapon, and brown hair, wiry as beach grass. His eyes were blue, blue, blue. I fell for him right away.

It must have been obvious. "Tread lightly," a friend told me a few days later. "Rob's wife Felicia died of leukemia a couple of years ago, and he's still working through his grief." And from observations I made from time to time, I wondered if he ever would. The two had been married only seven years when Felicia died.

But I could deal with that. I thought.

Augusta leaned forward slightly. "I'd like to hear about him," she said over Noodles's purring.

"Not much to tell," I lied. "We saw each other for about two years, and I thought . . . well, I thought this was it. And then last summer he was offered a job with CNN's London news bureau, and off he went. He called, of course, and we kept in touch on the Internet, but he never said anything about joining him there."

"That must have been disheartening." Augusta's eyes clouded in sympathy.

"I was going to break it off with him, and then Dad died. Rob came back for the funeral, and he really was a help. I don't know what Mom and I would've done without him." I accepted a fresh hankie from Augusta. It smelled of sweet grass. "That's when he asked me to go back with him."

"I'm afraid I don't see the problem." Augusta spoke softly.

"Don't you see? It was for the wrong reasons. He was lonely, he felt sorry for me. Besides, England's a long way away, and I couldn't leave my mother just then. Dad's death took us by surprise and she wasn't up to handling it alone. And Maggie—well, we didn't even know where Maggie was."

"But surely your young man would understand this. He wouldn't expect to whisk you off and marry you right away." Her sea-green eyes met mine. "Would he?"

"Well . . . no. That's just it, you see . . ."

She frowned. "I'm afraid I don't."

"The problem," I said, "is that he's never mentioned marriage—or even love. Not an ideal arrangement."

Augusta rocked silently, her lovely brow knitted in thought. She would give me a righteous explanation, and everything would be okay, even better than okay. Life would be good again.

"I see," she said, and she might have said more, but just then Deputy Weber pounded on the back door with a jarring that shook the house.

He stood on the porch with his hat crushed against his stomach and his face was smoky gray.

"What is it? What have you found?" Whatever it was, I knew it wasn't good.

It wasn't. They had found Uncle Faris's casket in the shed behind the barn, he said, and Uncle Faris wasn't in it.

But someone else was.

CHAPTER THREE

It was a woman, the deputy said, probably in her sixties or older, slightly overweight with bleached hair and bright red nail polish. Wearing only panties and bra, she had been wrapped in a cheap muslin sheet before being deposited mummy-style in what had been my uncle's former resting place.

"Does that fit the description of anyone you know?" Donald Weber asked. I stared at him, unable to speak. Why would anyone leave a body in our shed? "She might be one of Jasper's acquaintances," I said finally. "Has she been dead very long?" Maybe some other long-deceased relative had been uprooted as well.

I felt my bones go cold when he shook his head. "Happened fairly recently I'd guess." He wiped his face with a handkerchief, but he couldn't wipe away the horror. "The coroner should be able to tell us how she died."

"What on earth's going on? Is an escaped lunatic on the loose? A serial killer? And why *here*?" I thought of all those movies I'd seen about maniacs dismembering people with chain saws, and came close to grabbing him by the lapels.

"Not that we know of; at least there've been no reports." Donald Weber was trying to speak reassuringly, but I could tell he was almost as shaken as I was. We don't find dead bodies lying around just every day here in Liberty Bend.

But where was Uncle Faris? And how was I going to tell Aunt Zorah that what remained of the man she knew as her husband, fool though he might have been, had been displaced by a strange woman?

The earth-stained vault containing the casket was found beneath bundles of straw in the shed where Dad's tractor used to sit. The small storage room behind it was littered with empty beer bottles, cigarette butts, and a can that once held pinto beans. And according to Sergeant Sloan, it was ripe enough to sprout legs and walk in there. Jasper Totherow wasn't noted for exemplary hygiene.

"I don't suppose you'd remember if you saw that straw stacked up back there when you ran Totherow off the other day?" the deputy asked.

A rabid rhinoceros couldn't chase me into an empty building with Jasper Totherow. "I didn't go inside," I explained. "He was sneaking around the back of the barn, hoping I wouldn't see him, I guess. Do you think he might've put her there?" It made me shudder to think about the woman lying dead in our shed while I was alone in the empty house.

"I honestly don't know," Donald Weber said, "but I had Sergeant Sloan make some inquiries when I learned he'd been hanging around. His wife said she hasn't seen him—and she'd have no reason to lie, and he hasn't turned up at his usual haunts. Ralphine Totherow might be able to shed some light on this. Maybe she can tell us who this woman is.

"Jasper may be half a bubble off plumb, but he knows how to make himself scarce," he added aside to me. "And if he didn't have something to do with all this, you can bet he knows who did."

He turned to Sergeant Sloan. "Mike, get on the radio and see if you can find somebody to locate Mrs. Totherow. Maybe we'll get lucky."

But Ralphine Totherow had never seen the shrouded woman in our shed and had no idea who she was. She didn't know where her husband was either, and from what Donald Weber let slip, didn't care if he never showed up.

For the rest of the morning our place was invaded by a team of investigators. Ugly orange crime-scene tape crisscrossed the barn lot where Maggie used to ride her pony; detectives and photographers tramped about. The coroner did a preliminary inspection, and finally an ambulance came and took the pitiful remains away.

Since I was told in polite, but specific, terms to stay away from the grisly goings-on in the shed, I was glad to remain inside with Augusta's tranquil presence.

"I wish you'd ask somebody to stay with you, Prentice, at least until we can locate this Totherow guy," Don Weber said as they started to leave. "Meanwhile, you can rest assured we'll keep an eye on the place. You will call us at the first sign of trouble? Right?"

"You don't have to worry about that!" I promised as I watched them drive away.

The phone was ringing as I stepped inside. "How's it feel to be a woman of leisure?" Dottie Ives wanted to know.

"Depends on how you define leisure," I said, and told her about the body in Uncle Faris's coffin.

Dottie isn't easily shocked, but she drew in her breath so hard I thought she'd inhale the receiver.

"Dear God! Are you serious?" My friend gasped when she finally was able to speak. "And your uncle—what happened to him?"

"That's what we'd like to know. At first I thought there might be some kind of weird ritual going on, but this puts a whole new slant on things."

"And you don't know who she is?"

"Haven't a clue. No ID on her, no clothes either except for underwear. I heard the sergeant say the sheet she was wrapped in looks like the commercial kind you'd find in a cheap motel or some place like that. Somebody had cut a strip from the bottom—to get rid of any labels or markers I guess."

"Prentice, this is positively ghoulish! Do they know how she died?"

"Don Weber—he's one of our deputies—said she had abrasions, bruises like she'd been dragged, but of course they won't know for sure until the coroner completes an autopsy," I told her.

"Aren't you terrified out there by yourself? Why not hang out with me awhile? You'll have to bring your own hot dogs though. The larder's getting low around here!"

She was joking, but I knew it wasn't much of an exaggeration. I had a well-stocked freezer and no rent to pay. Dottie wasn't as fortunate. "You can't imagine how tempting that sounds, but I'll wait till Mom's spaghetti sauce runs out. Don't guess you've had any luck with the job market?"

This provoked a growl. "Not a lot, but I have an idea I'd like to kick around with you when we get a chance. How about you?"

"Haven't had time to look into it yet. Just being back in this house without family is adjustment enough without all the gory excitement."

A brief pause followed this. "How is your mom?" Dottie knew our relationship was about as strained as an old rubber band.

"Okay, I guess. I phoned her soon after I got here. She's playing in a swank restaurant three nights a week and taking in piano students."

"Her heart must be breaking."

"I know. Mine too."

"Well, that's one reason I called. I talked to Rob last night."

My heart raced like I'd been in a marathon and all the blood rushed to my head. I couldn't speak.

"He doesn't understand. He misses you, Prentice. Why won't you talk to him?"

"What doesn't he understand? Don't they use the same language in England?"

"I guess some men just aren't demonstrative, but he cares about you. I know he does." She sighed. "Maybe it's some kind of hangup about his first wife. He might not even be aware of it. Won't you at least give him a chance?"

"Dottie, tell me you didn't call him."

"He tried to call you at your apartment and learned the phone was disconnected. Didn't know about the *Journal* folding of course. That's when he called me."

"I suppose the phones in London have all been out of order since October. I haven't heard from Rob since he went back after Dad's funeral. Surely you must remember that."

"Prentice, he asked you to come back with him; you turned him down. He admits he didn't handle it well."

"You didn't say anything about my reason, did you? About what he *hasn't* said."

"That's between the two of you. I'm only a lowly messenger . . . and a lonely one if you must know the truth. I'd hate for you to make the same mistake I did."

Dottie and her husband had divorced when their son Luke was twelve and the boy chose to live with his

35

father. Luke was now in college and mother and son seemed to have a good relationship, but I knew she regretted missing even a portion of his growing-up years.

"Rob knows where I live," I said. "And I'm sure you gave him the phone number."

Now I would have to worry over whether Rob McCullough would call or not.

Thank goodness Aunt Zorah telephoned soon after I spoke with Dottie and gave me an excuse to get out of the house. The two policemen had been by to tell her about the unexpected guest in our shed and Uncle Faris's wandering ways. Now she expected me on her doorstep with my suitcase within the hour. "Don't know what we'll have for supper, but I'm sure I can scratch up something," she said.

"Absolutely not," I said. "I'll come on one condition, that you'll let me pick up a pizza." The last time Aunt Zorah scratched up something I lost three pounds, and the very thought of her meat loaf made me weak all over. "But just for tonight," I added. I didn't like to leave the house empty too long with whoever killed that woman spooking about.

"Whatever," my aunt said. She didn't specify a certain kind of pizza, but I didn't order meat toppings in case she was still in her vegetarian stage.

She wasn't. "Where's the pepperoni?" She looked in the box and frowned.

"The last time I was here, you wouldn't touch meat," I said.

"Oh, that. Well, never mind. I have some leftover tuna casserole if you want it."

My stomach quivered. "This is plenty, thanks." I followed her into the kitchen where we shared the pizza at her small round table covered with a yellow-fringed cloth. My aunt likes fringe. It dangles from her lampshades, her curtains, even from the vest she wore over a multicolored blouse. When Aunt Zorah was in college, my mom told me, only her strict upbringing prevented her from becoming a beatnik. They preceded the hippie movement, she said, and were what my mother referred to as "artsy." Aunt Zorah took to wearing berets and writing long poems nobody could understand that she read in coffee houses, but she never could let go and become a free spirit, Mom said. My aunt got rid of the beret, but she still writes poetry, and her mode of dress is something out of the ordinary. She'd probably spit nails if she knew Mom told me about her almost-wild college days. What would the Daughters of the American Revolution think? Of course they might guess . . . today she wore dangling metallic earrings shaped like the sun and a necklace of orange beads and string.

I told her I was sorry about Uncle Faris.

"It's a bad thing, Prentice. I reckon they picked him because he was so far removed from the rest, and some of the soil had washed away, but I worry more about you than what happened to Faris. The old fool's long dead. They can't hurt him now." She used her "I don't care" voice, but when she stood to throw her paper plate in the trash, I saw sadness in her eyes.

"You said they couldn't identify the woman. What'd she look like?"

I shuddered as if a snake had shimmied up my back. "Didn't see her, but she was about your age or older." I gave my aunt a brief description and she shrugged. "Must've been somebody passing through. Homeless maybe; you're right on that main highway." She shook her head. "But I can't for the life of me imagine how she ended up where she did!"

"The police think this happened recently," I said. "I'm sure when they learn who put her there, we'll know what happened to Uncle Faris." My pizza looked back at me with olive eyes and I shoved it away. I was just making things worse. Where in the world would you hide a body that had been buried all those years?

"Maynard Griggs said they buried him with his Phi Beta Kappa key. I told him it was a good thing, because Faris wouldn't want to be parted from that. Lord, he was proud of that thing! Fool didn't have a lick of practical sense, but he was book smart. Read all the time. That was what we had in common." She filled a glass from the tap and stood with it in her hand. "About all we had in common," she muttered.

I wanted to go to her and put my arms around her, smooth her bottled auburn curls, but I didn't dare. In all the years I'd known her, I'd never heard my aunt admit that she loved her husband, but I knew she did, and the memory of his disgrace still hurt.

"What do you hear from your mother?" she asked, finishing her water.

"Not much. She seems to like it there. At least she's staying busy."

"I'm glad to hear that. Virginia needed this, Prentice. She had to get away. Losing Maggie on top of your father's death was more than any woman should be expected to deal with, and she's handling it the best way she can."

"We had already lost Maggie," I reminded her. "I didn't even know how to get in touch with her to let her know Dad died." I wish I could forgive my sister for that.

"Your mother used to hear from Maggie from time to time, but she never knew where to find her." Aunt Zorah switched on a light in her living room and moved a stack of books from a chair.

"She didn't want us to. Wouldn't use a return address," I said. "There were a couple of letters from different places in Alabama, and a postcard from somewhere in Tennessee, but she didn't stay anywhere long enough for us to find her. We didn't even know she was married until the accident."

And I still wasn't sure it was an accident. My sister and her husband, Sonny Gaines, had died violently when their car tried to outrun a train while crossing the track. Sonny had been driving.

"Mom got a phone call from Maggie last summer," I said. "Sometime in July, I think, and for some reason Mom was under the impression Maggie was living alone, that she was trying to get her life back together. And maybe it was just hope and imagination, but I think she got the idea Maggie was thinking of coming home."

"She didn't end up with that rough-looking man she ran off with, did she?" My aunt pulled off clunky shoes and made herself comfortable in the recliner.

I shook my head. "That didn't last. I think this Sonny came along soon after, though. They were together for over a year." I closed my eyes, tried to shut down my thoughts. If only Maggie had come home! A few days before my sister left, we'd had a terrible argument and I'd told her she was being selfish and rotten, tearing our family apart. "When are you going to grow up?" I said. "I think you must get some kind of weird satisfaction out of worrying Mom and Dad!"

What a first-class jerk I was! No wonder Maggie left home. I wished we could have talked once more, made our peace. But she was probably afraid our dad would throw her out. And I guess I didn't give her much of an incentive either.

The people in the car behind them had said they couldn't believe it when Sonny accelerated just as the train approached. Surely he hadn't meant to kill himself and my sister as well!

When Aunt Zorah offered a glass of wine, I took her up on it. I could use a little help in getting to sleep that night.

Despite my aunt's protests, I left after breakfast the next morning. (There's not much you can do to screw up cold cereal.) And because I had to pass there on the way home, I stopped at Simmons and Griggs Funeral Home to see if Clyde Simmons had heard about a body turning up in my uncle's casket in our shed. Mr. Simmons was out, so I passed the information along to his partner, Harold Griggs, whose father, Maynard, had started the business, but was now semi-retired. To be honest, I didn't see anything semi about it, as every time I passed there during warmer weather, the older Mr. Griggs was asleep in a rocking chair on the front porch. To get away from his wife, Aunt Zorah said. "If I were married to Ernestine Griggs, I'd stay away too. An Abercrombie before she married, you know. Came from money—which is probably why Maynard married her in the first place. Penny-pincher if there ever was one, and that's not all he's pinched!" My aunt had hinted old Mr. Griggs used to be bad about women. Again, likely because of that "cold fish" Ernestine. "Don't ever give him a chance to be alone with you," she cautioned. But I couldn't imagine the old coot having a go at it with anybody! Today I found him napping on the sofa in the small back office and for a frozen second I thought he was a corpse lying there—until I heard a definite snore. His son and I whispered so we wouldn't wake him.

"Sheriff Bonner told me about it," the younger Griggs said, looking suitably despondent. "I hope they find whoever's responsible soon." He pumped my hand heartily, practicing, I supposed, for his upcoming political campaign for a seat on the state senate. "If we can do anything, anything at all, you just let us know, you hear?" As I left, I realized he'd slipped a card in my hand promoting himself as a candidate.

I hurried home, hoping Augusta would still be there. I needed an angel "fix." Turning into our driveway, I met our letter carrier, Suzie Wright, who was just leaving, and she stopped and rolled down her window to talk.

"Don't want to alarm you, Prentice, but I saw a strange man walking down the road near here as I started out this morning. Acted kind of peculiar when he saw me watching him—cut back into the woods like he was trying to hide. After what's been going on around here, I thought you ought to know."

"It wasn't Jasper Totherow, was it?"

"Lord no! I know that snake. This man had a beard, wore a cap—purple, with earflaps. Say, they haven't found out any more, have they? About who that woman was, I mean?"

I told her she knew about as much as I did, and Suzie frowned. "Prentice, you really shouldn't be out here by yourself. It's just not safe with all this going on."

I didn't tell her about my heavenly companion, but did say the police had promised to keep an eye on the place. "I'll call the sheriff right now and tell them what you saw. Could be just a hitchhiker passing through, but they'll want to check it out."

"I left a package on your back porch," Suzie said. "I was kinda worried about leaving it there after seeing that man, but I guess it'll be okay."

I thanked her and waved as she drove away, meaning to call the sheriff as soon as I got home. They had promised to get somebody to haul away that gruesome coffin in the barn. I didn't want it there any longer than it had to be, and bodies appearing and disappearing shook me up more than I cared to admit—Augusta or no Augusta.

But the package I found on the back porch made me forget everything else. It was postmarked from Athens, Tennessee, the town where Maggie died.

CHAPTER FOUR

I heard Augusta singing as soon as I stepped inside. The song was a favorite of hers, "Coming in on a Wing and a Prayer." She had learned it, she said, while on assignment during World War II. The silver-toned notes resounded from what used to be Maggie's room upstairs, accompanied by some kind of whirring noise like a blender breaking the sound barrier.

The box was about the size of a computer terminal but it wasn't heavy. With the package under my arm, I raced upstairs to find Augusta at my mother's old sewing machine. Folds of vividly patterned cloth in red, green, yellow, and white swirled at her feet, and she turned and smiled when she saw me. "Hope you don't mind, but I found this fabric in your mother's sewing cabinet. It was labeled *kitchen curtain material,* so I thought I'd zip them on up, add a little color around here."

For a minute I stood and stared at the obstinate old sewing machine my mother had referred to as "Jaws" because it ate cloth by the yard and shredded the rest. Now it hummed along so smoothly it might be singing backup.

Augusta draped a sample from her arm for my inspection. "What do you think? I measured the windows, and there was enough for the breakfast room too."

"Perfect," I said. And of course they were. She had even lined them and scalloped the hems. "Mom was going to do something about those windows last fall, and then Dad died, and I guess she just didn't care anymore." I put the package on my sister's cherry sleigh bed. "This just came in the mail from that town in Tennessee where Maggie was killed. I didn't want to open it alone."

Augusta snipped one last thread and folded the fruits of her labors, then sat on the bed beside me. "Then I guess there's nothing for it but to look," she said.

I tore apart the corrugated flaps to find a receipt listing the contents and a note from the police department there. They apologized for taking so long to return Maggie's effects, but in cases of accidental death, they were required to hold a victim's possessions until after an investigation. Which must mean the investigation was over and the police were satisfied with the outcome. I wasn't.

The letter rested on top of a cheap brown plastic purse and a square bubble-wrapped bundle. I guessed what I was going to find as I peeled away the wrapping and lifted the lid of the box. My sister's pearl ring, the one our parents had given her for her sixteenth birthday, lay inside. And next to it was the dainty gold wristwatch that had belonged to our grandmother. Maggie had always admired it, and Mom dangled it like a carrot to encourage my sister to graduate from high school. Maggie got her diploma and the watch just a few months before she roared out of our lives on the back of a Harley.

I picked up the watch and held it in the palm of my hand, remembering the day our mother presented it to Maggie. Mom had cried with pride, while Maggie, acting cool, pretended nonchalance. I slunk into the bathroom and pouted because I had wanted the watch for myself. Now it was mine—crushed crystal, broken catch and all. And it was my turn to cry. Again.

"I think there's something in the handbag," Augusta said, offering her ever-present hankie.

The purse was scuffed and dirty and one strap hung loose. I unzipped it to find my sister's worn red billfold, a present from me the last Christmas she'd spent at home. Tucked inside were a ten-dollar bill, four ones, and fifty-eight cents in change. It also held Maggie's driver's license still in her maiden name; her eighteen-year-old face grinned at me from the plastic. That had been how the police knew to locate us after the accident. I blotted my tears and stuffed the license back into its compartment. Mom mustn't see this. Not now. Maybe not ever.

I was about to put it away when Augusta stayed my hand. "Wait. There's a card or something."

The corner of something white protruded from a crevice behind a folded coupon for diapers, and I slipped out a small wallet-sized photograph of a baby who looked to be about three months old. There was also a picture of my sister holding the same child, along with a small color snapshot of our parents in front of the Christmas tree.

Feeling almost guilty for invading my dead sister's privacy, I reached again into the bottom of Maggie's purse, and as soon as my fingers closed around it, I knew what it was. A baby's pacifier!

I passed the pictures to Augusta. "It's Maggie's! I know it is. What a beautiful baby! What do you think? Boy or girl?" I spoke in a whisper because it seemed almost irreverent to use my normal voice after what we had discovered. My sister had had a child, and we would have a part of her once again. A new chance. I felt as if I had found a rosebush blooming in midwinter.

Augusta smiled. "Does it matter?"

It didn't. However, since the baby in the photo was wearing blue, I assumed it was a little boy—at least until we found out otherwise.

But where was he? There had been no mention of a child involved in the wreck that killed Maggie and her husband. "We have to find him," I said.

"What about her husband's parents? Do you know how to locate them?"

"Maggie wasn't living with Sonny Gaines when this happened. When Mom spoke with her last, she said something about not needing a man in her life."

Augusta looked at the baby's picture and smiled. "Seems as though she might've gotten one."

"She must've been pregnant when she called home," I said. "I wonder how old the baby is now."

"There's a possibility your sister's husband didn't know he had become a father," Augusta said. "And if so, she must have had a reason to keep it from him."

"I don't even know where—or when—this baby was born," I said. "Where do we start?"

Augusta let the long strand of beads shift through her fingers and I watched the colors change from indigo to dazzling purple. "Begin at the end, I think. The place where she died."

"Athens," I said. "It's somewhere between Chatta-nooga and Knoxville." I sat at Dad's old roll-top desk in the upstairs hall and stared at the telephone. The telephone stared back.

"There must be a hospital there." Augusta's light touch on my shoulder seemed to clear my jumbled thoughts. Of course. I called directory assistance.

But the hospital in Athens couldn't and wouldn't give me the answers I wanted. They weren't allowed to give out information on a patient, I was told. However, they could tell me the date of dismissal if I knew when my sister was admitted there. But of course I didn't.

I examined the photograph again. "This looks like it's been in her billfold for a while," I said. "If he was three months old when this was made, he might have been born in the summer, or even before."

Augusta nodded. "Before she came to Tennessee, you mean?"

"Or at least to the Athens area. The last card Mom got from Maggie was postmarked in some little town in Tennessee I've never heard of. Funny name . . . Three Oaks. I remember Mom calling there, trying to find her, but Maggie wasn't listed. Probably didn't even live there. My sister covered her tracks well—mailed things from different places so we couldn't find her." I thought of the hurt and disappointment in our mother's face, and once again anger at Maggie flared like heartburn. How could she do this to people who loved her?

Still, it wouldn't hurt to try. I asked the operator for the number of the hospital in that area, only to be told there wasn't one. A spokesman in the mayor's office in Three Oaks told me that most people there used the small hospital just over the Georgia line.

I felt as if I were trying to write a letter with alphabet blocks, but if I could just get one lead, it would be worth the effort.

The woman at the community hospital in Catoosa County repeated what I'd been told at the Athens facility: no information on a patient except for date of dismissal. "And when was your sister admitted?" she asked.

"Sometime in July, I think." It was as good a guess as any.

"July." Pause. "And her name?"

"Gaines," I said. "Or probably Dobson. Maggie. Margaret Dobson." If Maggie didn't want her husband to know about the baby, she might have used her maiden name.

The woman sighed. I was ruining her day. "I'm sorry," I said, although I wasn't.

"I don't see any record of either a Margaret Gaines or a Margaret Dobson as being a patient here in July," she said.

"Try August then . . . please. I wish I could give you more to go on, but it really is important." I tried not to sound as impatient as I felt; after all, she was doing me a favor.

"Just a minute. I'll see." The woman's voice sounded more cordial, downright pleasant. Maybe it was Augusta's influence as she was hovering over my shoulder.

"Right. Here it is. A Margaret Dobson was released from Community General last August seventeenth."

"And the baby?" I held my breath.

"Ma'am, we can't give out your sister's reasons for being admitted."

"I know, but this is different. Maggie was killed in an accident last month, and we don't even know the baby's name, much less where to find him."

"Births are a matter of public record in the state of Georgia," the woman said finally. "You might try the courthouse in Ringgold."

If I could have kissed her, I would.

A few minutes later I learned I had a nephew. Joseph Scott Dobson was born August 15 weighing seven pounds five ounces and was twenty-one inches long.

Our father's name was Joseph. "She named him after Dad," I told Augusta. "And he has my middle name!"

It took less than five minutes after another call to learn my sister had never lived in that area. If she had, she had never owned property, subscribed to a phone service, or voted.

"Sounds as though she kept on the move," Augusta said, "and if, as you say, Maggie wanted to keep the baby's birth a secret, I'd think she'd move on soon after his birth."

It made sense, yet there had to be some other trace of them in the area where Joseph was born. "A doctor!" I said. "I know Maggie would see that her baby had medical care."

It took another three calls to find the right pediatrician, and a long wait while the phone charges mounted as the receptionist scrolled her records. As "Margaret Dobson," I asked if they had sent my son Joseph's records to the doctor in Athens. "I'm almost sure I requested them," I gushed, "but during the move and all I might not have gotten around to it."

"Ms. Dobson, we faxed those records to Athens back in September. Doctors Huntley and O'Hara, wasn't it? If they didn't receive them, I'm sure we would've heard by now." She spoke as if she couldn't believe anybody would be as irresponsible and dimwitted as I appeared. I didn't blame her.

"Yes, I'm sure they must have. Just wanted to make certain. I'm trying to keep a complete record of Joseph's immunizations—for his baby book, you know."

"You'll need to check with the doctors there about that," the woman told me. "They should have all that information."

"Good grief!" I heard her utter as she hung up. It sounded like a prayer.

"What if he's living with his father's people?" I said. "The baby might not be in Athens now." I told Augusta about the pediatricians there where Joseph's records had been sent. "They should be able to give me an address," I said, reaching again for the phone.

"I'd go easy there." Augusta spoke calmly. "Remember, they don't know who you are."

Athens was a fairly large city. I wondered if the baby's doctors had learned of my sister's accident.

"Just give me a minute," I said to Augusta. Then, taking a deep breath, I picked up the receiver. "I'm going to gamble on the assumption that they still think Maggie's alive," I told her.

"This is Maggie Dobson, Joseph's mother," I said to the receptionist who answered. "Joseph Dobson . . . that's right . . . Joey. I'm afraid we missed an appointment—when was it?" I glanced at Augusta who was rolling her eyes heavenward. "My goodness! Two weeks ago? I'm terribly sorry, but we've been in the process of moving and I'm afraid I let it get by me. I'd like to reschedule if I could . . . You don't have anything until the end of the month? Oh, dear! Well, would you call me if you have a cancellation?" I looked at Augusta who perched on the window seat watching me. "I'm not sure I gave you my new number," I told the receptionist. "Would you mind . . ."

I wrote down the number as the woman read it to me. "Yes, thank you. That's the one!" It was all I could do to keep from jumping up and down, but I waited until I replaced the receiver to pull Augusta to her feet and swing her around the hall, her filmy scarf billowing. "She called him Joey!" I sang. "Joey!" At least we had somewhere to start. But what if no one answered?

Weakness overtook me as I moved back to the desk. My whole body felt hollow from my toes to my head, and my hand shook when I picked up the phone.

"Close your eyes," Augusta said, and I felt her standing behind me. Her hands touched my shoulders so lightly they might have been butterflies resting there, and I began to breathe calmly again.

A woman answered. "Ola Cress." She sounded like she wasn't one to put up with any dilly-dallying, so I came right to the point.

"Ms. Cress, I'm calling about little Joey," I began. "Joey Dobson. His moth—"

"What's wrong?" Augusta asked.

"She hung up. Wouldn't even let me finish. She just hung up!"

"I expect you startled her, calling out of the blue like that. She didn't know who you were, what you wanted."

"If she'd given me half a minute, I would've told her. She has no right to keep that baby from us!"

Augusta remained serene. "You mentioned a name?"

I nodded. "Ola. Ola Cress. Who do you suppose she is?"

"I don't know. Housekeeper. Baby-sitter. Maybe a relative of the Gaineses." She smiled. "Tell you what, let's go thaw some of that vegetable soup I saw in the freezer. You'll think better with something in your stomach. Let things settle a bit and we'll try her again." She shrugged. "Maybe she thought you were selling magazines."

But when I tried to call her after lunch, Ola Cress either wasn't at home or she didn't answer the phone. "I'll just have to go there," I told Augusta.

"*We'll* just have to go there," she said. "And what about your mother? Aren't you going to mention this to her?"

"Of course I am, but I don't think she could stand the emotional stress if we don't find Joey right away." From the way Ola Cress had reacted, I was afraid of some kind of snag, and it was about all I could do to keep my own feelings under control. But then I had Augusta. "I'll tell her as soon as I know something for sure."

I smiled, imagining Mom's response to hearing the news. If you could capture hope in a bottle, she would have enough to last a lifetime. Maggie was my mother's baby who came along when I was almost six. Her pictures lined the walls: Maggie in her pink tutu for her first ballet recital; her flag uniform in the junior high band; her high school cheerleading outfit. The blue china tea set that had belonged to my sister sat on a tray on the dining-room sideboard. The tiny red chair Dad had made for her doll, Miss Mary Priscilla, named for Maggie's first Sunday school teacher, waited in the hall upstairs. Maggie had taken Miss Mary Priscilla with her when she left.

I was going to phone the sheriff's office and let them know I would be out of town for a few days when I remembered I hadn't yet told them about the man Suzie saw.

"I was just going to call you," Deputy Weber said. "We picked up a vagrant near your place this morning and put him on a bus to Atlanta, which is where he claimed he was headed. Don't see how he could be the one who killed that woman we found or tampered with your uncle's grave. No record, and he says he got here yesterday from North Carolina. Story checks out."

"Did he have a beard and earflaps?" I asked.

The deputy laughed. "I'd say he looked kind of scruffy. Hadn't shaved in a while, if that's what you mean. I didn't notice his hat."

"What about Jasper?"

"We haven't turned up anything there either, but

he'll surface. Jasper always does. Just lock up tight when you leave, and we'll be out to look around as often as we can."

"I don't suppose you've learned anything more about the dead woman?" I asked. "Or my uncle Faris?"

"Still no lead on the woman, but we're working on it. One will lead to the other. I'm sure of it.

"Oh, and don't be alarmed if you see a truck backing up to your barn. We'll store that casket down at the county barn until . . . well, until we know what's going on."

I was ready to leave that very day for Ruby, Tennessee, which turned out to be the area of Ola Cress's phone listing. According to the map, Ruby was less than fifty miles from Athens, where Maggie was killed, and if we left right away, we should be there by dark. But Augusta convinced me I needed a good night's sleep and a fresh start in the morning.

And how did she expect me to sleep, I wanted to know, with the wicked things going on in our backyard and the prospect of finding my sister's baby on my mind? But I packed a small bag at Augusta's urging (You never know how long you'll be gone, and the weather is so unpredictable this time of year!), and tumbled into bed.

The phone rang before my head even warmed the pillow.

"Prentice? Hey, you weren't asleep, were you? Don't know how you can with all that going on over there." My cousin Be-trice paused for a snuffling breath. She has chronic adenoid problems. "Have they found out who that body is yet? You must be a nervous wreck! Why would anybody want to dump the poor soul there?"

I told her that as far as I knew, the woman's identity was still a mystery, but I hoped the police would know something soon.

"Is it true that somebody made off with Uncle Faris? I heard they sacrificed a goat or something, smeared blood everywhere!"

Our uncle's grave was empty, I said, but as far as I knew there had been no animal sacrifice. She sounded disappointed.

"I'm going to have to be out of town for a couple of days," I said. "Would you mind feeding the cat?"

I knew my cousin would pounce on an excuse to see what was going on, and I'd found out long ago the best time for Be-trice to visit was when I wasn't around.

That night I dreamed I heard a baby crying and the sadness of it pulled at my heart. I wandered about in the dark following the sound, only when I thought I was getting closer, the crying stopped. When I opened my eyes, my face was wet. It was morning. The morning of the day I hoped to meet my nephew.

CHAPTER FIVE

The image of little Joey traveled in front of me as we drove to Tennessee that morning. Of course it was only the Joey I imagined. Would he have long lashes like his mother's? Her dark, sparkling eyes? He looked blond in the photograph—like his granddaddy and me. Maggie had our mother's rich brown hair.

Augusta sat up front with me and sang—not always on key, but somehow it didn't matter. She liked the old ones best, she said, songs from as far back as the twenties and thirties. I learned the words to "Side by Side," a Depression song, and some silly thing from the forties about little lambs eating ivy. Her favorite, of course, was "My Blue Heaven."

The singing helped to keep my mind off what we might find—or not find when we got there. What if

Sonny's family had reached Joey first? In spite of the cheery songs, a dark thought slipped in, and I couldn't help but think of a frightened toddler crying for a mother that never came. A tear slipped down my face.

"None of that," Augusta said. "The time for crying is past. Tears won't help your sister or her little boy now."

"What tears?" I blinked away a shimmery haze. She was right, although I hated like the dickens to admit it. "What if Sonny's relatives have Joey?" I said. "I don't even know where they live."

"It might be a good idea to find out." Augusta leaned back in her seat and shook loose her hair. Today she wore a gauzy dress of turquoise and lilac with a scarf long enough to circle the state. She fingered the necklace as she spoke, and it shimmered like fiery opals. "You might check with the police in the town where the accident happened."

I frowned. "But if we tell them about Joey, they might not let us see him. Sonny's people could have legal custody." The thought turned my insides to mush.

Augusta's eyes were closed and she was so quiet I thought she'd gone to sleep. "What about the people at the funeral home there? Do you remember which one it was?"

"Clark and Clark." I would never forget it. I had to deal with them over the phone to have Maggie's body shipped home. "Ruby's on the other side of Athens; it wouldn't be out of the way." I looked at the clock on the dashboard. "Shouldn't take too long if we hurry." I glanced at my seraphic passenger. "What do we do about lunch?"

"I'm rather fond of barbecue. With pickles. And some of that wonderful stew. Brunswick stew I think it's called."

"I thought angels only ate ambrosia," I said.

She closed her eyes and smiled. "Only those who haven't tasted Brunswick stew."

We saw a likely looking spot on the other side of Chattanooga and I ordered our lunch from the drive-through. Augusta gave it her blessing, proclaiming the sweetened tea close to her own.

It was midafternoon by the time we reached Athens, and I stopped at a gas station to look up the address of the funeral home. Fortunately, it wasn't far away.

"What should I say?" I asked Augusta as we pulled into the parking lot a few minutes later.

"You could start with the truth." Her tranquil gaze gentled me. "Don't worry; you'll be fine."

And I knew I would.

The junior partner of Clark and Clark looked to be about seventy and walked with a cane. If his father was around, I didn't want to meet him.

Yes, of course he remembered speaking with me, he said after we were seated in a small hushed room that smelled heavily of carnations. "Such a tragedy about your sister, a young life cut short."

I let him finish his spiel. "I'm trying to locate my sister's husband's family, the Gaineses," I said. "To tell the truth, I didn't know Maggie was married until the accident. I'm afraid she wasn't much for keeping in touch," I added, seeing his long face grow longer, and maybe I was mistaken, but I thought I detected a slight expression of distaste at the mention of the family's name.

"Yes, I remember the family," he said. "The young man's father came for his body. There were several brothers as well, I believe."

"Do you know where I can find them?"

"Not right offhand, but I can look them up."

I trailed after him into an adjoining room where he seemed to move in slow motion as he switched on a computer, then hesitated before punching a few keys. "Right. Here it is: Pershing Gaines, lives over in Sleepy Creek. That's about thirty miles the other side of Knoxville."

Sleepy Creek. That sounded peaceful enough, I thought. He wrote something on a card and gave it to me. It was a business card promoting the funeral home and on the back was an address, *278 Wildwater Road.*

"Do you remember if the family had a child with them?" I asked. "A small boy?"

The man switched off his computer and stood slowly, bracing himself against the desk. "A child? I don't think so." He shook his head. "No, I'm certain of it. I would've remembered that."

I was so relieved to hear the Gaineses didn't have Joey with them, I thanked the man at least three times on my way out.

"Ma'am?" Mr. Clark spoke as I reached the door. "I'd tread lightly with those folks if I were you."

"What do you mean?"

"From the way the young man's father talked when they were here, I think they blame your sister for their son's death. The autopsy showed he had drugs in his system."

"Drugs? Why blame Maggie for that? Sonny Gaines was driving. He certainly had no business behind the wheel of a car—he didn't even try to stop! We're the ones who should be upset."

"I wouldn't call them upset," Mr. Clark, Jr., said. "I'd call them foamin' at the mouth mad."

I caught Augusta sneaking a peek at herself in the car mirror as I started back to the parking lot. With a quick little tweak here and a pat there, she repaired whatever she imagined was wrong with her image and seemed pleased with the result. I told her what Mr. Clark had said as she adjusted her scarf.

"I must say, you don't seem worried," I said as we drove away.

"Being worried won't do us any good. Being prepared will."

"You sound like a Boy Scout," I said.

"I once filled in as Juliette Low's angel for a brief period a few years back," Augusta said. "Founded the Girl Scouts, you know. About wore me out, that lady did! Crossing foot bridges and driving like a wild woman. I can assure you I was relieved when *that* assignment was over." Augusta took a deep breath. "As for the Gaineses' ill will, *forewarned is forearmed*, that rascal Cervantes said."

"You read Cervantes?" All I could remember was *Don Quixote*.

"Read him? I knew him. Only fleetingly, mind you. Too adventurous to remain in one place long."

"I wish all I had to fight were windmills," I said. The Gaines gang didn't sound like anyone I'd like to have in my neighborhood, much less in my family. How in the world did Maggie let herself get mixed up with somebody like that? And I found myself getting annoyed with my dead sister all over again.

Augusta leaned forward and looked at me. "Scowling doesn't become you, Prentice." She examined the passing landscape of grazing cattle before speaking again. "I assume you worked things out with your young man?"

"Huh?"

"That night you spent at your aunt's. He telephoned, left a message."

I groaned. In all the excitement of learning about Joey, I hadn't had time to check the answering machine. "I don't suppose you heard what he said?"

"I couldn't very well avoid it since I was right there in the room. Seems he wants to talk rather urgently and begs you to please get in touch."

"I haven't talked to Rob since early October," I said. "Guess he'll keep a little longer."

About ten miles outside of Ruby I began rehearsing what I would say to Ola Cress. I had even brought pictures of my sister and myself together to prove our relationship, but what good would they do if I couldn't find her, or if she wouldn't give me a chance to speak? Anxieties, along with the slaw and barbecue I'd had for lunch, played leapfrog in my stomach, until finally I stopped at the edge of town just to get some air.

"Breathe deeply and think blue," Augusta said as I stood beside the car.

"Blue?"

"It's a tranquil color. Restful. Just close your eyes and relax. You'll see."

I pictured a summer sky with white clouds drifting, a sapphire lake dotted with swans. And maybe it was the blue, or maybe the barbecue made friends with the slaw, but I felt much better when I got back behind the wheel again. A few miles down the road I stopped at a convenience store with a telephone out front and looked up Ola Cress's address. Thank goodness she was listed!

The woman behind the counter directed me to Cinnamon Street, which was about four or five blocks to the right after you passed the post office. It was a little after four o'clock, and if Ola Cress worked during the day, chances were she might not be at home. Fine, I thought. That would give me an opportunity to look around.

Ruby wasn't a big town, but the streets were clean, the buildings seemed to be well taken care of, and it had been there a long time. The rambling frame houses would be almost hidden from the street when the oaks came into leaf. Had my sister lived in this town? If so, I hoped she had found comfort here.

At the corner, one little girl pushed another in a rope swing. Farther down the street, a group of young boys, who looked to be about Cub Scout age, tussled on the lawn of the Methodist Church. Several older men clustered in front of the downtown bank. I could hear their laughter as I stopped for the light. A young mother passed by pushing her baby in a stroller, and my heart did a double flip because she looked a little like Maggie. But she wasn't Maggie. Maggie was dead, and I was going to find her little boy and bring him home where he belonged.

I turned right at the post office and passed an elementary school of worn red brick, a row of shops: florist, cleaners, bakery, then drove through a residential area of smaller homes set close to the street. "There's Cinnamon," Augusta said, pointing to a street sign, and we turned and made our way slowly up the narrow winding road looking for the number of the house where I hoped to find my sister's child.

Number 106 Cinnamon Street was a duplex on a slight hill surrounded by bushy shrubbery that would soon come into flower: quince, forsythia, lilac. I recognized them because we had some in our yard at Smokerise. Maggie should have felt at home here.

The house seemed to have been a one-family residence, converted to house two families. I parked the car out front and climbed the five steps to a broken cement walk that led to the porch. I couldn't see a light in any of the windows, and it didn't look as if anyone was at home. On the porch a metal glider sat against the wall, and two folded aluminum lawn chairs rested on top of it waiting out the season. Letters fanned out from the mailbox by the door, and I brazenly read the front of an envelope. It was addressed to Ola Cress.

I knocked at the door, but no one answered. I didn't expect them to. After waiting for what I thought was a reasonable length of time, I wandered around the outside of the house looking for any sign of Joey. The other duplex didn't seem to be occupied, and the shades were drawn on Ola's side. A big yellow cat rubbed against my legs as I skirted the back porch. A stack of terra-cotta pots leaned against the steps waiting for spring, and a plant that looked like oregano tumbled from a circle of stones nearby.

Okay, so Ola Cress had a cat and cooked with herbs. But was she kind to children? I ducked under the bare limbs of a dogwood tree and started back to the car. That was when I saw the blue canvas baby swing at the far end of the back porch, and in the seat, my sister's beloved rag doll, Miss Mary Priscilla.

CHAPTER SIX

hey're not at home right now. Can I help you?"
Ola Cress's neighbor from across the street
stood on the sidewalk, arms crossed. At a guess, I'd say
she weighed over two hundred pounds, and that's being
polite. I wasn't going to tangle with her.

I offered my hand and a smile. "I'm Prentice Dobson.
Ola doesn't know me, but she was a friend of my sister's, and I've been trying to find her. Do you know
where they went?" *She had said they, hadn't she? Which
must mean Ola didn't live alone.*

"Went to visit her brother, I think. Somewhere near
Chattanooga." Her little brown eyes locked in on me
and she wrapped her bright pink sweater around her
and shuffled her feet. I saw that she wore slippers that
used to be white and used to be fuzzy.

"Do you know when they'll be back?" I said.

"Couldn't say. Ola works part-time over at the phone company. Had a big job there, but she cut back when her health got so bad."

"Really? I'm sorry."

"Practically ran the place. And ran herself ragged! I said to her, I said, 'Ola Cress, you'd better slow down. Gettin' too old to be pushin' yourself like that.' And sure enough, she had to have that *anglo plastic*—you know, where they put them balloons in your veins."

I nodded. Ola's neighbor was getting downright blabby. I was dying to ask her about Joey, but I knew she'd be waiting to tell Ola Cress everything I'd said, and I'd already said too much.

"When you see her, tell her I'm sorry I missed her," I said.

"You're not stayin' then?"

"Not long I'm afraid. Just passing through." I offered my hand again. "Thanks for your help Mrs.—"

"Grace. Grace Pittman." She stood watching me as I got behind the wheel of the car and drove away. I guessed she'd been looking out the window the whole time I was prowling around across the street.

"Any luck?" Augusta wanted to know.

"I think Joey's been there, but where he is now is anybody's guess." I told her about finding the swing with the doll in it. "I led the neighbor to believe I wouldn't be back; don't want to scare our friend Ola away. I have a feeling she doesn't trust anybody."

"I suspect she has reasons," Augusta said. "Did her neighbor know when she might return?"

"If she knows, she's not saying. I think we should find a place to stay for the night, then drive by Ola's a little later, see if there are any lights."

The Berry Patch Cafe on the corner of Main and Nutmeg offered a great hamburger and blackberry cobbler every bit as good as Mom's, only I wouldn't tell her that. I got an order to go for Augusta. My waiter's name was Justin. He had red hair, a huge smile, and a great big yearning to get out of Ruby. As soon as he graduated from high school, he told me, he was going to get a job in Nashville and live with some cousins. Life in Ruby was about as exciting as yesterday's oatmeal, and he was ready to move on.

"And here I was thinking it was kind of a nice place," I said. "Thought I might even spend the night. Are there any motels close by?"

"Nothing like that, but there's Mr. Humphreys's place a couple of blocks down from the library. It's an old white house—kinda sits back from the road. He'll give you breakfast and everything."

"A bed and breakfast. Sounds great. Think he might have room for me?"

Justin shrugged. "Don't see why not. Nobody much comes here unless they have to. You can call if you want. He left us some cards."

The name *Nightingale House* was printed with a lot of curlicues, and beneath it *Tisdale Humphreys, Proprietor*, with the address and phone number. Mr. Humphreys, when I called, said he would have the Azalea Room, along with tea or sherry, ready when I arrived.

On leaving, I asked Justin if he knew Ola Cress and if she had a little boy staying with her, and I think it kind of took him by surprise because he frowned and shook his head.

"Oh, I know who she is all right, used to come in once in a while, but I haven't seen much of her lately. Don't know anything about a little boy." He totaled my bill and stuck it under my plate. "Funny you should ask, though. You're the second person wantin' to know that this week."

"I should've asked him if he knew my sister," I mumbled as we drove away.

"What's that?" Augusta was looking out the window and it bothered me a little that she wasn't listening to what I said.

"That young waiter back there. He might've known Maggie, but I was so surprised by what he said, I didn't think to ask." I told Augusta that somebody else had been asking questions before us.

"Did he have a beard?" Augusta asked.

"Who, the waiter?"

"No, the person asking questions, because there's a man behind us in a dark-looking car who seems to be following closer than I'd like. Looks like he has a beard."

I started for Mr. Humphreys's and as we passed the town library, I pulled in without signaling and parked out front. A light still shone from inside and I could see somebody at the front desk. The car that had been behind us passed without slowing. "False alarm," I said.

Augusta didn't blink. "Maybe."

We waited a couple of minutes longer but the car didn't come back. Since it was dark, I decided to try Ola's again just to see if there was anyone there. Maybe her nosy neighbor wouldn't notice me at night. But the windows were still dark at Ola Cress's, and across the street at Grace Pittman's the only things that moved were the story-tale figures on the television screen.

The streets of the little town were empty as we drove to Nightingale House, and only an occasional street-lamp splashed the sidewalks with a pale yellow light. A wooden sign bearing the name of the establishment swung from a post by the gate. It was meant to look weathered, I think, and did. A vine, probably wisteria, twined overhead on an arched trellis, and I followed a brick walk to the wraparound porch where a welcoming light beckoned. Augusta, I noticed, had done her disappearing act, but I knew she was around somewhere.

"Please come in, and here, let me take that bag." Tisdale Humphreys was sixtyish, trim, and more well groomed than any winner of the Triple Crown. I felt downright shoddy in my wrinkled pants and baggy sweater, but I let him relieve me of my overnight bag and plodded along after him into a room he called the front parlor. I expected stiff Victorian, but this room was bright and elegant with a comfortable-looking sofa and two armchairs on either side of a marble fireplace where a cheery fire burned low in the grate. When offered a chair, I accepted gratefully and cozied right up to the warmth. I accepted the sherry too, and hoped my host would join me. I had a feeling he knew just about everything going on in Ruby and would be glad to share it under the right conditions.

Naturally, he had the same idea. "And what brings you to Ruby?" he asked, passing a tray of fruit and cheese, and every fabricated story flew right out of my head. I told him the truth.

If my candor surprised him, he recovered quickly. "I'm sorry about your sister, but to discover she had a child—how wonderful! You must be excited."

"If I can only find him." I told him about getting Ola Cress's number from the pediatrician in Athens, and how she had reacted when I called. "She acts like she's afraid of something, and I don't want to frighten her away."

He refilled my glass and his own. "Yes, Ola would be careful. I don't know her well, but I can see why she might be inclined to shy away. A bit of a loner, I think."

"Did you know my sister, Maggie? I think she might've lived here awhile. Her name was Dobson, like mine."

"I've seen her, of course, walking dogs for some of the neighbors now and then. I believe she offered some sort of pet care service when their owners were out of town."

I smiled. "That was Maggie all right."

"Unfortunately, I never met your sister." My host stood to stir the fire. "I only bought this place a few years ago. You should've seen it . . . a disaster, I assure you!

"Now Ola, I understand, was for years the backbone of the telephone company and I knew her in that capacity, but for the last couple of years she's had to take it kind of easy I believe. Stays to herself mostly."

"So you never saw her with a small boy, a baby?"

He smiled. "I can't imagine Ola Cress with a baby, but she had that house made into a duplex not too long ago. Needed the extra money I suppose. Your sister lived there for a while, I know, and there might have been a child as well. Neighbors might know."

I knew one who would, I said, but this probably wasn't a good time to ask her. And I told him about Grace Pittman.

"Ah, yes, Grace! Well, you were wise to tiptoe around that one. Anything you said would get back to Ola and everybody else in town."

I barely sipped my sherry. I wanted it to last as long as possible, not because I particularly like the taste, but because I was reluctant to leave a comfortable chair and pleasant company. "I'll try again tomorrow," I said. "I guess I'll just have to hope she'll be back by then."

He set his glass aside. "And if not, what then?"

"I understand she has a brother somewhere near Chattanooga. Maybe the people at the phone company can give me an idea where to find her."

But from the look on Tisdale Humphreys's face, I had a feeling I was chasing smoke dreams.

Tired from the long drive, I climbed into the big mahogany four-poster, plumped the downy pillows, and pulled the covers up to my chin. "Good night, Augusta, wherever you are," I whispered before I dozed off. I slept well that night snuggled under hand-stitched quilts that smelled of lavender. Mr. Humphreys had done a beautiful job of decorating the room with hooked rugs in soft shades of rose and green on the polished oak floors, and white embroidered curtains that let in the light.

That light woke me gently the next morning and I lay in bed trying to think of what I would do if Ola Cress eluded me again, until the aroma of something wonderful lured me downstairs. My host had prepared thick slices of French toast served with orange marmalade and just-right bacon at a small table in front of the fire. It was going to be difficult to leave here, I told him.

"Whenever you want to come back, I'll have a place for you, and if there's any way I can help, just let me know," he said, wishing me luck as I told him good-bye.

Augusta waited in the car rubbing her hands together. "I thought you'd never come," she said. "It's freezing out here."

"Don't tell me you've been here all night."

"Only for a little while, but I could do with some good hot coffee. Does this heater work?"

"I didn't know angels cared about the temperature," I said, turning on the heater.

"Actually, I don't think we're supposed to, but my last assignments happened to be during the warmer months, and I'm afraid I've become acclimated to it." Augusta wrapped her long scarf about her until she resembled a brilliant cocoon.

I couldn't work up the nerve to look when we passed the house on Cinnamon Street, so I asked Augusta to see if there were any signs of life.

"I'm sorry, Prentice, but it doesn't seem as if she's there. I don't see a car, but it wouldn't hurt to look."

"Let's try the phone company first," I said. "At least they might be able to let us know when she'll be back."

The receptionist at the Ruby Telephone Company, who looked to be about ten, didn't seem interested in anything I had to say, but I told her anyway. "I'm looking for Ola Cress," I said, "and I understand she works here at least some of the time. Can you tell me when you expect her?"

The receptionist didn't know, but somebody named Willene at the desk behind hers said Ola had taken some time off to be with her brother who had been in poor health. "Frankly," Willene said, standing to lean over the counter, "I think Ola needs looking after as much as he does. That poor girl getting killed in that train accident just about tore her up."

I held to the counter for support. "Are you talking about Maggie Dobson?"

"Maggie. Yeah, I think that was her name. None of

us really knew her, but Ola—well, she got real attached to her and that baby."

Joey. "The baby. Do you know what happened to him?"

Willene shook her head. "I reckon the poor little thing went to live with his mama's folks, or his daddy's. Pity both his parents gettin' killed like that."

I didn't know whether to shake her or to hug her, and worse still, I started to cry. That seemed to stir up even the indifferent receptionist who offered a chair and a tissue.

Willene brought water. "Here, sip on this, honey, and try to get yourself together. I didn't for all the world mean to upset you like that."

Finally I was able to explain my relationship to Maggie and her little boy. "I was hoping Ola could help me find him," I said.

"I don't know how to reach her at her brother's," Willene said, "but the people at The Toy Box Child Care Center might know where the little boy is. Your sister worked there for a while. I bet one of them could at least give you an idea where to look."

I ran all the way to the car before I thought to go back and ask for directions.

CHAPTER SEVEN

The Toy Box Child Care Center was not hard to find. A multicolored sign about the size of a bread truck hung in front of a small frame house painted daffodil-yellow. It must have been outside play-time when we arrived because bundled-up toddlers were being pushed in swings or pulled in wagons while older children rode tricycles or climbed a jungle gym. Two young women, obviously supervising the activities, stopped talking as they watched my approach, and one of them stepped forward to meet me.

"Can I help you?" She stooped to wipe a little girl's nose but the child ducked her head and ran away.

"I hope so. Are you the director?"

"That would be Jackie. You'll find her inside."

I thanked her, stepped over a plastic pail, and dodged a rubber ball on my way to the door. I found Jackie in the tiny kitchen pouring juice into training cups while something that smelled like chicken noodle soup simmered on the stove.

"Excuse the clutter. You've caught me at lunchtime." She offered a hand. "Jackie Trimble. Are you here to enroll a child?"

"I hope I'm here to find one," I said. "I understand Maggie Dobson worked here for a while."

"Yes, she did. That was the saddest thing. So tragic! We all hated to lose Maggie, and the children miss her too." She turned to take sandwiches—tiny triangles oozing jam—from the refrigerator. Jackie Trimble wore her brown hair in bangs and a long pageboy that hung about her face. She had the faintest trace of a mustache and dark-rimmed glasses that she kept shoving back in place. She didn't look at me.

"I'm looking for Joey," I said. "Do you know where I can find him?"

"Lord, I wish I did!" She lifted the lid of the soup pot and glanced back at me. "You related to Maggie?"

"Her sister."

"Oh. Look, I'm sorry about Maggie. Joey too. I'm afraid Ola Cress has carted him off somewhere. Thinks she's hiding him, I reckon."

I frowned. "Hiding him from who?"

She shrugged. "From anybody, I guess. I could see Ola was getting too attached to that baby; never had any of her own, you know. Course I don't know what Maggie would've done without her."

"You mean she wants to *keep* Joey?" My composure

flew out the window and I know my voice went up an octave. "Do you know where she went?" I clenched my fists so tightly my nails bit into the flesh. Was I chasing a mad woman? "I think it's time to call the police," I said numbly.

"Oh, no, don't do that! Not yet." Jackie stopped in the middle of stirring the soup. "If you frighten her, there's no telling what she'll do." She lowered her voice. "Look, Joey's fine. She loves him, she'll take care of him, and she's got to come back to Ruby sooner or later. It's the only home she has. That's when you need to confront her. She's probably frightened now and on the run. You might lose that little boy forever." Her voice said, *Trust me!* But I couldn't see her eyes.

I could almost believe her, but not quite. For some reason, I kept thinking of Snow White being offered the apple. *Have a bite, won't you, dearie?* But I needed some questions answered.

Joey was born in August before Maggie came to Ruby, Jackie confirmed as she filled small bowls with soup. My sister started helping at The Toy Box in September, and it worked out fine, she said, because Maggie could bring the baby with her.

"Maggie and I became good friends, and I don't mind telling you, I've been worried to death about Joey." Jackie followed me to the door, wiping her hands on her apron. "If you find where Ola Cress is keeping him, how about giving me a call? And I'll do the same for you. I feel like we oughtta keep in touch, and heck— I don't even know your name." She tore off a sheet of tablet paper. "Here, write your name and phone number on this."

I stopped to write something down and gave it to her just as the children romped in from outside, then thanked her and backed my way out the door.

"That woman thinks Ola Cress plans to keep Joey," I told Augusta as we got under way.

"How do you know she doesn't?"

"I don't, but there was something about Jackie Trimble I didn't quite trust. She never would meet my eyes, and she acted like she was going to burst a seam to find out where Joey is. Besides, if she and my sister were such good friends, why didn't she know Maggie had a family?"

Augusta nodded. "I see. But still you gave her your name and number."

"Ah! You saw, but you *didn't see.*" I found it a relief that angels don't always know everything. "That's not what I wrote on the paper."

"What did you write?"

"Before I started working for *Martha's Journal,* I filled in as an office temp," I said. "For about three months I worked as a receptionist for a podiatrist in Atlanta, and his phone number just popped into my head." I laughed. "I'm afraid they're going to be upset if she calls. I told her my name was Ophelia Foote."

Before we left Ruby, I wanted to make one last stop at Cinnamon Street, just in case we might catch the evasive Ola unaware, but the house still had an abandoned look, and the mail that had been there the day before still jammed the letter box. Just to be sure, I pulled the car in the driveway and looked to see if it was the same correspondence I'd seen the day before. It was, and there had been no delivery since, so it appeared that not until recently had the local post office been notified to hold or forward her mail. Ola Cress had left in a hurry, I thought—probably after my call. I could almost feel two peering eyes from across the street fastening on me like bright brown leeches. Oh, well, let prying Grace have her excitement, I thought. And I looked shamelessly in Ola's windows where the shade wasn't lowered all the way.

What I saw was a teddy bear as big as a five-year-old staring at me from the corner of the sofa.

The rest of the room was neat, but drably furnished, and other than the bear, I didn't see any signs of a baby.

"I think she's packed up all the baby's things and plans to stay away awhile," I told Augusta. Except for the teddy, the room looked as if no one ever lived there.

But the canvas swing with Miss Mary Priscilla in it remained on the back porch. I wanted that doll. I considered prying open the screen door and snatching it from that cheerless place, but I couldn't take a chance on setting off an alarm and summoning the police—or worse, Grace Pittman. I remembered how I used to tease Maggie about Miss Mary Priscilla. Once I even threatened to throw the doll from the barn loft because Maggie had eaten my chocolate Easter rabbit. My little sister went crying to Mom, and for punishment, I had to stay home from the church Easter egg hunt. *Oh, Maggie, I would give you a million chocolate rabbits if I could!*

"We have to think of a way to get in touch with Ola Cress," I said, keeping one eye on the house across the street. "The post office won't give out information on a forwarding address, but what if I wrote her, gave her my phone number? Do you think she'd call?"

"It does seem as if she has us between a stone and a very firm object. But didn't you say someone had been asking about Joey at the restaurant? Who do you think that might be?"

"Probably Sonny's father. The people at the funeral home said he blamed Maggie for Sonny's death."

"I wonder why." Augusta thought about that for a minute. "Still, I wouldn't risk giving her your phone number, Prentice. The mail Ola received several days ago is still in her box. Anyone could read it. I'd be a little more careful I think."

"Then what? I would call and leave a message, but she doesn't have an answering machine."

"We need an intermediary," Augusta said, turning the heater up a notch as I backed out of the driveway. "Why not write and explain who you are. Have her call someone you both trust."

"It would have to be somebody local, and I certainly don't trust that woman at The Toy Box. I'm sure she knows more than she's telling."

"What about the gentleman at that lovely place you

stayed last night? The—what do you call it—bed and breakfast?"

"Tisdale Humphreys. Of course. He offered to help if he could." Well, he could, and I told him that when I called from the convenience store on our way out of town.

"Well, of course, I'll be most happy to relay your message," my new friend said. "I haven't had such a clandestine adventure since poor old Ernest Witherspoon hid out here when his third wife Opal Mae was on the warpath."

And so it was arranged that I would write Ola and explain who I was, asking her to call Mr. Humphreys if she wanted to get in touch. All I could do now was wait.

"Surely Maggie must have mentioned her family to Ola Cress," I mused as we started back to Georgia. "My sister kept in touch with Mom from time to time and even had our parents' picture in her billfold. I can't believe she didn't make provisions for her baby if anything happened to her."

"People your sister's age seldom believe anything life-threatening will happen," Augusta said. "But I agree. This woman shouldn't be surprised at your inquiries. Something's not quite right."

"You don't think she'd hurt Joey?" I almost rear-ended a truck.

"No, no. Nothing like that. But I believe she's afraid. Terribly afraid, and I don't know why."

"Maybe it's Sonny's father. From what Mr. Clark, Junior, said, I'm scared to death of him myself."

Augusta didn't answer.

The closer we got to the Georgia state line, the more I worried about what was happening back home. Or in my case, not happening. I had been doing some freelance writing to bring in a little money until I could find another job, but a *little* money is exactly what it brought in. I was going to have to start sending out résumés in a big way if I wanted to cover the job market, and I hadn't even had time to update mine. "By the way," I said, turning to my resident angel, "I don't suppose you're familiar with computers?"

"You mean that thing that looks like a little oven with a keyboard? One thing at a time." Augusta turned in her seat to look behind us. "Right now I think we're going to have to deal with that car that's been on our bumper for the last twenty miles."

"That's what you said last night, remember? Are you sure you're not imagining things?"

"I'm not imagining the driver is the same man I saw yesterday, and the car's the same too. Dark blue. I'm not familiar with manufacturers, so don't ask me the make."

I glanced in the rearview mirror. The Buick was about two car lengths behind and from what I could tell, the driver seemed to have a beard. "Must've been back there all along. We'll have to ditch him somehow—don't want him following us home."

"Isn't that a restaurant up ahead?" Augusta asked. "And it's crowded too. Good! Turn in here."

"I can't believe you're thinking of food with the bearded avenger on our tail."

"This might be our chance to give him the slip. But you'll have to hurry. No, don't park out front! Find a place in back."

I followed Augusta's directions and watched the blue Buick turn in behind us. "He stuck right with us," I said. "What now?"

"That's exactly what we wanted!" Augusta's face was flushed. I think she was actually enjoying this. She lowered her voice as if the man in the blue car might hear her. "Now here's what I want you to do . . ."

I hoped it would work.

With the strange man watching, I walked calmly around to the front of the building and went inside, giving him plenty of time to follow. I was led to a small table in a corner of the busy restaurant where I pretended to study the menu while my stomach turned to stone. The man at the table across from me was putting away french fries as if he were in some kind of contest, and the smell of them made me green. The man with the beard was seated three tables away. I couldn't see his face, but I could feel him looking at me. If he approached me, I would scream—right after I threw up from fright.

When the waitress came I ordered a glass of tea and a salad, slid a bill under my napkin to pay for it, and took my compact from my purse, frowning at what I saw. The ladies' room was in the rear and I avoided eye contact as I walked past the man who had been following me, aware that he watched my every step.

A couple of minutes crawled by before I worked up enough courage to peek around the door. The bearded man, his back to me, was tucking into a bowl of something, probably chili, and I slipped quickly and quietly out the back door, into the car, and out of the parking lot. While my heart thudded out of my chest, Augusta leaned back and laughed. "Fooled him that time, didn't we? Wonder what he'll do when he realizes you've gone?"

"I just hope I can put enough miles between us so I won't find out," I said. "I wish I knew what he wanted. If he had something to say, all he had to do was open his mouth."

"I think he wants to find out where you live," Augusta said.

I drove a little faster.

CHAPTER EIGHT

It was dark as I turned into the long drive approaching Smokerise, and I could see a glimmer of light from inside the house. I had meant to leave a light burning to discourage unwanted visitors, but we left in such a hurry I couldn't remember doing it.

But I did remember leaving Noodles inside, so why was she curled up on the back porch?

"That silly cat's out," I said to Augusta. "Be-trice must've let her out when she came to feed her." I tried the door and found it firmly locked. Except for Be-trice, Mom, and Aunt Zorah, no one else had a key.

Inside I turned on a light in the kitchen and sniffed. Bacon. Augusta had whipped up a cheese omelet the morning before we left for Tennessee, but we hadn't cooked any bacon, and bacon hung heavy on the air. A plate and flatware sat in the sink, and one of the placemats appeared to be streaked with jam. My cousin, for all her faults, was a neat freak. She would never leave a kitchen like this.

"Somebody's been here," I said, "and I don't think it's Goldilocks."

"Somebody's still here," Augusta said. "Get out."

That was when I heard a creak from the sitting room, as if somebody was trying to be quiet. The phone was in the sitting room.

If I could just get to the telephone upstairs, I would barricade myself in the bedroom and lock the door! Augusta gave me a shove in the right direction, and I could sense more than hear her close behind me as we ran through the dark dining room and up the stairs. We had almost reached the landing when I heard the back door shut softly.

"Whoever it was is gone now," Augusta whispered in what I supposed was an effort to assure me. I was not assured. I slammed the bedroom door behind us, and sat on the floor leaning against it. Augusta knelt at the window looking out. "I can't see who it is, but I hear somebody running."

"Jasper Totherow," I said, and reached for the phone.

"I don't know. Come and look at this." Augusta, who had wandered into the bathroom, beckoned to me from the doorway.

There was a ring around the bathtub the color of red Georgia clay, and a puddle on the floor beside it. A damp towel oozing water hung over the side. Thank heavens for 911, because I was too rattled to look up the sheriff's number and my hands too shaky to dial it.

It took the sheriff ten days to get there. Well, actually it was about ten minutes, but it seemed like ten days, and this time the big guy himself showed up, along with a young sergeant who stuck to him like chewing gum, and couldn't be more than nineteen.

"It sure does look like somebody made themselves at home here," Sheriff Bonner said after a preliminary look around. "Have you found anything missing?"

I hadn't had time to look, but with the sheriff and his shadow following me around, I checked the family silver, which is about all we had that was worth anything, except for a few family heirlooms, and they all seemed to be here. The worn velvet jewelry box that had belonged to my great-grandmother was still inside an empty box that once held sanitary napkins. Mom always called it "the family jewels" and kept it on the top shelf of her closet. She must have forgotten the box in her hurry to put Smokerise behind her. If whoever had been "boarding" here meant to steal something, the misleading box had put them off, or they hadn't had time to find it.

"I couldn't find any evidence of a break-in," the sheriff said. "At least not at this point in time. Are you absolutely sure that door was locked?"

"Unless she's a lot smarter than I think, that cat can't open a door," I told him. "My cousin came by to feed her yesterday, but she swears she locked the door.

I just spoke with her on the phone. The cat was inside when she left."

Sheriff Bonner was a big man. The sofa groaned when he sat on one end of it, and I almost expected the other to seesaw up. "Besides you and your cousin, who else has a key?" he asked.

"Just my mother, but she's in Savannah. And Aunt Zorah."

"Better call her and see if she still has it," he said. "My deputy tells me he was out here yesterday to look around and didn't notice anything out of the way."

That must've been a shock, I thought. "Have you been able to identify the dead woman yet? And what about Uncle Faris? Has he—"

Sheriff Bonner rubbed his eyes, as if he hoped it would make him see clearly. And I could clearly see he didn't have anything new to tell me. "Not much success there, I'm afraid. The woman's not from around here. We've sent out inquiries of course, but so far no one of that description has turned up missing."

"What about Jasper Totherow? Have you been able to locate him?"

When the sheriff shook his head, his ruddy jowls swayed with the motion. "Not at this point in time. He's a sly one, Jasper is, but he'll turn up sooner or later. I don't believe this is Jasper's doing, though."

"What makes you say that?"

The sheriff smiled at the skinny sidekick who accompanied him. "Took a bath, didn't he?"

Aunt Zorah found our door key in the bottom of her ironing basket where she always kept it. Nobody was likely to bother with her ironing basket, she said. (And neither was Aunt Zorah.)

"I wish you'd just come and stay awhile," she said. "You know I'd love to have you, and I don't for one minute like what's going on out there."

I told her I didn't like it either.

"I'm just about to sit down for supper. Stuffed peppers. Got plenty, so you come on."

"Oh? Stuffed with what?"

"Whatever was in the refrigerator. Pour enough ketchup on it and who cares? I'll save you a plate."

I made my excuses. A virus. A bad virus. And very contagious too. I promised to bolt all the doors, and the sheriff was sending a car to check periodically during the night.

"First thing tomorrow, I want you to get your locks changed," Sheriff Bonner said as he left. "I don't know what's going on out here, but I mean to find out. Meanwhile, I'd feel a lot better if you were to stay with your aunt."

"The sheriff's right," Augusta said after he left. "I do what I can, but a little common sense is in order here, Prentice Dobson."

I had bolted all the doors from the inside and stacked trash cans full of canned goods in front of them. "There are some things worse than intruders in your bathtub," I said. "Obviously you've never eaten Aunt Zorah's stuffed peppers."

She laughed. "Well, no and I don't intend to. At least *not at this point in time!*"

I slept that night on the sofa in the sitting room with Augusta blessedly nearby. I didn't remember till morning that my sister had rumbled out of our lives with a key to our house, and I didn't recall seeing it in her purse.

I found Maggie's scuffed brown purse wrapped in tissue upstairs in her chest of drawers where I had left it, but there were no keys in it, not even a key to the other side of the house she shared with Ola Cress. The '83 Dodge involved in the accident at the railroad crossing had belonged to my sister, and I imagine she used it only for errands; it was too old for much of anything else. Any keys she might have had would have been in the ignition at the time of the impact, and I didn't want to think what might have happened to them. If the key to Smokerise had been with them, there was no way to know it now.

Remembering the jewelry box, I decided to check it again to see if everything was there. My great-grandfather Scott had given a strand of pearls to his bride on their wedding day, and I knew how much the necklace meant to Mom. It was the only piece of jewelry she had that might be considered valuable, and she only wore it on special occasions. Sitting on my parents' bed, I held the box on my lap and opened it to find other treasures inside: Granddaddy Scott's gold watch fob, a Masonic ring from Grandpa Dobson,

Grandmother's sapphire pin, and the small diamond earrings that had been Mom's twenty-fifth anniversary gift from Dad. But no pearls. If someone had stolen the necklace, why didn't they take the other things too? My mother must have taken it with her, I thought, and prayed I was right. The idea of that shiftless Jasper Totherow with the family pearls in his pocket made me sick with rage.

The first thing after breakfast I called for a locksmith to change all our locks and he promised to take care of it right away. While I waited, I wrote to Ola Cress and tried to explain the urgency of my situation without spooking her completely. As far as I knew, the woman had no reason to distrust Tisdale Humphreys. I just hoped the post office in Ruby was forwarding her mail.

Maybe Ola would be able to tell me why Sonny Gaines was driving my sister's car. And what were they doing in Athens, Tennessee? She had her purse with her and had left Joey either at day care or with Ola Cress, so she must have been going somewhere. But for the life of me, I couldn't understand what she was doing with Sonny after she'd made it clear to our mother she didn't want any men in her life. Unless Maggie had been coerced.

While in town to mail the letter, I was conscience-driven to stop by the library to let Aunt Zorah know I was still among the living.

On my way inside I was almost knocked sideways

by Maynard Griggs, the elder of the funeral home Griggses, who came scurrying out with an armload of books.

"Oh, my goodness, I beg your pardon," he huffed as a thick volume slid to the sidewalk.

"That's all right." I tried to regain my breath and my composure as I stooped to pick up a copy of *A Collection of Works by Charles Dickens*.

"My granddaughter's writing a term paper," he said, hurrying away. I smiled. I didn't know the man was capable of moving that fast.

Aunt Zorah gave me the evil eye from her desk on high. "Well, I see you're still with us. Can't say I'm not surprised with all the goings-on out there. What do you suppose these people are after? You don't have hidden treasure you haven't told me about, do you?"

"If we do, it's hidden from me," I said. "And I'd probably be safer at home than here. Mr. Griggs just about bowled me over out there with all that literature he's lugging around."

Aunt Zorah made a face. "Spoils that Cynthia rotten! And that snobby Ernestine's just as bad, if not worse. Spent all that money to send that girl to prep school, and what does she do? Flunks out before the term's half over! What is she now? Sixteen? Seventeen? Old enough to go to the library on her own." She snorted. "It doesn't help a child to do too much for them. She'll pay for it in the long run."

I thought of the papier-mâché hand puppet Mom sculpted for Maggie's book report in the fourth grade, the excuses she made for her poor grades. Maybe Aunt Zorah had a point.

"I don't guess you've heard any more about what happened to Uncle Faris," I said, hesitating to bring up the subject.

My aunt obviously couldn't restrain a sneer at Becky Tinsley's selection of romances but checked them out anyway. "I don't think the sheriff and his gang know how to put on their drawers in the morning," she said aside to me. "Don't have a lead, they say. Why anybody would want to dig up a corpse is beyond me, and they don't seem to have a clue about that poor woman they found! That Fool Faris wasn't any good when he was alive, and he sure isn't going to win any prizes dead."

"They mentioned something about a cult, some teenagers—"

She shook her head. "Didn't find out anything there, but I don't think that's who did it. And frankly, neither does the sheriff."

For all her blustering, I noticed my aunt's lip trembling, and when she said his name, *That Fool* came out a little softer than usual. Aunt Zorah never stopped loving Faris Haskell, and you can take that to the bank!

When I got home, I found Augusta gathering armfuls of sunshiny forsythia and bright coral quince. One pinkish blossom tilted over a dainty ear, and the necklace trailed against her breast like a string of violet stars. She looked like a perfume ad in a pale fluted chemise with a rose-splashed overlay of sheerest gossamer that flowed behind her when she walked. Augusta wouldn't fit today's idea of a model. There was a roundness to her arms, and her shoulders weren't even close to being bony, but her goodness made her beautiful, and her clothing seemed to have been cut from a bolt of cloth that was part sea and part sky.

After a season of cold and rain, the day was warm and sunny, and since the house had strong new locks, we decided to take some of the flowers to Maggie's and my father's graves. I changed into boots and a sweater, and off we went across the dried winter grass and around the wooded hill where new leaves budded. I could smell spring, feel it, not only in the flowers we carried, but in the awakening earth itself. There was hope for my mother, hope for me, and its name was Joey. It made me want to sing. So I did. It was a song I'd learned long ago in grade school: *Welcome sweet springtime, we greet thee in song* . . . and Augusta with her (sometimes) soulful voice joined in.

The gaping rectangle where Uncle Faris had been was still there. Uncle Faris himself, if we ever got him back, would be reburied in higher ground, and the new road would slash the gentle hillside below where he once lay. Already bulldozers waited to peel back the earth in readiness for the new homes to march in ordered lines where my granddaddy planted corn. The developers had promised to rebuild that part of the stone wall at the bottom of the old family graveyard. Even the dead deserve privacy, and I don't guess the new home owners wanted to be reminded of the fate that awaits us all.

I mixed daffodils with the other blossoms and found the fruit jars we kept there for that purpose, but first I had to get water from the creek. Even though the day was mild, the brown water rushed cold and deep and I walked along the banks looking for a gradual slope where I could reach it without slipping.

Augusta trailed along in her own time, laughing at a family of rabbits, admiring a squirrel's nest high in a sycamore tree. When we reached the old homestead, she stayed behind to run her fingers over the moss-covered stones, examine the pit that was the root cellar, touch lightly the place where the fireplace had been. She had lived in such a house, she said, and it made her think of the people there.

"Do you miss them?" I asked. "Will you think of me when you go?"

Augusta smiled. "I'll carry you in my heart."

But I could see she wanted to stay behind, and so I left her there. There was plenty of daylight left, the sun felt warm on my face and I must have walked for a half mile or more. If it had been warmer, I would have taken off my shoes and waded to dip up water, but today I was careful not to get my feet wet. I had started back to the cemetery, a dripping jar in each hand, when something caught my eye about halfway through the trees on the side of a hill. I set down the jars and moved closer. Fresh red dirt was mounded beside a crude trench. *Oh, Lord, please don't let me find Uncle Faris here!* I was afraid to look and afraid not to. For all I knew, whoever dug this thing might still be around. I stepped forward to take a quick look when a crow cawed with his loud sore throat voice from a limb above me and scared me clean into next week.

I turned and ran, crashing through the underbrush like a frightened animal, and raced across the pasture to the old homestead where Augusta sat quietly on the hearthstone. The trench had been empty, but I knew it was waiting for somebody.

CHAPTER NINE

I guess you're thinking you might as well set up camp here," I said to Donald Weber when he came out to look at our latest mysterious hole in the ground.

"You're not far from right, because that's kind of what I had in mind," he said. "We've tried to keep an eye on your place, but this is so far from the house, they could have a square dance out here and nobody would see it. Hear it either. Of course whoever's doing all this digging knows that. Tonight, by golly, we'll come in the back way and see what happens."

"You mean like a stakeout?" I asked.

"I guess you could call it that." We stood back from the trench because the area was trampled with footprints and we didn't want to disturb them by adding ours. Sergeant Sloan leaned over to look into the oblong hole. "Maybe somebody's planning to bury an animal. Big dog or something. Know of any neighbors who've lost a pet?"

I shook my head. "If they had, they'd bury it on their own property. I think whoever dug this means to put a person here." Probably Uncle Faris—or what was left of him, I thought.

"Looks like there were two of them." The deputy pointed out two distinct sets of prints—one a little larger than the other. "And I suspect at least one of them borrowed your bathtub the other night. A lot of red mud, Sheriff Bonner tells me."

The idea of it made me feel like somebody had tied a string to my backbone and jerked me inside out. I immediately thought of Jasper. "Ralphine Totherow used to do some cleaning for us," I said. "Mom could've given her a key."

But Sergeant Sloan shook his head. "Already checked on that. She says not. She did tell us that Jasper has been after her for money. Found him sittin' on her doorstep yesterday; said he was broke and hungry and didn't have anywhere to go."

So the elusive Jasper had turned up at last! I could have told him where to go, and I hoped Ralphine did. "What did she do?" I asked.

The sergeant grinned. "Gave him a box of crackers and some peanut butter and sent him on his way."

I frowned. "Where is he now? Did you get a chance to question him?"

"Ralphine called us as soon as he left, but the son

of a gun seems to have disappeared altogether. His wife thinks he was on the run, said somebody was after him."

"He was telling the truth that time," Deputy Weber said. "That man has more hidey-holes than a rabbit."

"Or a snake," I said.

"Some of the sheriff's men are going to be watching that back part of the property tonight to see if the grave diggers return," I told Augusta later. "I hope they clear up all this mess before Mom learns about it. We've been lucky so far she hasn't seen it in the papers."

Augusta nodded but didn't answer because she was standing on a chair hanging curtains in the kitchen. Already the room looked transformed. Mom would be pleased if she ever came back home. But I doubted if she would. Of course she'd never be able to find anything because Augusta had put a lot of her cooking utensils in all the wrong places. I found Mom's egg-shaped timer in the refrigerator and those little plastic things you stick in the ends of corn on the cob were pinning up grocery lists on the kitchen bulletin board.

Funny. It couldn't have been five minutes before my mother phoned to ask if I was all right. "I've had you on my mind all day and just wanted to hear your voice. Is everything okay? How's it going with the job hunting?"

"I'm working on that," I said. How could I admit I hadn't even updated my résumé? How I wanted to tell her about Joey! But there were too many "ifs" to get into that just yet. I looked forward to putting that baby in my mother's arms, bringing feeling back into her heart. And to seeing her eyes come to life when I did it.

"By the way, I had the locks changed," I told her. "I'll send you a key."

"Why did you do that? Prentice, is something the matter out there?"

Thanks heavens Mom rarely watched television, and newspapers would collect for days before she'd get around to reading them. "Of course not," I lied, "but I didn't know how many people had keys, and it kind of made me uneasy."

"Besides the two of us, I can't think of anybody but Be-trice and Zorah," she said. "And there's that extra one in the garage."

"Where in the garage?" I hadn't thought about that.

"Your dad kept one hanging under a shelf just to the right of the door. Never carried a house key. Said he was afraid he'd lose it."

I had lived with my parents eighteen years before I went away to college, and I never knew that about my father. We had been like strangers to each other since Maggie rode out of our lives. I wondered how many other things I never took time to know.

"So Ralphine never had one?" I asked.

"Heavens no!" My mother laughed. "Not that I'd object to giving her one, but I wouldn't want that Jasper getting his hands on it."

My mother paused, and I knew something was up other than my welfare. "Are you sure you're all right?" she asked again.

"Mom, I'm fine. Really. What is it?"

"You're not still upset with me about leaving? About what happened between you and Rob?"

"You mean what *didn't* happen?"

"Oh, dear! You are upset. Prentice, I'm sorry. I don't know what else to say. Would it make you feel better if I came back home?"

"No! No, it wouldn't. Please don't!" I realized I really didn't want my mother to come home. But I did want her to make the offer. "I think it's good for you to be away, for a while at least. And I guess I need to work out some things on my own too." The fact that I had a bit of heavenly help would have to be my secret.

I could hear relief in her breathing. "Oh, I'm so glad to hear you say that! Elaine has persuaded me to take a little cruise, says a vacation would do me good. Your father and I never really went anywhere, you know, and now that I've sold the property, I can afford to travel once in a while."

"That's good, Mom. Sounds wonderful, and you deserve it. Where will you be going? When?"

My mother would be leaving in a couple of days for a ten-day cruise in Alaska, she said. I surprised myself by wishing her bon voyage and meaning it. Must be Augusta's influence.

"By the way," I said, "you do have the pearls, don't you?"

"Pearls?"

"Your grandmother's pearls. Mom, please tell me you have them! They're not in the box."

"Oh. The pearls. Well, of course, don't worry about that. Now, honey, I must run. My four o'clock piano student's here—"

I wondered why my mother would take the pearls and leave the other keepsakes behind, but at least that sneaky Jasper Totherow hadn't gotten his filthy hands on them. While it was still light I went to the garage to see if Dad's key was still there. I found the nail where he had kept it beneath the shelf by the door, but the door key wasn't there. I felt the shelf to be sure, checked the floor underneath . . . nothing!

As I started back to the house I heard something that made my heart drop like a rock. It sounded like a dentist's drill at high speed hitting bone, or a prehistoric creature from a science fiction film. Was Noodles stuck in the drainpipe again? Silly cat! It wouldn't be the first time. I ran toward the awful caterwauling that was now reaching a crescendo. Who or whatever was making that noise must be in horrible pain.

Inside, Noodles cringed underneath the sitting-room sofa with only one black ear and a pink nose protruding. The sound vibrated all around me until even my teeth screamed for mercy. And it was coming from upstairs.

"Augusta?" Surely this must be a beastly demon sent to overpower my guardian angel, and they were locked in some kind of otherworldly battle between good and evil. What could I do? Probably nothing, but I had to try. I raced up the steps, scared to death of what I might see, but prepared to face the devil himself.

Augusta stood by a floor lamp in my parents' room with a music stand in front of her and my father's fiddle tucked under her chin.

She looked up and smiled at me. "I hope your mother won't mind, but I found this in the hall closet when I was looking for curtain rods, and I've always wanted to learn how to play."

I didn't have the heart to tell her how hopeless that seemed. "Lessons might be a good idea," I suggested, trying not to shudder at the thought.

"You can see why that would be awkward in my position. Requires personal contact. Line dancing I learned from a video . . . and what a wonderful gadget that is!" Augusta whirled about and performed a sample step. "But this . . . I don't suppose you—?"

"Oh, no! That was Dad's fiddle. Used to play for square dances." Dad had tried to teach me to play, but I lost interest after a while and never pursued it. I wished now I had at least made more of an effort.

Augusta again tucked the instrument under her chin. "I thought if I could just practice enough, I might have a chance for the Heavenly Orchestra. We have some great composers up there, you know. Why Beethoven just finished another symphony. Number 473, I believe."

I hoped Beethoven was still deaf if he had to hear Augusta audition. I'm afraid I snatched the instrument from her. "I'll just show you a few scales," I said, stepping in front of the stand. "Where on earth did you find this music? I'd forgotten all about it!" There were sheafs of music on the stand, songs I'd learned to play years ago, and before I knew it, I had fiddled away almost two hours.

When Augusta called me to supper, it was after seven o'clock and nearly dark. It made me feel a little safer to know policemen stood watch over that troublesome area on the other side of the hill behind us. Augusta and I ate our supper of baked potatoes and salad in front of the fire while Noodles stretched out in Dad's chair, and it was the first time I'd consciously relaxed since I learned Uncle Faris had vacated the premises. I had eaten two of Augusta's blissfully delightful brownies for dessert, and was about a nod away from dozing off when the ringing of the telephone jerked me awake.

"Prentice? Are you okay? Any more bodies turn up out there?" Dottie Ives wanted to know. "Look, Rob's been on my case again, and I'm beginning to feel like *Dear Abby*! Didn't you get his message?"

"Well, yes, sort of, but I haven't had a chance to get back to him . . . Dottie, I've learned I have a nephew! Maggie had a little boy!" I told her about my trip to Tennessee and the phone calls that led to it.

"Maggie? Oh, Prentice, that's grand! But don't you have any idea where he is?"

"Not yet, but we're tracking down every possible lead. Right now all we can do is wait."

"Wait for what? How can you bear it? You must be going nuts not knowing where that baby is."

"Don't remind me. But you can see why I've had to put Rob on hold," I said.

"Absolutely! But do give him a call when you get a chance. I'm running out of excuses." Dottie laughed. "Guess I'd never qualify for a job on the psychic hotline. I thought you'd be bored to death by now, just sitting by the fireside watching smoke roll up the chimney."

"I could use a little boredom right now," I said.

"Don't tell me they've found another body!"

"As we speak, police are staking out the family cemetery to see if they can catch whoever's playing some kind of grisly game with Uncle Faris's coffin. It looks like somebody's hollowed out another grave up on the hillside, but we don't know who they're planning to plant in that one."

"You lie."

"Well, sometimes, but not about this, and I don't want to leave home until we hear from Ola Cress."

"You keep saying *we*. Is somebody there with you?"

I glanced at Augusta who was reading my old copy of *Tom Sawyer* and laughing now and then. "No, of course not. It's only a figure of speech."

"I can't believe that woman just disappeared with Maggie's child! She must be crazy."

"Please don't say that! I don't think she realizes who I am," I explained. "I mailed her a letter this morning and we—I—hope to hear something soon."

My friend said one of her favorite words, which you

won't find in a church newsletter. "Prentice, it's unreal how calm you are," Dottie said. "Are you sure you're all right? You sound different somehow."

I smiled. I was different. I didn't even want to think how the old Prentice would've reacted in the same situation. The Prentice before Augusta. "I'm fine," I said. "And I'll let you know what happens. Honest."

"Let me know nothing! I'm coming to Liberty Bend!"

"No, really, Dottie, I'm perfectly okay. There's no need to worry."

"Worry my ass! I just don't like the idea of something happening to my future business partner."

I laughed. "Future what?"

"You heard me. I've been thinking about it, Prentice. We could start our own public relations firm! Why not? We both have the background for it, and I have a few contacts. Just think about it, okay?"

I promised her I'd give it some thought, and she promised to stay where she was unless I hollered for help. Right now the only things I wanted to do were find my sister's baby and learn the police had arrested the person who had invaded our property and our lives.

Well, maybe one more thing. Immediately on hanging up, I replayed Rob's message on my answering machine and his voice had the same effect as hot buttered rum. My middle went all warm and mushy, and throwing all reservations aside, I dialed his number.

CHAPTER TEN

Let him be out on assignment, I thought as I placed the call. *Please Rob, don't answer!* I would leave a message, and then the ball would be in his court again. It was Saturday here in the States, and in England as well if I calculated right. Most people didn't go in to work on Saturdays, especially at this strange hour, but Rob McCullough wasn't most people and he didn't work at just any job. I wanted to hear his voice so much I could almost taste the words, and yet I had to force myself not to hang up the phone. What kind of wishy-washy dishrag had I become?

"Rob? I'm sorry I didn't—"

"Prentice? Is that you? I was about to walk out the door, but something just told me to hang around! How's that for a lucky hunch?"

"So, how've you been?" I asked. *Prentice, Prentice, what a brilliant thing to say!*

"Missing you. Honey, it's great to hear your voice."

"Yours too." Silence. What was the matter with me?

"But I want to do more than hear you. Prentice, I want to see you, need to see you." Rob hesitated. Was he waiting for me to speak? "I heard about Maggie. What a god-awful thing to happen! Why didn't you call me?"

"It happened so fast. There was nothing we could do, nothing anyone could do. I guess I'm not dealing with it very well, but I'm trying."

"I understand. Believe me, I've been there, and I didn't mean to put you on the spot." Rob paused and I could imagine him hunched over with pencil and paper, doodling as we spoke. He kept a pad by the phone and decorated the margins with pastoral scenes that could have come from a child's storybook: a barn, a tree, a rabbit, a squirrel with a nut in its paws, a road winding over a bridge. Maybe you were meant to be an illustrator, I used to tell him, but he only laughed. Now I pictured him in a London apartment, much like the one he'd had in Atlanta, filled with serviceable but comfortable furniture, every surface covered in books, papers, and coffee cups. If a person stood still in there long enough, I warned him, he might disappear forever.

"Dottie told me about *Martha's Journal*, Prentice, and I'm sorry. I can only imagine what you've gone through lately. And look, here's the thing—I know how you loved what you were doing, but before you get involved in anything else, why not make a trip over here?"

"Rob . . . I do want to see you but—"

"If you're worried about your mother, bring her along. I have a friend who's a travel agent, and I can get a good price on the tickets. My treat. I want to do this for you, and it would probably be good for your mom to get away for a while."

"It's not that, Rob. Some things have come up, things I have to take care of before I do anything else."

Silence. He was frowning now, I knew it, as his pencil moved rapidly across the page: the brook would overflow its banks and wash away the bridge; the playful squirrel would froth at the mouth and bite the rabbit.

"I just found out my sister had a baby," I said. "A little boy."

"Maggie? No kidding? Where is he?"

"That's the problem. I don't know. I'm doing my best to find him."

"My God, Prentice! Don't you have any idea who has him? Where he might be?"

"Yes, and I'm working on it. It's too complicated to go into over the phone right now, but I hope to hear something soon."

"Good, good. You will let me know, won't you?" Rob said. "Leave a message if I'm not here."

I noticed he didn't offer to come over and help.

Aunt Zorah arrived without notice the next morning in that ancient green trucklike machine she calls a car and announced herself with a token "you-hoo" before making herself at home.

"I'm hiding from Be-trice," she confessed, "and if you have any compassion at all, you won't let on I'm here. She's about to drive me crazy wanting to know what's going on out here, and if I've found out what happened to Faris—as if I'd tell her if I knew!" My aunt stomped into the kitchen and tossed her pocketbook on a chair. She hadn't had breakfast, she said, so the two of us sat in the kitchen and finished off the batch of waffles Augusta had stirred up earlier. Augusta disappeared upstairs. I just hoped she wouldn't decide to practice the violin again.

"These are the best waffles I ever put in my mouth," Aunt Zorah said. "You'll have to give me the recipe. And where on earth did you get that heavenly strawberry syrup? Don't tell me it came from anywhere in Liberty Bend, because I've never seen it in the stores."

Since our little town had only two grocery stores, I knew not to argue with her. And I suspected the syrup didn't come from anywhere on earth. "Made right here in this kitchen," I bragged. "Ready for another?"

She held up an empty plate. "You've certainly been hiding your culinary talents," my aunt said. "But I suppose I shouldn't be surprised. It runs in the family, you know."

I almost choked on a big gulp of coffee.

After breakfast my aunt pulled on brown rubber boots I'm sure she must've worn in high school for a tramp around the yard. "Told your mother I'd keep an eye on her azaleas," she said. "And that dwarf gardenia by the front walk oughtta be covered up if it gets down to freezing."

"If you want to walk over to the cemetery, I'll go with you," I told her. I didn't want her coming upon that grim scene alone.

But she waved me away. "Maybe later."

I gave her a couple of old sheets to cover the plants and watched from the living-room window as she puttered about the lawn.

"That's thoughtful of her," Augusta said, pulling aside the curtain to look. I didn't answer. As well read as my aunt was, she knew p-turkey squat about gardening, and I was almost sure Aunt Zorah would have been the last person my mother would ask to look after her plants, especially since she knew I was perfectly capable of doing it myself.

Later in the morning Deputy Weber called to tell me they had kept their vigil in vain the night before, but were going to try again tonight. "Just wanted to let you know in case you happened to run across one of our men—although you shouldn't if they stay out of sight the way they're supposed to. And I guess you know not to say anything about this to anyone else."

I didn't mention Aunt Zorah was there because I wasn't going to tell her. Maybe it's all those years of having to be quiet in the library, but she could out-talk a preacher at an August camp meeting. My own daddy said it of her and I know it's true.

Later that morning we did walk over to the family graveyard and I stood off by myself for a few minutes while Aunt Zorah examined her late husband's former resting place. She didn't say much, just wandered around and looked at the ground like she expected to find Faris Haskell's footprints there.

The trench on the side of the hill was still there and still empty. I had to remind myself not to say anything about the police coming back, so I got a jolt when Aunt Zorah decided we needed to fill it in. "This is an eyesore and an abomination," she said. "And if you'll get a couple of shovels, we ought to be able to fill this hole in no time."

But I finally convinced her the sheriff was still investigating and didn't want the evidence tampered with. "Actually some of his men will be watching this place tonight," I admitted.

"Thornton Bonner wouldn't know evidence if it jumped up and snatched off that silly rug he wears on his head!" my aunt snorted. But she gave in about the shovels. I can't say I wasn't relieved to see her drive away soon after we got back to the house.

Inside I found Augusta watching *Casablanca* featuring Humphrey Bogart and Ingrid Bergman on the old movie channel. She looked up misty-eyed and silently made room for me on the sofa.

"What happened to your aunt's husband—I mean before this latest unfortunate incident?" she asked after the film was over. "Were the two no longer together?"

"He was involved in some kind of crooked scheme," I told her. "Dad never would talk about it around us, but I think he embezzled a lot of money. According to Mother, Uncle Faris never would admit it, but he didn't get away with it either. If he hadn't driven his car off Poindexter Point, he would've gone to jail for a long, long time." I shrugged. "Still be there, I guess. Aunt Zorah never could forgive him."

Augusta made a little shame-shame sound. "Still, suicide is a no-win solution."

"It was either that or face Aunt Zorah," I said. "He must've thought he was taking the easy way out."

"Prentice Dobson! Shame on you!" Augusta laughed in spite of herself. "Your aunt seems a bit of a free spirit as well, or I imagine she was in her younger days."

"Mom said she was sort of a beatnik-wanna-be; you know—funky clothes, weird poetry, and all that. Of course she'd never do the least thing scandalous. My heavens!"

She nodded. "Still, she doesn't seem all that prim and proper."

"Aunt Zorah was never what you'd call prim and proper, but she follows a rigid code of ethics, and don't dare mess with her family honor! If there's an organization of descendants of *whoever*, my aunt belongs to it. Dad used to call it 'The Sons and Daughters of I Will Arise'—made Aunt Zorah spittin' mad." I laughed. Sometimes I forgot what a sense of humor my father had.

Augusta had left some of my mother's cookbooks out

on the kitchen counter, and that afternoon while she caught up on her reading, I flipped through a few and rediscovered some familiar favorites. When I was about ten, Mom taught me to prepare a simple pork chop meal with onions, rice, and canned tomatoes, along with corn bread baked in a black iron skillet. For years it was the only thing I knew how to make.

And there was no reason I couldn't make it now. I found pork chops in the freezer, a canister of cornmeal in the refrigerator, and the other ingredients in the pantry. I smiled, remembering how my mother greased the skillet and heated it before pouring in the corn bread batter. "Now be careful, honey, it's hot! Don't let it spatter and burn you." And after a few tries, she claimed my corn bread was every bit as good as hers. I stood on tiptoe to reach the blue striped bowl Mom always used to mix corn bread, found the old tin measuring cup and spoons we'd played with as babies. I almost sensed my mother beside me saying, "Go easy now. Don't get heavy-handed with the salt." And even though she wasn't here at Smokerise, a little part of her remained.

For dessert I made a pudding cake Mom always called "lemon mystery," and it tasted every bit as good as I remembered.

"I believe being here brings out your domestic side," Augusta said after her second helping of dessert. "No wonder you don't want to sell Smokerise. It's beautiful here, Prentice. Have you considered staying?"

"What would I do with it? I can't commute from here. And then there's Joey. I have to think of him."

She frowned. "What about Joey? Have you considered who's going to raise him? You? Your mom? And don't forget the other side of the family. I assume he has other grandparents too."

"Whose side are you on? Believe me, I don't need reminding! I'm sure it was Sonny's father, Pershing Gaines, who tried to follow us home from Ruby."

I tried to picture Sonny's father's face, although I'd never seen it, and I always came up with somebody with bad teeth and a beard who probably carried a club to keep defenseless females in line.

"The weatherman mentioned the S word tonight," I said as we cleared the table after supper. "This time I hope he's wrong."

"The S word?"

"*Snow.* They think there's a chance of snow. Can you believe it after that great weather we've been having? I feel sorry for whoever has the duty out there tonight."

I automatically checked our supply of milk and bread, which is what most Georgians do anytime there's a hint of bad winter weather. Then we all rush out and strip the grocery stores of about a month's supply of perishables, even though the snow rarely stays on the ground for more than a day or two. This time, though, it looked as if we had enough food to get us through.

I tried not to think of Deputy Weber or whoever was crouched out on that cold muddy hillside. After a relatively moderate morning, the temperature had inched downward throughout the afternoon, and it was supposed to drop below freezing by morning. If the person who dug that grave meant to bury somebody tonight, they'd have to move fast before the ground froze.

Later, at Augusta's suggestion, I picked up Dad's old fiddle and played around with some of his favorite square dance tunes: "Turkey in the Straw," "Skip to My Lou," and the one I always liked best, "Ol' Dan Tucker." The fingering came back to me bit by bit, and I could almost hear Dad's voice encouraging me. "Let the fiddle know you love it, honey. Snuggle it under your chin, stroke it tenderly, and it will love you back." I closed my eyes, and the polished smoothness of the instrument against my cheek gave me a few minutes of something close to peace.

It didn't last. Not long after midnight Augusta woke me from a sound sleep to tell me she'd looked out the bedroom window to see somebody moving around our barn lot with a light.

CHAPTER ELEVEN

I sat up dazed. "What kind of light?"

"Flashlight I guess. Like a torch, moved around a lot. I wouldn't have noticed it, but I thought I heard something out there and went to the window." Augusta stood in my bedroom doorway wrapped in an enormous blue plaid robe of my father's she'd found in the closet. The dim lamp in the upstairs hallway cast a halfhearted light on her sock-clad feet. "You don't want to miss this! Hurry, you'll see what I mean," she urged in a loud whisper.

I yawned, scrambling for my shoes in the dark. I wouldn't be the least bit upset if I did miss it, but sleep was impossible now. "What time is it? Seems like I just got to bed."

"Almost two." Augusta crept across the hall looking kind of like a cartoon cat sneaking up on a cartoon canary. Of course I laughed.

"What's so funny? Will you be quiet? And for heaven's sake, keep down. Do you want them to see you?"

"Good grief, lighten up! It's probably one of the sheriff's men. They're supposed to be out there tonight. Remember?"

"But aren't they watching behind that far hill, on the other side of the cemetery?" She knelt by the window. "Look, there it is again. See . . . just beyond the barn."

For a fraction of a second a faint light wavered, hardly longer than a firefly's glimmer, only there aren't any fireflies in February.

"What in the world do you think they're looking for?" Augusta crouched beside me even though whoever was out there wouldn't be able to see her. She smelled like sheets dried in the sun.

"Don't know. Maybe it's Uncle Faris hunting for his coffin." I crawled away from the light and edged into the hall.

"That's not funny, Prentice . . . Prentice, where are you going?"

"To call the sheriff. Maybe somebody can tell us if that's his man out there or one of the creeps who killed that woman and made off with Uncle Faris."

But the dispatcher who took my call said she would have to get back to me on that.

"How soon will that be?" I asked. "Because if it isn't one of them, somebody's prowling around our barn who isn't supposed to be there."

"What'd they say?" Augusta asked from across the room.

"That she'd get the message to them as soon as she could, and for me to keep my doors locked." I found myself whispering too. "Can you see anything else?"

"Snow. At least I think it's snow . . . it is! Prentice, look! It's beginning to *snow*. How lovely!" Suddenly Augusta sobered. "Except that it reminds me of that awful winter at Valley Forge."

"Valley Forge? You were *there*? With Washington?"

She nodded solemnly. "For a while. They got across the river, didn't they? Why do you think I don't like the cold?"

I tiptoed clumsily to the window. I couldn't see anyone moving around, but as we watched, snowflakes, sparse at first, began falling thicker, swirling in the back porch light.

Augusta and I padded downstairs in the dark and I put on the kettle for tea. Thank goodness Mom was a creature of habit and the canister sat in its usual place on the countertop, the mugs on the shelf above it.

The phone rang as we sipped our hot drinks in the darkened sitting room, our hands cupped around the familiar brown mugs for warmth. The light we saw was *not* one of the sheriff's men, the dispatcher told me. Sergeant Sloan and another policeman were on their way to check it out, and I was to keep the house dark and remain inside. *Not a problem here*, I thought.

"We'll do our best to keep you informed as soon as

we know anything," she said. "And the sergeant says not to answer the door unless you're sure it's one of them."

"That's comforting," I said, relating this to Augusta. She balled into a blue plaid wad and rolled herself cocoonlike in my grandmother's afghan. I wrapped a scratchy blanket that smelled of mothballs about me and snuggled in Dad's big chair. I wished we could have a fire, but that would give off too much light.

About an hour later, Sergeant Sloan knocked at the back door to tell us they had found tracks in the barn lot and followed them partway to the road before they were obliterated by snow.

Cottony blobs fell silently around us shrouding the landscape in a cold, soft cloak. The policemen's boots were caked with clumps of muddy snow, and even their shoulders wore epaulets of frosty white.

I shivered in the doorway as the two men stood on the porch stamping their feet, their faces red from the cold. "You must be freezing . . . come in and get warm," I said. "I'm sure you could use some coffee."

But they didn't want to track up the floor, they said, and besides, they had to get back to file a report. I noticed by the kitchen clock that it was almost five. After a night of tramping around in the cold and slush, I'd imagine the two would be ready for a hot shower and a big breakfast.

"Somebody will be out when it's lighter to see if we can track this fellow down," the sergeant said. He slapped his gloved hands together and showered me with crystals of snow. "I doubt if he'll be back, but be sure and keep your doors locked."

"Do you think it could be Jasper Totherow?" I asked.

"Could be, but I can't imagine what in tarnation he's looking for."

I couldn't either. My uncle's coffin had been in the shed until it was hauled to the county barn. Had there been something valuable in the coffin that Jasper—or someone else—knew about? And if so, how did it get there? Faris Haskell was supposed to have embezzled a lot of money before he died. I had always heard you can't take it with you; maybe Uncle Faris was the exception.

Sheriff Bonner came out later that morning to tell me that "at this point in time" they hadn't been able to locate the trespasser who'd been waving around a flashlight in our barn lot. "But we did find tire tracks just off the main road," he added. "Looks like he must've parked there and walked to your place, or else somebody was waiting for him there."

"Great. Now they think there could be two of them," I said after the sheriff left.

"What about your friend in Atlanta?" Augusta suggested during lunch. "Do you think you might feel safer there for a while?"

"Probably, but I'm still hoping I'll hear from Ola Cress. I'd better hang around here for a while at least."

"And what if you don't hear?"

"Then I'll have to report Joey missing and call in

the police, but that would give that rotten Pershing Gaines an equal claim."

Augusta crumbled crackers into her tomato soup. "And the young man in England? I don't suppose you've spoken with him."

"Then you suppose wrong. Are all angels this nosy? As a matter of fact, we had a long talk just the other day."

"And?"

"And what? We talked, that's all. *Miss you . . . how are you . . .* that kind of thing. He said my friend Dottie had told him about Maggie."

She nodded. "I imagine he's hurt that you didn't let him know."

"We don't always follow the rule book at times like that," I said.

"So what now?"

I shrugged. "What do you mean?"

"I mean, do you care about this man? Because if you don't, I don't think you should rope him along."

I thought about that for a minute, then laughed. "You mean *string* him along! You sound like Dottie."

"He isn't going to wait forever," my friend had told me during our last conversation together. "I guess you'll just have to decide whether or not you really give a damn."

"Well, thank you, Rhett," I had replied. I couldn't say more because just then I was too confused to think. I still was.

The temperature hovered around freezing and snow

124

still covered the ground that afternoon. I braved the cold long enough to bring in wood for a fire, then popped corn and ate it in front of the cheery blaze while I tried to get interested in the latest best-seller. But the fire was the only thing that was cheery, and I couldn't concentrate on the book.

Would the person who had been roaming around out there come back tonight? If he did, he'd be in danger of breaking a leg on the icy crust of snow—and it would serve him right! I couldn't imagine anyone being fool enough to try, still I made sure the doors were double locked and drew the curtains across the sitting-room windows so I wouldn't be on display. Now and then I took a quick peek at the white expanse of snow and watched the gray-blue dusk seep gradually across it until everything glowed with an eerie light. And I thought of the day when Maggie and I, half-sick from winter colds, had sneaked outside to gather a dishpan full of forbidden snow while Mom was upstairs sewing. Later she tracked us down in the kitchen where we were attempting to make snow ice cream with milk, sugar, and vanilla. I was inspired to dribble in about half a bottle of green food coloring that spattered the countertop, floor, *and* our clothing, so our efforts didn't remain a secret long.

"Now you've done it!" Maggie fumed at me. "Mama told us not to go outside and you've gone and dyed the whole kitchen green. She's gonna kill us!" But our mother only laughed and shook her head. "If I didn't know better I'd think I was in Oz!" she said, and even helped us save some of our ghastly concoction in the freezer where it stayed until we threw it out to make room for peaches the following summer.

But she never knew what happened to her china girl with the kitten.

Poor Mom! For weeks, even months after it disappeared, she fretted over the missing figurine, and even as recently as the summer Maggie went away, wondered aloud what had become of it.

"I've always kind of suspected your sister broke my little porcelain girl. The one with the kitten, remember?" Mom sat at her piano aimlessly walking her fingers up and down the keys. Maggie had been gone less than a month, and neither Mom nor I had stopped hoping she'd come home. It was late afternoon, usually the time we started preparations for supper and Dad was soon due in from the fields, but my mother showed no inclination to do anything about it. I recognized fragments of a tune: "My Darling Clementine." It was the only song my sister ever learned to play and she almost drove us crazy with it.

I shrugged. "Why do you think that?" I asked as she repeated the tune.

"She looked guilty every time I mentioned it," Mom said. "Maggie never was a very good liar." Suddenly she brought her hands down with a discordant crash, dropped her head, and cried, "Oh, Prentice, why doesn't she come home?"

I stood behind my mother and encircled her in my arms. My tears slipped into her hair as I bent to kiss her. "Just give her time," I said. "You know Maggie, Mama. She'll probably turn up when you least expect her."

I lied, of course. Maggie wasn't coming home until our father made amends, but Joseph Winston Dobson wasn't going to welcome home his wayward daughter. He was too damn stubborn! I think Mom knew this as well as I did, but neither of us wanted to admit it.

I also knew what had happened to the china figurine. Maggie was about seven and I was thirteen when we knocked it off the console table playing at "Peter Pan" in the living room, and both of us were horrified at what we'd done.

The porcelain girl with the kitten had been a gift to our mother from her first piano teacher, the one who had encouraged her, and it was one of Mom's most cherished possessions. Even today I can remember watching helplessly as the figurine crashed to the floor and broke into two jagged pieces.

Immediately my little sister started to howl. "Look what we've done! Mama's gonna kill us! Prentice, what are we going to do?"

"Hush now," I told her, scooping up the pieces. "Maybe we can glue it back together so she won't notice. Hurry! Help me find the glue before Mom gets back from the store." We had been warned about running in the living room, but I had been reading the story to Maggie, and today, caught up in the thrill of the tale, my little sister "flew" too close to the table.

But the glue wouldn't hold no matter how much we

applied, and when we heard Mom's car in the driveway, I guessed how a deer must feel when caught in the headlights.

"Ohmygosh, here she comes! What'll we do with it?" Maggie wiped gooey fingers on her shirt.

"We'll have to hide it," I said. "Let's hope she won't realize it's gone—for a while anyway." Maybe by that time I could think of an excuse.

"But where?" Maggie's lower lip started to tremble. "Prentice, you won't tell, will you?"

"I'm not gonna tell . . . hurry now, help me clean up this mess and wash your hands." My sister had been the one who crashed into the table and made the china figurine totter and fall, but she wouldn't have been running in such a blind panic if I hadn't been close on her heels, "tick-tocking" like the dreaded crocodile that swallowed the clock.

"Promise?" Maggie stared at the broken halves of what once had been a pink-cheeked child holding a gray kitten. The kitten was forever batting at a ball of blue china yarn. It wouldn't bat it anymore.

"I promise," I said, hastily sponging off the countertop. "Tell you what, let's each keep a half. It will be a token of our pledge to each other—just like couples exchange rings when they get married."

Maggie almost smiled. "Really?"

"Really. Only this means we promise to be loyal as sisters." I snatched a couple of plastic grocery bags from the pantry and wrapped a broken half in each, then gave one to my sister. "Careful now, don't cut yourself.

Put it in a place Mom would never think to look, and I'll do the same with mine. But we'll have to hide them somewhere really good." From the kitchen window, I saw our mother, arms filled with groceries, approaching the house. The two of us fled upstairs.

"If she asks, just say you don't know anything about it," I warned breathlessly, "and I'll do the same. It will be our secret."

She turned to me at the top of the stairs. "We'll keep them always and never, never tell?"

"Always," I said.

I stuffed my half of the evidence inside a sock, then tucked it away in a lunch box I'd had since grade school. It was still there.

I never knew what Maggie did with hers.

When the phone rang, it startled me so I must have jumped because Noodles sprang yowling from my lap.

"Anything happening out there?" Aunt Zorah wanted to know.

Good. She hadn't yet heard about last night's excitement, and I didn't mean to tell her. As town librarian, if Aunt Zorah didn't know about something, it hadn't happened yet, and apparently the news hadn't made the rounds.

"Did Bumbling Bonner bring justice to Liberty Bend?" I heard my aunt's beaded earrings rattling against the receiver when she laughed.

"Too cold," I said, keeping my tone light. "Guess the snow kept our ghoulish vandals away."

"So nobody showed up, huh?" I could tell she was making an effort not to sound interested.

"If he did, they didn't see him." At least that part was true.

"I reckon you're better off staying there than trying to drive on these slick roads," she said. "They closed the library today, and I doubt if we'll be open tomorrow either. You okay for milk and bread?"

I assured my aunt I was fine and hoped she was the same. "Don't go out unless you absolutely have to," I said. "There's ice everywhere." I hoped the library would stay closed for a few more days so there would be less chance for her to hear what else had been going on at Smokerise.

I was putting another log on the fire a few minutes later when the telephone rang again. Aunt Zorah had probably forgotten to tell me something, I thought as I watched red sparks fly up the chimney.

But it wasn't Aunt Zorah.

"Is this the Dobson place?" a man's voice asked.

"Who's calling please?"

"I'm trying to locate the Dobsons in Liberty Bend. *Who is this?*"

"I'm sorry, I don't believe I got your name," I said. And then the line went dead.

Awareness flared like a cold flame inside me and I slammed down the receiver as if it had been scorching hot. I had a nasty feeling I had just been talking to Pershing Gaines.

What would I say if he called back? And where was he? If he knew my phone number, then chances were he also knew where I lived.

Within three minutes I had turned on every light in the house, plus the radio in Mom's room and the television downstairs. Pershing Gaines mustn't know I was here alone.

I was sitting at the foot of the stairs with my chin on my chest thinking it couldn't get any worse than this when all the lights went out.

"Oh, hell!" I said.

"Oh, Prentice!" Augusta echoed. "Is that a mature and responsible solution to your problems?"

"Don't talk to me about being responsible," I said. "Just what were you doing while somebody dug up Uncle Faris and put that woman in his place? Where were you when that fool with a flashlight prowled about our property in the middle of the night? What kind of angel are you, anyway?"

"Prentice dear, surely you must know I'm always close by."

"Well, that's just great, but can't you do anything about *anything*?"

She looked at me sadly. "I think you forget. I'm a guardian angel, not a bodyguard. I can only advise, help you to work things out for yourself," Augusta reminded me. "And right now I advise you to look around for a flashlight or maybe a few candles, and it wouldn't hurt to add some wood to that fire. I believe this house is getting cold already." And although she tried not to show it, I detected a slight angelic shiver.

How could she possibly be cold? Augusta had traded her bathrobe for a long skirt of shimmery violet that contained enough material to make curtains for Buckingham Palace. Her silvery blouse was as soft as clouds with billowing sleeves and violet-lined hood.

For supper, Augusta and I ate scrambled eggs and toast by candlelight in front of the fire and I couldn't help but think how nice it would be if Rob were there instead. At least I supposed it was Rob. I hadn't seen him in so long, whenever I tried to picture his face, he looked a lot like Harrison Ford in 1930s archaeological attire—but without the bullwhip.

Augusta looked at me and smiled. "That ocean's not as big as it used to be," she said. "He could be here by tomorrow."

"I know, but right now I think I need you more." I hoped Rob would wait, but at the present I had more urgent problems.

When the telephone rang again, I didn't answer.

CHAPTER TWELVE

Ma'am, do you recognize this hat?" Deputy Weber stood on our back porch in a puddle of melting snow holding a soggy, mud-caked cap that on closer inspection appeared to have once been purple.

I shook my head. My dad would have rather been chased barefoot through a briar patch by a swarm of yellow jackets than wear a thing like that. "If I knew whose it was, I'd be embarrassed to admit it," I said, smiling. I felt much better since the power had come on during the night, and Augusta rose early to bake her apple cinnamon loaf that now smelled good enough to entice a lame man to walk. It enticed Deputy Weber.

"Somebody's been baking mighty early," he said with a couple of gentlemanly sniffs.

"And it's still hot, and so's the coffee. I was just

about to have some." I held open the door. "Come in and join me."

He held the dripping cap away from him, then laid it carefully on the doormat. "Well, thank you, I believe I will."

The temperature had been rising since daybreak and only patches of snow remained, leaving a gooey landscape of mud. As the deputy wiped his feet, I looked again at the dirty purple hat. It had earflaps.

"Suzie Wright," I said.

"What about her?" The policeman looked up as I filled his coffee cup.

"She saw a man wearing a hat like this walking near our property the other day, and he ran into the woods when he saw her coming." I cut a thick slice of the loaf and set it in front of him. "I reported it, remember? You said you'd picked up a vagrant near here and put him on the bus to Atlanta. Do you think that cap might have been his?"

He frowned. "I doubt it. Somebody would've noticed it before now. We found this hanging from a bush between here and the road like it had been snagged when somebody tried to duck underneath. Too dark to see it last night, but it waved at me like a flag this morning."

I watched the deputy's face as he took a bite of the apple loaf, then followed it with deep swallows of coffee. His eyes were closed and his mouth had that same slaphappy expression most men get only after watching a weekend of continuous football. If Augusta could market her recipes, they would probably be illegal, I thought.

"I'll try to catch Suzie back at the post office," he said after seconds all around. "Maybe she can tell me if this is the cap she saw."

How many men actually go out in public wearing purple hats with earflaps? And what was this one doing hanging around our property?

"Maybe one of Sonny Gaines's clan," I suggested to Augusta after the deputy left with a third piece of cinnamon loaf swaddled in a napkin. (For his *partner*, he *said*.) "Probably one of his brothers. Wonder how many there are?" I pictured a slovenly line of them—kind of like the seven dwarfs, only much bigger, all wearing ragged overalls and carrying shotguns. " 'Purple Hat' was probably assigned to 'case the joint' and see if we had Joey—which should mean *they don't*."

"I wouldn't be too sure, Prentice," Augusta said. She sat at the foot of the stairs with her frothy skirt spread about her and examined the notebook she carried in her bottomless tapestry bag. "It might turn out that this man has no connection with the Gaines family. I wouldn't put all my chickens in one sack if I were you."

I smiled. "You mean eggs in one basket?"

"That either." Augusta looked briefly at me with her calm-sea eyes, then turned to a fresh page in her notebook. "Do you suppose your sister might have mentioned Ola Cress to your mother, perhaps in a card or a letter?"

"I don't think so. She didn't write much, and she had only been living there a few months before she was killed. We didn't even know how to find her when Dad died."

"Still, we might be overlooking some clue—maybe something in your sister's things that came in the mail. Do you mind if I have another look?"

"Of course not, but you were there when I opened the package. There isn't anything else to see."

I hovered close as Augusta combed almost reverently through the pitiful remnants of Maggie's life, hoping she would find something I had missed. Perhaps a business card, an address, or a book of matches that had slipped behind the lining of the handbag would lead us to Ola Cress's frequent hangouts and ultimately to Joey. That was the way it happened in books, and after all, Augusta *was* an angel. Surely she must have some sort of heavenly radar to put us on the right path to finding my sister's baby. But it didn't take long to learn there really wasn't anything to discover, and I think Augusta was even more disappointed than I was.

I carefully rebundled the things that had belonged to my sister and tucked them into a dresser drawer in what had been Maggie's room, concealing them under a tissue-wrapped parcel so my mother wouldn't see them.

"What's that?" Augusta wanted to know, indicating the package swathed in crinkly white paper. Her eyes glowed with anticipation. "Is it something that belonged to Maggie?"

"I doubt it," I said. "After Maggie left, Dad gave most of her clothes to charity. Mom used this chest of drawers for storage mostly, although she did keep some of my sister's things from childhood. It might be something Maggie wore in a ballet recital or her flag girl uniform from the year she stuck it out with the junior high band." It seemed as if Mom was forever sewing things for Maggie to wear only once or twice.

I shrugged. "It won't hurt to look," I said to Augusta, aware that she was fairly ready to explode with curiosity.

It took me a minute or two to recognize the sheer white dress trimmed in scallops of lace that Augusta held before me. Tiny pearl buttons strung together by nylon thread cascaded in loops and swirls from bodice and waist. A dainty tiara was covered in more of the same.

"My goodness," Augusta said. I had never known her to be at a loss for words. "My goodness," she said again.

I giggled. "I can see you haven't a clue as to what this is," I said.

If Augusta Goodnight had wings, she would've fluttered them in vexation. She was annoyed, I could tell. Only slightly, but still annoyed. "Well . . ." she said.

"Mom made it for me when I was in the second grade," I explained. "I played the Tooth Fairy. See all the little buttons? They're supposed to be teeth. See, the Tooth Fairy collects them."

"I see," Augusta said. But I could see she didn't. "It

must've taken your mother hours to do all this. It's really a work of art."

I remembered only slightly my mother's labors over the frilly dress. I was seven. What did I care? But I did remember the pride I felt in wearing it, and in bravely speaking my small part on a stage that seemed bigger than the whole state of Georgia.

My best friend, Bunny Feldman, had sulked for a week because she had to be a tube of toothpaste and wear a bulky cardboard box. I smiled.

"What is it?" Augusta wanted to know. "What's so funny?"

"Nothing," I lied, and smiled again.

"We're almost out of milk," I said to Augusta that afternoon. "If I don't hear from Ola Cress soon, I'm going to have to run some errands and risk missing her call. Besides," I added, "I'm running out of things to do."

"You might give me a violin lesson," she suggested. "Or you *could* start updating your . . . what is it you call that thing you need to apply for a job?"

"Résumé," I said. "You're right. I've put that off far too long."

I had been at my computer for less than an hour when Ola Cress phoned.

She spoke scarcely above a whisper and I found myself almost shimmying through the phone lines to hear her. "Mr. Humphreys gave me your number," she began. "I understand you spoke with him recently."

"Yes," I said. "You received my letter then?"

She made some sort of sound that I took to be affirmative.

"Maggie Dobson was my sister," I said. *And I want my nephew back! I want him back now! Don't you dare play games with me, you batty old woman!*

I am not by nature a patient person, and I had to mentally gag myself to keep from demanding news of Joey, where he was, how he was, and, for God's sake . . . when did she intend to let me see him. *Careful, Prentice. Tread lightly. She hung up on you the last time, remember?* My breathing dragged as if there were no room in me for air, and my mouth tasted like it had a sock stuffed in it as I waited for her to speak.

And then I felt Augusta's cool touch on my shoulder and remembered to think *blue.*

"Maggie was the only sister I had," I said calmly. "My mother and I are devastated at losing her. There's been an estrangement between Maggie and my parents since she left several years ago, and I imagine you were the closest person to family she had. I want to thank you for that, and for your kindness to my sister."

"Oh." I heard a quick intake of breath on the other end of the line. At least she was alive. "Maggie was . . . I was fond of your sister," Ola Cress said. "Any real happiness I've had was because of Maggie and that sweet baby, and I'll live the rest of my life regretting how she died."

I could tell in the silence that followed the woman was obviously struggling for composure. "If I could go back and change what happened that day, it would be me in that car," she announced. "I should be the one who was killed by that train!"

"Why do you say that? Sonny Gaines was driving, wasn't he? Surely you weren't there!"

"I should've kept him away from her. I tried, but it wasn't enough. I'm sorry, so sorry . . ."

A baby cried in the background, and I knew it wasn't just any baby. It was my nephew, my mother's first grandchild, my sister's own little boy. "That's Joey, isn't it?" I whispered.

"Yes. He's rolling over now, but he hasn't figured out how to get back on his tummy again." There was pride in her voice. "Aggravates him something fierce . . . here, sweetie, Aunt Ola's coming."

"I'd love to see him," I said. "Do you think we might arrange a—"

"Look, I know I have no right to Joey, but it seemed my only choice at the time. I suppose you know about Sonny's father?"

"I've heard," I said. "Does he have any idea where you are?"

"I don't think so; not yet, anyway, but I've had to stay a jump ahead. He has friends, family. You can't trust anybody." Her voice trembled. "I'd rather die than let that man have this baby."

"My goodness, let's hope it won't come to that!" I tried to lighten things up a little, but Ola Cress sounded almost beyond comforting, and that scared me even more. "Could we meet somewhere? Wherever it's convenient for you." *Scrub your floors, mow your lawn, peel you a grape . . . ?*

"Are you sure those people aren't watching you?" Ola Cress asked.

"What people?"

"Sonny Gaines's family. Wouldn't put it past them to follow you, and that wouldn't do. That wouldn't do at all."

I couldn't think of an answer to that because I didn't know one. We would have to meet in some place with a lot of people around, a place that would be confusing to a man like Pershing Gaines.

"I think I have an idea," I said. "Do you like to shop?"

Now all I had to worry about was getting there without one of the Gaines clan on my trail.

CHAPTER THIRTEEN

W here's this place we're going?" Augusta wanted to know. The weather had turned springlike again and she had shed her multi-layers of fabric for a little green belted job with a swirly skirt. Now she topped her glowing locks with a crocheted raffia hat that could only be called "pert" and gave Noodles a good-bye nuzzle before gliding into the front seat beside me.

"Fawn Park Mall. Ola says it's a big new shopping complex this side of Chattanooga. She wants us to meet her there at the fountain."

"Fawn Park? Will there be deer?" Augusta blew Noodles a fleeting kiss as the cat, sprawled in what was left of my mother's pansy bed, watched us drive away.

"It's just a fancy name," I explained. "I doubt if

there've been deer around in years. Ola said to wait for her by the fountain near the concessions area. If she doesn't show up by one o'clock, I'm to call Tisdale Humphreys about an alternative meeting place."

Augusta gave an angelic snort. "For goodness sakes, why go to that extent? Couldn't the woman just tell *you* her second choice of a place to meet?"

"It's all very mysterious. Ola Cress teeters between eccentric and just plain nutty, and she's scared to death of Pershing Gaines. I'd call her neurotic if I weren't so afraid of him too. I'm almost sure he's the man who phoned the other night, and he might've been prowling around our property. Remember that purple hat the deputy found? Suzie Wright said it looked like the one that man was wearing the other day—the one who ran off into the woods."

"And you think it was Pershing Gaines?" Augusta glanced behind us as if she thought he might be on our bumper already.

"I don't know," I said. "I just know I feel threatened by him. Heck, I feel threatened by just about everybody—especially since that dead woman turned up in our shed. I can understand why Ola Cress isn't taking any chances."

"How long will it take us to drive there?"

"Less than two hours probably, if we don't hit any major traffic snags."

She pulled needles and embroidery thread from her huge tapestry bag and began stitching on something that looked like a pastoral scene. Her fingers, like hummingbird wings, moved almost too quickly to see. "And how will you know her?" she asked.

"Know her? Well, I . . . I guess I hadn't thought of that." I had no idea what Ola Cress looked like, had never even seen a picture of her. "I'll just have to hope she recognizes me," I said. "I haven't changed *that* much since the snapshot was made." The photo of Maggie and me I had mailed to Ola had been taken several years earlier. "And I imagine she'll have little Joey with her," I added. My heart leapfrogged at the prospect. I could hardly wait to see him!

But I did wait. And wait. While Augusta window-shopped, I sat on a bench by the fountain and watched the water splash, widen into circles and disappear. Toddlers threw coins into the sparkling blue basin, mothers pushed strollers about. Babies laughed and cooed and cried, but none of them was Joey.

Joey would be about seven months old, and from his earlier picture, round-faced and fair. He wouldn't know me, but I would know him. Some inherent instinct would tell me he was ours and I would love him immediately.

For about the tenth time I looked at my watch. Almost half an hour had passed. If no one approached me within the next fifteen minutes, I would telephone Tisdale Humphreys.

I found myself examining the face of almost every baby who might be Joey's age. Too old, too young, too dark, too slender . . . uh-oh . . . dressed in pink frills, obviously a girl. I noticed a father or two, but usually the babies were accompanied by mothers, grandmothers, or sometimes both. I smiled, thinking how much fun it would be for Mom and me to go on an outing with Joey, of all the things we'd do, and when the woman suddenly sat beside me on the bench, it jarred me into reality.

"You must be Prentice Dobson." She was not at all what I expected. Why, Ola Cress was pretty, and much younger than I'd thought. Surely not more than fifty! She wore her straight dark hair, streaked with gray, in a stylish cut that accented high cheekbones. A bright scarf, splashed with sunflowers, embellished her buttercup-yellow pants suit. Jaunty porcelain daffodils dangled from her ears.

I started to rise, then looked about. She hadn't brought the child. Of course she wouldn't—couldn't take the chance. One of us might be followed. "Could we go somewhere?" I said. "I think we need to talk."

The woman smiled. "I'm so glad you see it that way." She nodded in the direction of the concessions area. "If you'll grab us a table, I'll get a couple of coffees, okay?"

I nodded numbly and followed.

"How is he?" I asked as she sat across from me, steaming cups in hand. I could wait no longer. "Is he happy? Healthy?"

The woman tore open an envelope of artificial

sweetener and sprinkled it into her cup a few grains at a time. "You're asking me?" She stirred it before looking up at me.

"Well, yes. Who else would know? He is all right, isn't he?"

I never knew fear could hurt, but when she didn't answer, my entire body ached and I thought I was going to be sick right there. "Joey," I said. "Where is he now?"

She stiffened and leaned forward, clasping her hands on the table in front of her. "I believe we need to get some things straight," she said. I noticed her well-manicured nails polished with a slight pink gloss, her emerald-cut diamond that probably cost as much or more than my car.

This woman was not Ola Cress.

There was one quick way to know for sure. "I was beginning to think you weren't going to show." I spoke softly, remembering to breathe slowly and think *blue*. "I was almost ready to phone our mutual friend."

Her eyes narrowed. "Our mutual friend?"

"The person we agreed upon earlier," I said. "You know."

Her silence answered me. She didn't know. "Who are you?" I started to rise; coffee spilled onto my wrist, the front of my blouse.

"I thought you knew. My nephew said . . . I assumed he'd been in touch, and you didn't seem surprised to see me." The woman held out a hand, palm down, as if to delay my leaving. "I'm Sonny's aunt, Julia—"

146

"How did you know where to find me?" I pretended not to notice her hand.

I didn't wait for an answer, but turned and walked out quickly, losing myself in the crowded mall. Sonny Gaines's aunt had followed me here.

Thank heavens Augusta waited in the car. I didn't have time to look for her now. "You heard?" I said, and she nodded. "We have to get out of here before she can follow, then find a telephone fast."

We zigzagged through a maze of streets before we felt at ease enough to phone Tisdale Humphreys from an out-of-the-way pizza restaurant. He was waiting for my call.

"What took you so long?" he wanted to know. "Ola phoned more than an hour ago, said she was sure she was being followed."

"There must be more than one of them," I said, and told him about Sonny's aunt. "Probably a whole clan of them—human bloodhounds!" I shuddered at the notion and glanced at my watch. "We still have time to meet. Did Ola mention another place?"

"I wrote down the address. Cousin of hers, I think. Just a minute, I know it's somewhere on this desk . . ."

While waiting, I read the messages scribbled on the wall by the phone and hoped my straitlaced angel wasn't looking over my shoulder. It was much too warm in the restaurant, and the floor needed a thorough scrubbing. I looked at my watch again. Had our friend Mr. Humphreys forgotten all about me?

"Sorry! Place is a shambles here. I'm having the up-stairs hall repapered and you know what a mess that is!"

I didn't know and didn't much care, but he was such a good sport I pretended to sympathize. The address he gave me was in a nearby town of Jasper. "Won't take long to get there," my friend assured me. "Ola says it's small, so you shouldn't have much trouble finding the house."

But we weren't counting on the afternoon traffic and it was later than I anticipated when we finally crossed into the city limits of Jasper, Tennessee. Ola's cousin, Lydia Bosworth, lived on the corner of Willow Trail and Academy in what Ola remembered as a small yellow cottage with a big stone chimney. I found the house with the big stone chimney, but now it was painted white. Obviously it had been a while since Ola's last visit.

I didn't realize how long until I rang the doorbell and asked for Lydia Bosworth.

"Who?" The frowning child who answered the door looked to be about ten and I could see that I was interrupting her dinner.

"Lydia Bosworth. I was told I could find her here. Maybe your mother could help me," I suggested.

The girl shrugged. "Mom!" she yelled, revealing a mouthful of partly chewed sandwich. "You know any-body named Lydia—who'd you say?"

"Bosworth." I smiled at the child's mother who hur-ried from the back of the house.

"Lydia Bosworth? My goodness, I'm afraid she died a

couple of years ago. We bought this house from her estate." The woman reached out to touch my arm. "I'm really sorry. I hope this isn't too much of a shock."

I shook my head and mumbled thanks, then walked numbly back to the street. What was I to do now? Was Ola Cress playing cruel games with me?

And then as if the scene were being orchestrated from above, I heard the threatening rumble of thunder and looked up to see dark clouds gathering. And I sat on what used to be Ola's cousin Lydia's cold stone steps and cried.

A raindrop splashed on my nose and somebody started blowing a car horn nearby. Couldn't Augusta see I was upset? What was the matter with her? I darted a nasty look in the direction of my car, but Augusta sat patiently in the passenger seat working on her needlepoint.

"Over here!" A skinny white arm waved to me from the window of a car parked across the street and the horn beeped timidly once again. "You are Prentice Dobson, aren't you? Sorry about the mix-up. It's been a long time since I was here."

Oh, God, I thought, *this time please let it be Ola Cress!*

Chapter Fourteen

*S*he appeared to be in her sixties, maybe older, and I guessed that ill health, hard work, and probably something more had contributed to her drawn, troubled look. Life had offered no free lunches to Ola Cress.

The threatening storm had hastened nightfall and it was difficult to see well in the gloom, but the woman seemed harmless enough. Her hair, spiderweb gray, was pulled into a bun at the back, and the light from a passing car glinted off her bifocals.

"I'm afraid we're in for a storm," she said as I drew nearer. "Better climb in before you get drenched." And then she saw my face in the light of the open car door, and her expression stirred a memory. It was like that of a mother searching for a child in a crowd. I had seen it in my own mother's face from the window of a bus or at the airport gate on returning from camp or college. But Ola was clearly unfulfilled when she saw me. "You're not very like your sister, but I can tell you're kin," she said.

Then I heard a sweet murmur from the seat behind her and saw the sleeping child. He was in a child restraint seat, as he should be, of course. I hadn't thought of that, but even in the darkness I could see he was a Dobson. My sister's own child. Joey.

I reached out to him, spoke his name, swallowing my tears. If I cried it might frighten him.

"Shh! He's sleeping. Don't wake him." Ola glanced back at the little boy with such love and pride on her face, I realized Pershing Gaines might not be my fiercest opponent. "He's just getting over a cold, and he didn't take much of a nap." And then her voice softened as if she realized she might be treading on sensitive ground. "You know, I believe he looks a bit like you."

I closed the door behind me and sat in the darkened car with no sound but that of the rising wind and the rain thudding on the roof. I was really here within touching distance of my own flesh and blood! Maggie's baby. Finally. I had to let the reality sink in.

"Looks like March will be coming in like a lion," Ola said, breaking the silence. I could see she was struggling, just as I was, about how to approach the subject of Joey's future. "I hope that wasn't too much of a shock to you finding my cousin had died," she added with a nod toward the house across the street. "Believe me, I didn't know. She was one of those people you just assume will live forever, and I thought of meeting here as sort of a last resort. When I called to let her know we were coming, I learned that number was no longer in service. You can imagine my distress when I called my brother and he told me the poor soul had died!"

"I'll have to admit, it did shake me up," I said. "I'm sorry about your cousin."

"I shouldn't have been surprised. She was well into her eighties. I'm just sorry I didn't keep in touch. Life is all too brief and it surprises us around every turn . . . but then I think you know that."

The baby stirred before I could reply and Ola reached back and tucked a blanket around him. "He should be in bed. I've a room—a small suite really— in a little place not far from here. Could you follow me? Do you mind? We could talk there."

And you could lose me in the traffic and lead me up another blind alley. I looked back at Joey, his tiny fingers curled in a fist beneath his chin. We couldn't sit here all night. I would have to trust this woman. But I would follow so closely she'd think she had a Siamese twin!

"Don't worry. I'll drive slowly so you can follow," Ola said, as if she read my thoughts. "Wait, I think I have a card with the address." She fumbled in her purse and produced a business card with the name of a motel in a town not too far over the Georgia line. At least we would be on the way home.

"I'm going to need your help." There was an urgency in her voice.

I nodded, still reluctant to leave my nephew in her

care. Yet Joey was familiar with Ola Cress; for weeks she had been the only caretaker he knew. I was the stranger here.

The woman touched my arm. "I don't blame you for being concerned, but you're going to have to believe me. I want what's best for Joey. I just can't run anymore."

"You drive. I'll navigate," Augusta said when I scooted under the wheel of my car. "Get closer so I can read her license plate."

"Why, Augusta, I do believe you've been reading detective stories," I said. "You're getting to be a regular Sherlock Holmes."

"Hmm, well, Arthur had a few problems with that first one. Plot development and such. Don't mind saying I gave him a hint or two."

"Arthur . . . ?"

"Conan Doyle. You know. The man who wrote the series. Let me tell you, there were times when we both despaired, but it worked out well, don't you think? Only I do wish he'd left out that part about Sherlock smoking dope!" Augusta stuffed her needlework back into her bag and held onto the door grip. "She's turning right at the next corner. Step on it, Prentice, I believe we're gaining on her."

I was glad it was too dark for her to see my smile. Ola Cress wasn't driving above forty and I was close enough to read the name of the company where she'd bought the car.

Still, I was relieved an hour later when we pulled into the near-empty parking lot of The Dogwood Inn.

Since neither of us had eaten, I picked up sandwiches at the motel coffee shop while Ola got Joey ready for bed. Ola's rooms were as she had described them: comfortable but nothing fancy. The bedroom, just large enough for a double bed and the baby's crib, led off of a small sitting area and kitchenette. A playpen took up one corner of the living room, toys were scattered about, and a quick look in the kitchen cabinets revealed a good supply of baby food and formula. It appeared as if Ola Cress was prepared to stay awhile.

"Would you like to give Joey his bottle?" Ola asked. "You'll find one ready in the refrigerator. Just zap it for about ten seconds in the microwave."

I hadn't baby-sat since my college days, but I did remember how to heat a bottle, shake it, and test a drop on my arm. My nephew made his entrance howling and clung to Ola for dear life until he saw I had the bottle. I held out my arms and bribed him with milk, and from then on, it was a piece of cake. I sat across from Ola at the small kitchen table while Joey drained his seven ounces, burped obligingly, and dropped off to sleep in my arms. Finally, Ola, seeing I wasn't going to give him up voluntarily, picked up the sleeping infant and tucked him into bed.

"Thank you," I said when she returned.

"For what?"

"For letting me hold him, feed him."

Ola opened a couple of soft drinks and found plates for our sandwiches. "He has to get used to you. I can't just abandon him with someone he doesn't know." She pulled out a chair and sat across from me, but didn't touch her food. "I didn't know what else to do," she said, grabbing a paper napkin to blot her tears.

"You made the right decision, and we'll work things out, we'll have to. There's no reason you have to leave right away. Why not come back to Smokerise with me for a while? That's our home in Liberty Bend."

Ola Cress smiled. "I know. Your sister told me. She loved that place, missed it." She broke off a piece of her sandwich and looked at it, then put it back on her plate. "But we'll have to be careful of the Gaineses you know. It's only a matter of time before they trace me here; I expect they already have. I'm sure that was one of Sonny's family who followed me this morning when I was on my way to the mall. Had to go through all sorts of maneuvers to get rid of him."

I frowned. "Him? Are you sure it was a man?"

"Didn't let them get close enough to find out. Why?"

"Because Sonny's aunt met me there at the fountain. At first I thought it was you. She must have followed me there."

"Or somebody told her where to find you." Ola nibbled at her sandwich.

"But nobody knew." I looked up at her. "*Tisdale Humphreys!* But he wouldn't. I just don't believe it."

"Then who else could it be?" Ola asked.

155

"Maybe somebody overheard . . . the wallpaper hanger! He told me he was having the upstairs hall repapered. But why would a stranger care? He probably doesn't even know you."

"This one would. There are no strangers in Ruby, Tennessee, and there's only one person who's skilled enough to suit Tisdale Humphreys: Roy Henry Trimble, Jackie Trimble's brother."

Jackie Trimble. For a moment the name drew a blank, and then I remembered the woman who had worked with Maggie at The Toy Box Child Care Center, the one who wanted to find Ola Cress. "But I never told Mr. Humphreys we were meeting at the mall," I said.

Ola sighed. "I'm afraid I did. I just thought he ought to know—in case you had trouble finding it or something. And of course I didn't think about it, but Roy Henry must've been there then too. I heard Tisdale warn somebody about being careful with a mirror."

"I don't understand why Jackie Trimble would want Sonny's family to have Joey," I said. "Is she related to them or something?"

Ola made a face as if she'd eaten something rotten. "Money," she said. "Money pure and simple. If it's one of that Trimble bunch, you can rest assured the Gaineses have made it worth their while to snoop." Ola hammered out her words with obvious distaste.

I groaned. "They've probably followed us here too. Maybe I'm getting paranoid, but I feel like we're surrounded by a whole troop of Gaines spies on twenty-four-hour duty!"

"Then they must know where you live as well." Ola shoved her plate away. She looked like she was ready to cry. I wouldn't blame her.

"True, but once we get Joey on our own property we'll have a better chance of keeping him. They can't just march in and take him away from his own relatives."

Ola spoke quietly. "Prentice, they're his relatives too."

CHAPTER FIFTEEN

We left before dawn. Ola had loaned me a blanket, a pillow, and the small sofa in her sitting area for the night, but I think I would have been more comfortable in my car. From all we'd learned about the Gaines gang, I half expected them to come bursting through the door and snatch Joey away from us. And to tell the truth, I wasn't completely trusting of Ola Cress.

It was dark when we left The Dogwood Inn and headed for the Interstate, and I almost went cross-eyed trying to keep Ola's car in sight behind us.

Beside me Augusta yawned. "I could do with a cup of coffee. It's hard to keep that woman's car in view when I can't hold my eyes open."

"There's no place to stop," I said. "And besides, there isn't time. The Gaineses could be right behind us."

Augusta tweaked her cheeks, did something to her hair, and sat a little straighter. "You're perfectly right, of course. I'm afraid I'm a bit selfish when it comes to my morning coffee. We had to do without it, you know, during the war days."

"Which war days?" I knew ten times over, but I could tell she wanted me to ask.

"World War Two, of course, the last big one. So many things were rationed, hard to come by, but I especially missed coffee. Nothing makes you want something more than being told you can't have it."

"Uh-huh," I said. I sensed a lesson here—for my benefit of course, but the angel's words rang true. Did I want Rob McCullough because I didn't think I could have him? I didn't have time to dwell on it now because Ola was blinking her lights as a signal she needed to stop.

We pulled off into the parking lot of a fast food hamburger restaurant where Augusta got her wish for coffee while Ola fed Joey his morning bottle. "I'm supposed to be weaning him onto a cup, but the little tyrant won't have any part of it," Ola said, wiping the baby's mouth with a paper napkin. And I had an idea that if Joey had demanded his bottle served on a silver tray with orchestral accompaniment, Ola would have at least made an effort to comply.

It was getting light when we left the restaurant and turned south for home and I suspected every car that trailed us to have a sneaky Gaines lurking inside. Not until I glimpsed the comforting silhouette of Smokerise at the end of our long, curving driveway did I begin to allow myself to relax.

And then I saw the car parked behind the house where no car should be, and if Ola hadn't been close behind me, I'd have jammed on my brakes and turned around.

A small white sedan with Georgia license plates seemed to have made itself at home to the left of the back steps where Mom always used to park, and as peeved as I was with my mother, I still resented the impudence of this intruder. For a moment I even forgot to be wary of a Gaines ambush.

Whoever it was must be inside the house because a light shone from the kitchen and I thought I could see someone moving about. Was our mysterious prowler back for another breakfast and bath? But how did he get in?

I had one foot out of the car when Augusta put a hand on my arm. "Wait! Watch before you jump, Prentice."

I looked down to see what I should watch. "Meaning?"

"You don't know who's in there, and the child's safety must come first, so don't go looking for trouble. Signal Ola to follow, then turn around and find a place to call the police. Quickly now!"

Was Augusta getting bossier or what? But she was right. That might be one of Sonny's relatives in there, or the ghoul who made off with Uncle Faris and left another corpse in his place. We had to get Joey safely out of the way.

I heard the screen door slam and looked up to see a figure dash across the back porch and down the steps. Noodles streaked in front of me in a gray blur and almost used up another of her lives as I missed her by inches in my rush to get away.

"Prentice! Where are you going? Come back!" I looked over my shoulder at the woman pursuing me. Her short dark hair was trimmed just below the ears and bounced when she ran—just like my mother's; she wore my mother's ratty yellow bathrobe. She *was* my mother!

I decided to wait until we were all inside to introduce her to her grandson.

Mom wrapped me in her arms and held me for the longest time. "I thought you'd gone to Alaska," I said, crying in spite of myself.

"Got as far as Seattle, then turned around and caught a plane to Atlanta, rented a car, and here I am."

"But why?"

"Prentice, I can *read*. Grabbed a paper in the Savannah Airport to read on the plane, and there it was! Why didn't you tell me what's been going on here?"

"I didn't want to worry you. Besides, what could you do?"

"I could be here for you for one thing, at least give you moral support. Hey, who's the mother here?" She gave me a tight little smile and squeezed my fingers.

"Come on, let's go inside, then you can fill me in. Why, I had to jimmy a window on the back porch to get inside! Forgot you'd changed the locks."

Ola remained in her car with Joey, obviously not knowing what to do, and now my mother looked at them curiously, then smiled. "Have any of you had breakfast? I was just getting ready to stir up something, and I know you'll want to get that precious 'lamb-baby' out of this chill."

Lamb-baby. The almost-forgotten term made me lose my breath for a minute. It was what she used to call Maggie until my sister reached kindergarten age and begged her to stop. "I'm not a lamb, and I'm not a baby!" she'd say. But if Mother realized what she'd said, she didn't show it.

"Ola and the baby are going to be staying with us for a while," I said as we helped to carry Joey's things inside. A sense of quiet joy settled about me, and although I couldn't see her, I knew Augusta was there.

"How nice! I'm glad to have them." My mother's smile was genuine. She liked babies, all babies, and was she ever going to love this one! I smiled too.

Joey had rice cereal with applesauce while Mom served the rest of us scrambled eggs and grits. "What a healthy appetite he has!" she observed. "He really is a beautiful child." My mother smiled at Ola Cress. "Is this your grandson?"

Ola looked at me expectantly.

"No, Mom, he's yours," I said, and told her how I had found him.

Ola and I cleared away the breakfast dishes while Mom rocked Joey in the same cane-bottomed chair she'd used to lull my sister and me to sleep. Listening to her, for a little while, I didn't once think of Sonny Gaines's lurking relatives or the grisly episodes in our own backyard. My mother's happiness spread over me like balm, and if ever I sensed an angel's presence, I sensed it now.

A loud knocking at the door jolted me back into the here and now, and Mom appeared in the hallway with the sleeping baby on her shoulder. "Oh, I almost forgot," she whispered. "That must be Ralphine. I'd asked her to come over and help me clean this morning, but the house looks like somebody beat her to it."

I shrugged. "Had a little time on my hands."

"And these kitchen curtains—what a difference they make, Prentice! Honey, I didn't know you could sew like that."

Fortunately I didn't have to answer because Mom opened the door for Ralphine Totherow and immediately began telling her about Joey. "I thought we could get Maggie's old crib down from the attic and maybe fix up her room for a nursery," my mother said, ushering Ralphine into the house. "I think I still have that old high chair, Prentice—the one we bought for you."

"My gosh, Mom, it's not exactly an antique," I said.

"And of course we'll need curtains for the baby's room—a cute little nursery print, I think . . ." She flitted about like a butterfly, pausing now and then, but not lighting anywhere. "My goodness, I don't even know a good pediatrician!"

"Mom," I said, "settle down for a minute, will you? I'm afraid it's not as simple as that." I told her what I knew about Sonny's family—all of it, including what the funeral director back in Tennessee had said. "Somehow his aunt knew I was meeting Ola at a mall outside of Chattanooga," I said. "Knew who I was and why I was there. They want Joey too, Mom. This isn't going to be easy."

"Then we'll hire a lawyer—somebody good. I'll use the money from my land sale. We'll fight them, Prentice!"

My mother's eyes flashed danger and I fully expected her to begin snorting and pawing the ground. I glanced at Ralphine who seemed to understand, and together we persuaded Mom to sit in Dad's chair and put up her feet. "Now close your eyes and think blue," I told her.

Her eyes blazed open. "Think *what?*"

"Blue," I said.

"For heaven's sake, why?"

"Just do it," I barked. "It'll calm you."

Mom opened one eye and made a face. "Then maybe you'd better try it too. I don't remember your being so bossy, Prentice."

I waited until Ola tiptoed into the parlor, where Joey slept on a pallet, to tell my mother about the woman's friendship with Maggie. "She'll be able to explain better than I can about the problems with Sonny's family,"

I said. "Before we make any definite plans, I think the three of us need to sit down calmly and talk."

"I can come back later if you want me to," Ralphine offered.

"Good heavens no! There's always something to do around here," Mom told her. "Prentice, why don't you go upstairs with Ralphine and help her straighten that messy hall closet? It'll give me a chance to visit with Ola."

Augusta had tidied that same closet a few days ago, but obviously Mom hadn't looked in there yet, so I said okay and went along upstairs. I remembered seeing boxes of books in there that that nobody would probably ever read again, and thought Ralphine might like to take some home.

"Lord, yes, I do like to read a good mystery whenever I get the chance—but then people in hell want ice water!" Ralphine laughed. "Don't know when's the last time I actually had time to sit down and read, but miracles do happen. Hell, that shiftless Jasper Totherow's stayed outta jail for over a year now. That's a miracle in itself!"

"I don't suppose you've seen him lately?" I flipped through a well-read copy of *Little Women* and added it to my pile to keep.

"Lord, don't I wish I hadn't! Jasper doesn't come around much—'specially since I swore out a warrant against him." Ralphine slammed a book aside. "But if that man wants something, you can't run him off with a red-hot poker, and he stays about one breath ahead of the sheriff's bunch. Thought I was rid of him for a while there. Guess he's learned I'm not giving him any money, but he came by yesterday with some kind of little old dinky bracelet he wanted me to keep for him. Said I could have it if I dropped my complaint with the police."

"What'd you say?"

"Told him to take a flyin' leap into a bucket of shit. What would I want with that tacky old bracelet? Probably stole it anyway!"

"So you didn't keep it?"

"Didn't want anything to do with it. God knows where he got it, and Jasper's scared of something. I don't want to get mixed up in it. Found out later he'd passed it off on one of the girls. Gave Brandi Lynn a dollar if she'd hold on to it till he got back." Ralphine shook her head. "A whole dollar now! First money that kid's ever seen from her old man—and probably the last!"

I couldn't argue with that.

I picked up the last book in my stack and flipped through it to be sure there was nothing tucked inside. It was one that had been on the best-seller list several years back and I remembered giving it to Mom for Christmas when I was still in college. I assumed she had dutifully read it, then added it to her pile of "been there and done that." A small piece of paper drifted to the floor and I picked it up, meaning to throw it away, but something caught my eye: it was the logo at the top.

The paper was a receipt from The Quick Cash Pawnshop in Atlanta for my mother's heirloom pearls.

CHAPTER SIXTEEN

The digital tinkling of "Twinkle, Twinkle Little Star" came from the kitchen where Joey lay on his back in a playpen kicking a musical toy. The baby laughed and reached for the bright plastic rings suspended above him. My mother and Ola sat at the kitchen table, cups of coffee untouched before them. My mother's eyes were red, her cheeks wet with tears. Ola drooped in her chair with her head propped in her hands, her frail shoulders trembled. Sitting there like that, they might have posed for an artist's rendering of "Grief."

I tried to tiptoe past them, give them time to share the remnants of their memories of Maggie, but Ralphine in her size ten brogans thundered in before I could stop her.

Mom looked up and made an effort to smile. "Ola

and I have been filling in the gaps," she said and reached for my hand. "And oh, Prentice, there are too many gaps!"

Ola took a wad of tissues from her pocket and blew her nose, then wiped her glasses on the sleeve of her dress. "I'm sorry, I just can't help it." She looked about her at the big yellow kitchen, the worn oak floors dotted with gaudy rag rugs our grandmother made. "I've heard so much about this place from Maggie, I feel like I've been here before."

"Did she talk about it a lot?" I asked. "About us?"

Ola nodded. "Home was special to Maggie, and so were you. She meant to come back here, you know."

Mom and I looked at each other. "We didn't know," we said together. And wept. Ola Cress took off her glasses once again and joined us.

Poor Ralphine, left standing there, dustcloth in hand, turned her attention to Joey. While the three of us searched for composure, she plucked him from his playpen and cuddled him in her vast lap. "At least you have the baby," she said, in an obvious effort to comfort us. "And what a cutie pie he is! I'll swear, Miz Dobson, I think he takes after you."

"I believe it would be best," Ola said, still sniffing, "if you didn't mention anything about the baby. His father's family's been harassing us, and they're a pretty unsavory bunch. It wouldn't do for them to know he was here."

"Swear out an injunction against them," Ralphine advised, nodding sagely. "Wish I'd a done it long ago!"

"We'll cross that bridge when we come to it," Mom said. "Right now I think we just need time to get acquainted with Joey." She smiled at Ola. "Ms. Cress is right, though. I don't think it would be wise to say anything about having the baby here just yet."

"You got it," Ralphine promised, and I knew we could count on her word.

It wasn't until after lunch that I remembered the slip of paper in my pocket. I was putting away the dishes while Ola and Joey napped upstairs, and Mom sat at the table making a list of "baby needs."

"I suppose you left your pearls back in Savannah," I said, watching her face.

She frowned. "My pearls? Why would I need pearls here? Do you think they still make that baby shampoo? The kind that doesn't hurt your eyes. And those cute little towels with a hood?"

"You don't have them do you?"

"Have what, the pearls?" She sighed. "Well, of course I have them, Prentice! Surely you don't expect me to be like your aunt Zorah and carry the family valuables everywhere I go."

I smiled. It had always been a joke with us how my aunt took her silver chest along with her whenever she traveled out of town. Dad used to warn her she was taking a far greater chance of having it stolen from her car than if she'd left it at home.

I placed the receipt from the pawnshop on the table in front of my mother and waited.

She read the scrap of paper without touching it. "Where on earth did that come from?"

I told her.

"I could've sworn I threw that thing away. In fact, I meant to burn it. Prentice, I wish you hadn't seen that old receipt. I didn't mean for anyone to know about those pearls, especially you."

"Why not?" I asked, but she didn't answer.

I looked again at the date on the receipt. It was during my junior year in college, a lean year for selling crops and cattle. And for paying college tuition. My mother had sold her pearls to help pay for my senior year.

"Oh, Mama!" I knelt on the floor and put my head in her lap. "I don't know whether to say 'I'm sorry' or 'thank you,' or both."

Gently she stroked the hair from my face. "Honey, they're just beads. You and Maggie were all the jewels I ever wanted." She glanced again at the list she was making for Joey. "And now we'll have this little diamond chip . . . But for the life of me, I don't know how that receipt got inside that book."

I thought I knew. Somebody had wanted me to find it there.

"What are we going to do about Aunt Zorah?" I asked Mom later. "If we tell her about Joey, everybody in Liberty Bend will know it before the library closes for the day, and Be-trice is just as bad."

"Mercy! I didn't think of that." She looked out the window as if she expected to see our relatives driving up at any minute. "We certainly can't take a chance on that. What can I do to keep them from coming over? If Zorah knows I'm here, she'll want to hear all about Savannah."

"She might come over anyway just to check on Uncle Faris's grave," I said.

"I don't suppose you've heard any more about that poor woman they found?"

"Only they suspect she was killed by something called 'vehicular homicide'—meaning they think somebody ran over her with a car. Don Weber says they're trying to locate the vehicle. And as far as I know, Uncle Faris hasn't turned up yet."

"*Faris!*" My mother snorted. "Too bad they didn't make off with him a long time ago. Would've spared us a whole lot of grief." She shook her head and frowned at me as if it were all my fault. "That Thornton Bonner doesn't have the sense God promised a billy goat! Has no business being sheriff. Your dad went to school with him, you know; told me once Thornton flunked English two years in a row."

"The police seem to think they picked Uncle Faris at random—because he was buried apart from the rest," I said. "Maybe they thought we wouldn't miss him. Anyway, it doesn't look like they'll be back." I wanted to get her off the subject before it led to the bathtub invasion, the open trench in the hillside, and the barn lot prowler.

"That's disgusting—even if it was Faris," my mother said. "And you have no business staying out here a—"

"We could tell Aunt Zorah you're here recuperating from some kind of contagious disease," I said. "You know what a hypochondriac she is."

Mom smiled. "Your dad used to say Zorah never failed to come down immediately with whatever ailment they featured on the TV medical shows."

"There's a bad flu going around," I said.

"A new strain, I hear—and highly contagious." Mom felt her forehead. "I do believe I'm feverish. Don't I look feverish, Prentice?"

I agreed that she did. I just hoped our relatives would buy it.

"Poor Mom's just burning up with fever . . . aches all over . . . can't hold a thing in her stomach . . ." I had my speech memorized as I walked up the steps of the library a few days later. My three overdue books gave me a legitimate excuse for popping in with my distressing "news." Should I drag my feet and appear listless so my aunt would naturally assume that I, too, was soon to become a victim of this horrid, virulent strain?

Nope. Don't overdo, Prentice. Besides, I wasn't that good an actress. And my talents would have been wasted anyway because Aunt Zorah wasn't there. Instead, Miss Donna Appelbaum sat behind the big front desk frowning over a stack of books in front of her. She looked up at me over her little Ben Franklin glasses and frowned some more.

"Well, Prentice, I heard you were back in town. Things not work out in the city?" She shot me her illusion of a smile and it sent an icy dagger through me. Miss Donna had taught me in the fifth grade where we'd made each other miserable for a whole year, and the relationship hadn't improved since. I once made up a poem about her and passed it around in class: *Miss Donna the Piranha*, a fitting tribute still. She took up the poem, of course, made me read it aloud. Now she was retired and honing her teeth on library patrons when Aunt Zorah wasn't there.

I pretended I hadn't heard her. "Aunt Zorah's not sick, is she?" (Heavens, maybe *she'd* come down with the dreaded influenza!)

"Gone to one of those family reunions she traipses off to all the time. I should think you'd know, Prentice, being a Dobson and all. Somewhere in Florida this time I think."

I didn't know. The last time my parents took us to a family reunion, Cousin Hortense from Mobile and Great-Aunt Josephine from Augusta got into a shouting match over somebody not being asked to be in somebody else's wedding about a trillion years ago. We never went again.

But Aunt Zorah belonged to just about every family organization she could join. They sent out newsletters, elected officers, the works, and Aunt Zorah was the High Poo-bah in several, so I wasn't surprised to hear she'd taken off on another of what Dad used to call her "genealogical jaunts."

Miss Donna accepted my late fee, counting it twice just to be sure. "You'd think Zorah'd get tired of running around all the time to this that and the other—especially since she insists on lugging all that silver everywhere she goes. Asking for trouble is what she is! One of these days, she's going to be conked on the noggin!

"And how's your mother?" she wanted to know as I edged toward the door. "Thought I saw her in Clyde's Cupboard the other day picking up bread and milk."

"She's sick," I said. "Real sick. Some kind of virus. Can hardly lift her head."

"Some nasty thing she picked up in Savannah, no doubt. All that humidity. You won't catch me going off to live in some place I don't know anything about!" Miss Donna the Piranha thumped the stack of books in front of her. "Looks like old Maynard's planning a trip to Mexico." She made a sound that might be considered a giggle. "And you know what happens to you if you drink the water down there!"

"Maynard Griggs?" I said it aloud without even thinking.

"Only Maynard in town far as I know. Said he'd always wanted to go and decided to read up on it. Guess that stuck-up Ernestine will go along too, just so she can brag about it. If you ask me, people oughtta stay home where they belong..."

Then why don't you, you wicked old bitch? I wanted to say. But coward that I am, I just said good-bye and headed for the door.

"By the way," she called to my departing back, "did that man ever find you?"

"What man?"

"Some man came in here this morning asking if I knew where you lived. Had a beard."

CHAPTER SEVENTEEN

To tell or not to tell? I didn't want to alarm my mother and Ola. The three of us were already as "jumpy as a frog on a pogo stick," as Dad used to say, but if Sonny's father was that close to finding us, we had to be prepared. "What now, Augusta?" I asked aloud, but if she was around, she didn't answer. Yet I knew she couldn't be very far away.

I drove home by a route so complex and dizzying, I almost got lost myself.

"Are you sure it's Sonny's father?" Mom wanted to know.

"Who else could it be? I'm not expecting anybody with a beard."

"How old a person was this? Did Donna Appelbaum tell him where he could find you?"

I shrugged. "I don't know . . . I don't know."

Mom sighed. "Oh, Prentice, you didn't ask her? Why not?"

"All I wanted to do was get away from that woman before I said something I might regret," I told her. "Besides, I guess it kinda shook me up to know this—this spooky bearded guy is right here in Liberty Bend."

"I wish Wally would hurry back," she said. "He could tell us what to do." Mom grew up with Wallace Turner who practices law in Atlanta and handles her legal affairs. "He and his wife are in Europe and won't be home for another week. I have no idea how to reach him."

"He has several partners, doesn't he? Couldn't one of them advise us?"

But my stubborn mother shook her head. "They might not understand. I'd rather wait for Wally."

"Then I think we should find another place for Joey," I said. "I hate to keep moving him from here to there, but we're isolated out here, Mom, and who knows what that man might do?"

My mother started to answer, then held out her hand for silence. Joey was crying upstairs. I was learning his signals already. This one meant he was already hungry and working up to being mad.

"Bottle time!" Mom smiled and started for the stairs.

"Where's Ola?"

"Joey was running low on diapers, so I asked her to pick up a few groceries in town. Prentice, we need to talk about Ola," she whispered. "Something's not right. I'm worried about her."

I nodded. Augusta had said almost the same thing.

Mom changed Joey's diaper and reluctantly allowed me to give him his bottle. Earlier, under Ola's supervision, the two of us had bathed the baby in the same big plastic pan my mother had used for Maggie and me, only I think we got wetter than Joey did.

"I guess you've noticed how much time Ola spends at the cemetery," Mom said, reaching out to pat Joey's fat knee. "For some reason she feels responsible for Maggie's death."

"I know. I think she believes she could've stopped her somehow, kept her from going with Sonny. Whatever it is, it's eating her up inside."

"It isn't doing a lot for me, either," Mom said, shaking her head. "And it can't be good for Joey."

Soon after our arrival at Smokerise, Ola had asked me to take her to my sister's grave. Once there, I could see she wanted to be alone. I left her kneeling beside the stone while I walked past the old homestead and along the creek bank to the place where I had found the trench in the hillside. It was hard to see through the now-greening woods, but it looked as if the grave—or whatever it was meant to be—had been filled in. With *dirt only*, I hoped, and didn't waste any time getting back to the cemetery to collect Ola on my way to the house. I had found her crying there with her arms wrapped around the stone angel.

"She makes me uncomfortable," my mother said. "This morning she asked if I'd mind if she broke off some dogwood blooms and a few blossoms from that early white azalea for Maggie's grave. And of course I don't mind! Maggie could have every flower on this farm—but it's something I'd like to do myself."

I knew how she felt. Finding a comparative stranger weeping over my sister's grave had annoyed me as well. This woman had only known Maggie for a few short months. She had no right to grieve as we did!

I tried to think what Augusta would say. "Maybe it's just something she has to get out of her system," I said. "If it goes on, one of us needs to talk with her."

"But how?"

I didn't know, but I did know that when Ola returned from the store we were going to have to decide if or when to leave Smokerise.

But Ola herself decided that for us. "Somebody's watching this place," she said, dumping an armload of groceries in the middle of the kitchen table. "He's parked across the road in sort of a clearing under some pines—but back a few yards like he doesn't want anybody to know he's there." She twisted her hands as she spoke and seemed ready to cry if somebody said "Scat!"

"How can you be sure he was watching us?" I asked, although I had a hunch she was right.

"I noticed him when I left to go to the store, and he was still there when I came back." Ola sat abruptly at the table, and the pocketbook that had been hanging by a strap from her arm slid to the floor. "It's him! I know it's him—Sonny's father! Oh, dear God, what are we going to do?"

"First, we'll ask the sheriff's department to send somebody to check on him," I told her as I called the now-familiar number. "Maybe it's just a bird-watcher."

"And we're sitting ducks," my mother said. "I don't feel safe here, Prentice, even if this does turn out to be somebody perfectly harmless. Until we know we have a good chance of keeping Joey, I believe we should take that baby someplace else."

I tried to give her the "be quiet or else" look she used to give Maggie and me, but it didn't work. Meanwhile, I could see Ola was getting more and more agitated.

The dispatcher at the sheriff's office wanted to know what kind of car it was and if my friend could see who was in it. The car looked sort of blue, Ola said, but she couldn't make out who was behind the wheel.

While I was on the phone with the police, I asked about the trench on the hill behind our house and was told the sheriff had it filled in. Still, this didn't help to ease my anxieties. We needed to get out of here—and soon.

"But where on earth can we go?" I wanted to know.

"Elaine's family owns this old place outside of Savannah," Mom said. "Belongs to an uncle, I think, but nobody lives there now."

Elaine Fuller is Mom's old friend from college who had invited her to share her home in Savannah until she could get her life back together after Maggie died.

"What do you mean, 'nobody lives there'?" I asked,

picturing a crumbling old mausoleum of a house somewhere on the edge of a swamp.

"It's really just a guest house. The main house—Ellynwood, I think it was called—burned years ago. The place has been in the Hathcock family for years... Elaine was a Hathcock, you know."

I said I knew, but wasn't Elaine off cruising around Alaska somewhere? And didn't we need her uncle's permission?

She looked at me as if that was a "given" and if I had any sense I would've known it. "Well, of course. Just let me find my itinerary. Maybe I can catch up with her at that hotel in Anchorage."

While my mother made the call, Ola hurried from room to room, window to window, until she'd checked every one. Instinctively I held Joey closer. Is this how pioneer women felt as they circled the wagons for the night?

The baby slobbered on my cheek, pulled my hair, and laughed, and I kissed him and put him on his quilt to play. "He's getting ready to crawl," Mom pointed out. "Look at him rocking on his hands and knees." And from the pride on her face, you'd have thought Joey had discovered a cure for the common cold.

Elaine was expected at the hotel in Anchorage sometime today, Mom told us, and she had left a message for her friend to return her call. "But I don't think there'll be a problem about staying at the cottage," she added. "Elaine's uncle Albert lives in town and rarely goes to Ellynwood. His family only uses it once in a while when they want to get away."

I wondered just how far *away* that was, but then beggars can't be choosers, and until Mom could get in touch with her lawyer, Ellynwood would have to do.

When we heard a car approaching from the road, the three of us flew in different directions: Mom to lock the door, Ola to run upstairs with the baby, and me to draw the curtains. We were stumbling all over each other trying to crowd into the hall when someone knocked on the back door and called out to us. "Anybody home? Everything all right in here?"

I recognized Donald Weber's voice and hurried to let him in. "We're fine," I said, "but I think somebody's watching the house." I told him about the bearded man who had asked about me at the library. "Normally I wouldn't think anything about it, but after all the things that have been going on around here, it makes us uncomfortable."

"Not uncomfortable," my mother said. "Scared. Was the man still out there? Did you get his license?"

"Something must've spooked him," the deputy said. "He was gone before we could get over here, but we'll sure be on the lookout for him."

"Is that *all*?" Mom was using her "I've just about had it with you" tone of voice. "I mean, can't you *do* anything?"

"Not unless he breaks the law, and from what you tell me, he hasn't done that. Not yet anyway." The deputy started to leave, then paused and addressed my mother. "Ma'am, I don't blame you for being nervous, but if he comes up this drive, you'll hear him before you see him. Give us a call if you do. We'll be here in five minutes."

Mom followed him to the porch. "Donald, we're thinking of leaving tomorrow to visit relatives for a few days. I'd appreciate it if you'd keep an eye on the place while we're gone."

It would save the deputy time if he were to just move in here, I thought, and was grateful that he didn't mention the midnight prowler or bathtub caper. Mom had dealt with the unidentified body and Uncle Faris's disappearance better than I'd expected, but I didn't want to push my luck.

We were finishing dinner when Elaine Fuller called to say that as far as she was concerned, we were welcome to use the guest house at Ellynwood, but she'd have to confirm it with her uncle and let us know. A short time later she phoned again to give Mom directions and tell us where to pick up the key.

"Elaine says the place hasn't been used in a while, so it's going to need a good airing," Mom said. "Cleaning too, no doubt," she added with a sigh.

If only Augusta could lend a hand, I thought. Yet I knew she was near, and from time to time drew from the strength of her presence. I only hoped my angel would follow us to Savannah.

We decided to leave in the morning by the back route using the old cemetery road, in one car—Mom's—hoping that whoever was looking for us would be fooled into thinking we were still at Smokerise. I phoned Suzie Wright and arranged for her to feed the cat—this time we'd leave Noodles outside—and we spent the rest of the evening packing.

When the telephone rang earlier, the three of us agreed to ignore it. It might be Pershing Gaines. It might not. But why challenge fate? Maybe he would think we weren't at home. Twice more that night it rang, and the persistent caller let it go on and on for what seemed like forever before finally giving up. None of us was expecting any important messages—or any we wanted to hear—so I had turned off the answering machine.

It was almost midnight when the telephone shrilled again and I heard Mom shuffle into the hallway. "I've had about enough of this!" she said. "They're going to wake that baby.

"Who is this? Don't you know what time it is?"

This was followed by a pause and I expected her to hang up the phone in a panic. Then, "Who? Oh . . . that's all right. Yes, she's right here . . ."

I sat up in bed and tossed back the covers. It was probably Dottie, a dyed-in-the-wool night owl who never seemed to realize there were others who weren't.

My mother met me in the doorway and shrugged. "It's Rob. I think he's calling from London."

"Sorry if I woke you," he began. "Prentice, I need to see you."

How could I tactfully tell him his timing couldn't be

worse? "Rob, something's come up. We're leaving for Savannah in the morning."

"Is there any way you can hold off on that? Listen, I'm packing my bag as we speak . . ."

I heard what sounded like a drawer opening on his end of the line. "No, Rob, wait! I'd rather you come next week, or better still, the week after. We'll have more time to spend together. Let me call you."

"Prentice, what's going on?"

"It's too involved to go into right now. I'll phone you from Savannah. I promise."

"Not this time. I'm taking a few days off—catching the first plane for the States in the morning. Should be in Atlanta by this time tomorrow." There was a question in his voice and the silence stretched until I thought it would snap in two, zing me like a rubber band.

I felt a hand on my shoulder and turned to find my mother standing there. I could tell by her expression that she understood what was going on from hearing my end of the conversation. "We'll be all right," she whispered. "You can join us there later. A few more days won't matter."

And so I promised Rob McCullough I'd meet him at the airport in Atlanta when he arrived. It would be good, I thought, to have another warm "body" on our side.

Of course that was before I stumbled across the one in our barn. And this one was dead.

CHAPTER EIGHTEEN

My mother refused to leave under cover of darkness. "I'll be darned if I'll sneak out of my own house like some kind of thief!" she proclaimed, so it was well past dawn when they left the next morning with most of Joey's belongings and the two women's suitcases shoved into the trunk of Mom's rental car. I stood on the back porch and watched them bump around the bend and out of sight on the gravel road that led to the family cemetery and eventually through what would become Daisy Dell Acres, the soon-to-be-developed "community" behind our farm. Few people knew the two roads connected. We hoped one of them wasn't the stranger watching our house.

Just before leaving, Ola had shoved a small parcel into my hands. It was about the size of a grapefruit and was wrapped in layers of brown paper. "I found this in Maggie's things," she said. "Must be something special since she kept it in a drawer along with Joey's baby book and some pictures of her family. I think she wanted you to have it, Prentice."

I guessed, even before I unwrapped it, what was in Maggie's crude bundle. My sister had scribbled in ink on the masking tape that held it together: *For always, Maggie and Prentice,* and judging from the handwriting, I'd say she wrote it after she left home. Inside I found my sister's half of the broken figurine still shrouded in the plastic grocery bag where I had hurriedly placed it so many years before.

Upstairs in the silent house, I took my half of the china girl from the lunch box on my closet shelf and fit the pieces together. Someday I would have the keepsake professionally repaired for Mom. As for myself, the mending had already begun.

The house felt empty, oddly vacant. Except for Noodles, who was just beginning to tolerate me, I was alone. Really alone because Augusta had gone to Ellynwood with the others, only they didn't know it, of course.

Unable to sleep late, I had come down early planning to prepare an edible, if not substantial breakfast to start them on their way. I couldn't cook as well as

Augusta, but I could scramble a few eggs, and have been known to stir up a batch of pancakes now and then if there's a box of mix handy.

But Augusta beat me to it. The warm homey smell of just-baked bread wrapped itself around me and drew me into the kitchen where Augusta, enveloped in a posy-sprigged pinafore, lifted a crusty loaf from the oven. "A little something to start the day," she said. "I hope you don't mind."

"I mind terribly," I said. "I hate your cooking, Augusta. Is that hot chocolate I smell?"

"With just a whiff of cinnamon." She poured me a cup, then quickly whisked eggs and cheese together and paused to listen for footsteps upstairs. "I expect they'll be down in a minute. I see you've decided to stay."

I nodded between sips of chocolate. "For a day or two, but I'm worried about the others. I hope I'm doing the right thing."

"I wish I could assure you, Prentice. I can't. We just have to make our choices and do the best we can."

"What do you mean, *we*? This is my mother we're talking about! My nephew. What if something happens to them?"

The angel heated butter in a pan. "I believe your mother wants you to wait for your friend Rob. She seems to feel responsible for your turning him down before."

"I know . . . well, she was in a way. But I couldn't go running off to England and leave her here alone after Dad died."

I took blue-rimmed plates from the cabinet and set three places, put out Joey's small bowl with the kittens on it. "This place—this Ellynwood—I don't know anything about it. It could be in the middle of nowhere! I just hope they'll be all right."

Augusta spoke softly. "Would you like me to go along?"

"Would you? That would be great!"

"As you know, I'm limited as to what I can do, but perhaps I can be of some help.

"I believe your pan's ready," she said, putting the bowl of eggs into my hands. "Stir it quickly or it'll burn."

"What's that heavenly smell?" My mother stood in the doorway. "Prentice, did you do this? You must've been up all night."

I looked behind me, but of course Augusta was no longer there. "Pull up a chair and dig in," I said.

Now I took my time rinsing the dishes, wiping off the table, sticky with honey. Noodles curled about my feet and I treated her to a saucer of milk. Soon Rob would call from London to let me know when to expect his flight.

But it was well past noon before I heard from Rob. His flight had been canceled because of mechanical problems and he couldn't get another for several hours.

It would be sometime tomorrow before he'd arrive in Atlanta.

I was upstairs picking out tunes on the violin that afternoon when I heard somebody drive up behind the house. From my position at the window I couldn't tell who was driving, but the car looked like the one that had followed Augusta and me when we left Ruby, Tennessee.

Give us a call if you see or hear anyone drive up. We'll be there in five minutes, the deputy had said. But how could I be sure this wasn't someone on a harmless errand? If I didn't answer the door, maybe they would go away. I sidled up to one side of the window and watched a man get out from the driver's side. It was difficult to get a good look at his face from where I stood, but he moved like a much younger man than I imagined Sonny's father to be, and as he approached the house I saw that he had a beard. Not the long, bushy, trailing whiskers I'd imagined, but what appeared to be a neat, well-trimmed beard.

I heard his footsteps cross the porch and waited until he knocked on the door before I slipped off my shoes and crept as quietly as I could to the phone in the hallway. The sheriff's line was busy.

The knocking came again, this time louder, and after a few minutes I heard him move off the porch. Good. He was leaving! I listened for his car to start. It didn't. Instead the doorbell rang. The persistent man had walked around to the front. I could hear his feet shuffle impatiently as he waited. The sheriff's line was still tied up—and so was my stomach! What if he came through a window? Battered down the door? Was this the same person who had asked about me in the library? He didn't seem particularly threatening, but you can't always go by appearances. He seemed much too young to be married to the deceiving woman in yellow who had tracked me to the mall near Chattanooga. Of course he could be her son or a younger brother. Or maybe this was the nephew she mentioned.

Whoever he was, I was sure he was somehow connected to the Gaineses and that no good could come of that. I had my finger poised to call 911 when I heard him drive away.

"Why didn't you call like I asked you to?" the deputy demanded when I finally got through almost fifteen minutes later.

"I tried. Your line was busy." I attempted not to sound as exasperated as I really was. We needed these people on our side.

"You called 911?"

"Well . . . no. It wasn't exactly an emergency," I said. "But if he hadn't left, I was going to in another minute."

"If that man had really wanted to get inside your house, you might not have had another minute," he told me. "He could be miles away by now, but if he tries watching your house again from across the road, we'll find out what's going on. We can't arrest the man for knocking on your door." I could tell by Don's tone he'd probably like to put me away instead.

When Mom called a few minutes later to let me know they were safely at Ellynwood, I didn't mention my would-be visitor. At least our crafty little back road ploy had seemed to work, as Mom said that as far as she could tell, they hadn't been followed there.

"What time are you meeting Rob's plane?" my mother asked.

"There's been a delay. He won't be getting in until tomorrow."

"You aren't staying at Smokerise alone tonight?"

"Probably not. Thought I might spend the night with Dottie Ives in Atlanta." Actually I hadn't thought of it until just then, but the idea of a return visitor after dark didn't appeal to me at all.

"Good idea!" Mom said. "Have a good visit with Rob now, honey, and let us know when to look for you."

"Is everything all right there?" I thought I detected a false gaiety in her voice.

"Fine. House needed a bit of airing but it wasn't as bad as I'd thought. Elaine's uncle must've had someone clean it before we arrived. And, Prentice, we found fresh fruit, pastries, and a delicious green salad waiting in the refrigerator. So thoughtful, and I don't even know who to thank."

I was pretty sure I did.

Dottie wasn't at home when I called, but I knew she hadn't gone far. Like me, she was too broke to travel. I left a message that I hoped she wouldn't mind company for the night and went upstairs to add a few things to the bag I'd packed the night before. I tried to phone

Aunt Zorah to let her know I'd be gone for a few days, but nobody answered. Probably still "reunioning," I thought, although it was well into Sunday afternoon and those affairs were usually over by then.

If I hadn't wanted to be a thoughtful houseguest, I don't know when we would've found the body in the barn. But I remembered Dottie admiring a hand-carved picture frame in an antique shop once, and I was sure I'd seen one like it hanging in our loft. It had been carved by Great-Great-Uncle Edgar during his whittling period, my father said. My parents found the barn loft a convenient place to keep broken furniture you might want to repair someday, old radios (who knows what they might be worth eventually?), the set of dishes Mom got with Green Stamps, and not-quite-discarded picture frames.

Dottie had begun redecorating her small apartment, but had to stop when *Martha's Journal* folded. Maybe this gift, dusty though it may be, would renew her spirits. And it would be perfect, I thought, for that spot in the corner of her guest bedroom. I swung open the barnyard gate feeling proud of myself for having thought of it, but as soon as I stepped inside the building it became obvious something had died in there—and not too recently.

He lay as if he had been flung there about midway inside the barn, still clutching in one fist what looked like a handful of straw. His head was turned at a most peculiar angle, and the eye I could see seemed to be staring at my feet. Jasper Totherow hadn't smelled like a rose in the best of times, and this was definitely not the best of times. The stench of him made me gag and dash for air. I almost made it to the fence before I lost my lunch. Ralphine Totherow wouldn't be bothered by Jasper again.

CHAPTER NINETEEN

Something was dreadfully wrong, and Aunt Zorah wasn't talking. I had fled to her home from Smokerise as soon as the police were satisfied I hadn't put an end to Jasper Totherow and didn't know who did. I had an idea who might've though, and so did they. Jasper's wife Ralphine headed the list, although I doubted if she'd done it. If Ralphine Totherow was going to do away with her husband, she would've done him in long ago. However, she did have opportunity—and oodles and oodles of motives. And from the way the people investigating the crime scene scurried about with smug expressions, I had a feeling they knew more than they were sharing. Sheriff Bonner was also interested in my mysterious "bearded" visitor and took note of every minute detail I could remember about his car, his clothing, and the little I managed to see of his appearance. It wasn't much.

I left them photographing the pathetic remains in our barn and drove to Aunt Zorah's intending to spend the night. Our barn lot was becoming a much-too-popular spot for dead people, and after what had happened to Jasper, the idea of a night alone at Smokerise didn't seem at all beneficial to my well-being. The sheriff had asked me to stick around in case the bearded man turned up, so Dottie agreed to get word to Rob when his flight arrived the next day. They had rental cars at the airport, and Rob knew how to drive. I just hoped he remembered to drive on the right side of the road.

No one answered when I'd telephoned my aunt, so I assumed she hadn't yet returned from the big family whoop-de-do, but a dim light burned in the back of her house and I knew where she kept a key.

I found Aunt Zorah in the semidarkness of her sitting room, still in her hat and coat, luggage at her feet, and after discovering one corpse that day, I was horrified to think I'd found another. Fortunately this one spoke.

"Prentice, that you? I didn't hear you. What is it?"

"I tried to call you a couple of times but nobody answered. Did you just get in?" I couldn't tell if she was coming or going.

"A little while ago. Just had to sit down for a minute."

My aunt was practically mumbling and that alarmed me. Dad said she sounded so much like his army drill sergeant he'd felt right at home during basic training.

"Are you all right?" I felt her forehead. "You're not sick, are you? And it's freezing cold in here. I'll turn up the heat."

"Not sick, just tired," she said as I rubbed her cold hands in my warm ones.

"What's wrong? Have they found Uncle Faris?" Aunt Zorah seemed to be in shock. I gently removed her green knitted hat, slipped off her shoes, and placed a footstool under her feet, almost forgetting for a moment what I had found in my own backyard. I didn't know if I would ever be able to go inside that barn again.

I took a few deep breaths, thought *blue*, and made tea. My aunt took a couple of sips and said it was just what she needed, but I noticed that her hand trembled when she replaced the cup in the saucer. "Are you going to tell me what brought this on?" I said. "I thought you went to some kind of family reunion."

"Ran into some difficulty," she whispered, raising the cup again to her lips. "Rather unpleasant situation . . ."

"What kind of situation?" Did somebody get in a huff because they were left off somebody else's guest list? I didn't roll my eyes, but I thought about it.

"I'm afraid my silver was taken," she said.

"Your *silver*? All of it? Oh, Aunt Zorah!" *You see! We knew all along this was going to happen! Why, oh, why, did you insist on carting that stuff around?* The words came to my lips, but mercifully stopped there. It would only hurt to say it, and besides, she knew this already.

She closed her eyes and patted my hand. "It's all right. It was returned."

"Oh. Well, that's good. Where is it?"

Aunt Zorah nodded in the direction of her suitcase. "It's all there, I guess. Doesn't matter."

I shook my head. "It doesn't?"

"I'm really tired. Think I'll go on to bed," my aunt said. "It's been such a trying day. You just wouldn't believe it, Prentice."

"Try me," I said, but she didn't answer.

"My Lord, Prentice!" Rob McCullough said the next day. "What on God's green earth have you gotten yourself into?"

I didn't remember having a choice in the matter, but I decided to overlook his thoughtless remark since he'd driven, bleary-eyed from lack of sleep, straight from the Atlanta airport.

We sat in a dark corner booth in A Fine Kettle, Liberty Bend's only restaurant, and drank coffee—or Rob drank coffee. I had a ham sandwich and apple pie à la mode, since yesterday's lunch hadn't stayed with me, and supper at Aunt Zorah's had been tuna on crackers and a raw carrot.

"Now you know why I couldn't fly to London," I said, scooping up the last dollop of ice cream. "It's been a busy season."

"Sure seems like it." Rob reached for my hand and squeezed it. "But you're all right?"

"So far, so good." I smiled. I liked having him there, liked his holding my hand. "If we could just straighten things out with Sonny's hairy relatives and find out who did away with 'Madam X' and Jasper we'd be well on the road to almost normal."

"Sonny?"

"Sonny Gaines, the guy Maggie married. Remember? I told you about him." When Rob first arrived I'd tried to explain to him where my mother was and why.

Now he nodded. "Right. The little boy's father." He pulled a paper napkin from the dispenser and reached into his pocket for a pen. "So what now?"

"Now we keep our heads down and don't look up," I said.

"Huh?"

"Cousin Be-trice is headed this way," I muttered. "Maybe she won't notice us."

No such luck. "Why, Prentice Dobson, where've you been? I ought not even speak to you the way you've been ignoring me!"

I should be so lucky, I thought as my cousin swooped upon us, arms full of bundles, and plopped down beside Rob.

"And who's this handsome hunk? Have you been keeping secrets from me?"

"You remember Rob. You met him at Dad's funeral last fall." I introduced the two again and Rob twisted awkwardly in the small booth and shook her hand. Cousin Be-trice had large, bony hands, protruding teeth, and ears the size of saucers. In fact, when I was a child I always pictured my cousin as the wolf when my mother read the story of "Red Riding Hood."

Now she patted lank brown hair behind her ears and smiled at me over the bulging shopping bag. "Lotta excitement out your way, I hear. Is it true you were the one who found him? They say he'd been lying there dead as a doornail for who knows how long." Cousin Be-trice leaned across the table so closely I could count the hairs on her chin and spoke in a chilling whisper. "Mercy, Prentice! That must've been awful! What'd he look like?

"Over here, Inez!" She signaled to the waitress who was serving another table. "I'll have a cheeseburger and fries."

I kicked Rob under the table and gave him my slitty-eyed look. "Hate to rush off and leave you," I told my cousin, "but Rob has some phone calls to make, and I promised to go to the store for Aunt Zorah. She's not feeling so great."

Still Be-trice didn't budge. "That Zorah! She's been up to something this time—don't ask me what, but it wasn't any family reunion."

"Why do you say that?" I asked.

"I get the same information she does, although I usually don't have time for such foolishness with a job as demanding as mine." (Cousin Be-trice compiles the news of local social events every week for the *Liberty*

Bend Gazette, but you wouldn't want to believe everything she writes.) Now she smiled her rabbity grin and reluctantly slid over to let Rob out of the booth. "There was no reunion last weekend," she announced. "If there had been, I'd have known it."

Back at Smokerise, while Rob crashed on the sofa I phoned the number Mom had given me to reach them at Ellynwood Cottage. We'd be delayed a couple of days, I said, and explained about Jasper Totherow's unfortunate demise.

"My gracious, Prentice!" my mother gasped. "What's going on out there? Do they have any idea who did it?"

"Ralphine comes to mind," I said.

"Bosh! Not that Jasper wasn't a worthless piece of nuisance, but he really wasn't worth killing. Ralphine knows that better than anybody."

I agreed. "I think the police are on to something," I said. "They've searched our place inside and out, but I have no idea what they're looking for." I still didn't say anything about the man with the beard. After all, Jasper had been dead for at least a couple of days before the stranger showed up at my door. "How's Joey?" I asked, eager to change the subject.

"Brilliant. Prentice, he's starting to crawl. And I think he likes me," Mom said. "I'm sure he knows I'm his grandmother."

"And Ola. She okay?"

My mother hesitated. "Uh-huh."

"I guess she must be close by," I said.

"Why yes, that's right."

"And still acting weird?"

"Well . . . some of the time, but the weather here is lovely, Prentice, and the little house is charming. I don't understand it, but it smells like strawberries here."

Jasper had died of a broken neck, Deputy Weber told me when he came by later that day. Since Rob was still sacked out on the sofa, the two of us sat on the back steps in the fading afternoon sun. I tried to avoid looking in the direction of the barn lot.

"How do you know he didn't fall?" I said. "Maybe he'd been drinking."

"Of course we considered that," he said, "and as it turns out, he had been drinking a little beer."

"How much is a little?"

He smiled and shook his head. "Well, in Jasper's case, not enough to cause him to fall. Plus, in addition to a broken neck, he had a concussion that couldn't have come from the fall."

"You think somebody hit him? With what? What else did you find out there?" I'd seen them taking photographs and knew they had checked for fingerprints, but that wouldn't account for all the hush-hush and huddle going on. "Something must've turned up. I saw that detective crawling around in the muck out there. Come on, Don, you can tell me."

But the deputy clamped shut tighter than a miser's purse. He'd already said more than he should've, he told me.

He did say he thought it would be all right if Rob and I took off for a day or two as long as they knew where to reach me—just in case the bearded man turned up. And maybe it was my imagination, but there was something in the way he said it that led me to think they weren't all that sure there *was* a bearded man.

The next day temperatures were mild for March as Rob and I started for the mountains with a couple of overnight bags and a hurriedly packed picnic basket in the trunk.

Rob, in the passenger seat, leaned back and sighed. "What a grand idea, Prentice! You just don't know how many times I've thought of doing something like this." And he smiled at me with his blue, blue eyes. "Will it take very long to get there?"

"Not too long. There's a park just above Dalonega where I thought we'd eat our lunch. It's right on the river and there are hiking trails and cabins . . ."

"Forget the hiking trails," Rob said, reaching up to touch my neck. "Hey, where are we going now?"

"Into a ditch if we're not careful," I said. "Don't mess with me if you don't want me to run off the road!" I caught his hand and kissed it. "First, though, I have to stop at the library."

He grinned. "Don't tell me you plan to *read?*"

"Nope, but I do want to check on Aunt Zorah. She was acting stranger than usual yesterday, and I just want to be sure she's okay."

But my aunt hadn't come in that day, the Piranha said. "Says she wasn't feeling so good. I expect it's all that running around she does. Bound to take its toll, and Zorah's not getting any younger either!

"How's your mama today?" she asked as I was leaving.

"My mama?" I hesitated.

"You said she had the flu?"

"Oh. Right. A little better, thanks, but she's still running a slight fever." I had almost forgotten my mother's trumped-up illness.

Rather than use the phone at the library, I telephoned my aunt from a public booth on our way out of town. She sounded as if she'd been asleep a hundred years.

"Aunt Zorah? Did I wake you?"

"No. No, just resting. Can't seem to find the energy to get up out of this chair."

"Rob and I are on our way to the mountains. Are you sure you're all right? Can I get you anything before I go?"

"No, you go on. I'm fine, really. It's just old age creeping up, I'm afraid."

"Promise you'll call the doctor if you don't feel better." My aunt had a list of physicians beside the phone that would reach to Texas and back, and frankly I was surprised she hadn't called one already.

"I promise," she said. "But all I need right now is rest."

"Maybe you picked up some kind of bug at the reunion," I said. "Where was it this time? I forgot to ask."

"Sugar, I believe I hear my kettle boiling," my aunt said. "Call me when you get back."

Maybe this time Cousin Be-trice was right, I thought as I hung up the phone. But if Aunt Zorah hadn't gone to a family reunion, where on earth had she been?

I didn't worry about it long. I got back to the car to find Rob on the driver's side, and he leaned across to swing open the door. "Hope you don't mind if I drive," he said. "We have a lot of time to make up for and only a couple of days to do it. Now, which way are these cabins?"

CHAPTER TWENTY

We sat by a stream that sang of spring, our lunch on a blue flowered cloth before us, and Rob, who had said he wasn't hungry, ate two huge sandwiches, potato salad, a pear, and four peanut butter cookies. The blue cloth reminded me of Augusta. Or maybe it was the soothing sound of the stream. Trees were just beginning to bud into leaf, but the woods wore a winter look in soft shades of brown and gray like an old photograph. I could feel at peace here if it weren't for the car that had been behind us a few miles back and Rob's smug attitude.

"Okay," I said. "Maybe you were right."

He chose just the right pickle before answering. "Right about what?"

"Maybe I am being paranoid, but it looked like he was following us."

"If he'd been following us, why would he turn off before we did?"

I shrugged. "A trick? Maybe he knows a shortcut."

Rob shook his head and halfway smiled at me, as though I'd said I had been abducted by space aliens. "And you seem to see a beard around every corner. Prentice, that man didn't even have a beard."

"Then he had a bad case of five o'clock shadow!" I gathered up what was left of our lunch and jammed it into the basket. "Okay, so it probably wasn't him, but at this point I'd actually *like* to see the bearded man again."

Rob's hand closed over mine. "Hey, I'm on your side, remember? We're here for a picnic. I just want you to relax, forget about bodies, missing uncles, and sinister bearded men. Okay?"

"I'll try," I said. And for a little while I did. Our cabin was still being cleaned so we left our luggage in the car and climbed the trail to a clearing above the river where we could look across at the distant hills.

"It's beautiful here . . . and so are you." Rob wrapped his arms around me from behind and kissed the top of my head, my neck. He smelled of something wonderful and woodsy and I drew down his head and kissed him, delighting in the warmth and strength of his body against mine, the sweet closeness of his face. He spoke softly somewhere near my ear. "I've missed you, Prentice. God, it's good to be with you again."

"And I've missed you." I kissed him again and waited

for him to say what I wanted to hear. "I've thought of you a lot since you left. I know I didn't handle things too well. I'm sorry."

He held my hand against his chest. "Are you trying to tell me you've changed your mind?"

"About what?"

"About coming to England."

"Rob, there are too many things to deal with right now, too many ifs. I can't make a decision like that for a while." I turned, still holding his hand, to start back down the trail, but Rob stood firm.

"Then when, Prentice?" His blue eyes locked on to mine and held me there.

"You can't expect me to drop everything and go running off to England just because you're lonely," I said. "First we have to work things out about Joey. It's not just me anymore, Rob, and England's so far away. I couldn't do that to Mom—put an ocean between her and Joey." I smiled. "You should see her! She's a different woman since—"

"But I thought . . . I just assumed your mother would be raising Maggie's child." I could feel the tension like a current in Rob's fingers.

"His name is Joey," I said. "His parents are dead and his granddaddy's a lunatic. My mother and I are all he has, and she'll be sixty in November. I'm sure she wants to be a part of Joey's life, but she's already raised two children. Joey and I are a package deal—take it or leave it!"

I snatched my hand from his and ran down the path, stumbling over roots, shoving aside branches.

"Prentice, wait! Slow down, will you? Look, I wasn't thinking. Can't we just sit a minute and talk?" I heard him close behind me. My chest hurt from running, my eyes burned, and I had a pain in my side. I knew I wasn't being fair to Rob. I had thrust this upon him with very little prologue. What did I expect? I turned and waited for him, threw my arms around his neck and cried.

We sat on a stone outcropping and talked until the shadows began to grow longer, and what had been a refreshing breeze turned into a chilling wind. I shivered and pulled my light jacket closer about me as we renewed our descent. "You're cold. I'll go and get a fire started." Rob moved ahead of me on the path when we came within sight of the cabins. The small cottages were heated, but each was also supplied with a stack of wood for burning in the stone fireplace that dominated the main room. Our cabin, on entering, smelled of long-ago wood smoke and dark winter days, but the bathroom was clean, the sofa inviting, and soon bright flames fanned warmth and color into an otherwise dreary room.

While Rob drove a few miles for takeout from a restaurant we'd passed earlier, I showered and changed and opened the wine we'd brought, then added more wood to the fire and sipped some as I watched the flames leap and curl. I felt drained, limp, as if I'd been sick for a long time. During our conversation on the rock, Rob and I had "danced" around the topic of marriage. And as for the issue of raising Joey, Rob admitted he was hesitant, even afraid.

"It's not that I don't want children," he'd said. "Felicia and I talked about it, but then that never came about. And you know what my job is like. It's impossible to put down roots."

I didn't argue that other people with the news bureau had families, and that Joey, as a baby, would come to know him as his own father. If Rob couldn't see this for himself, he hardly needed it pointed out. We had, it seemed, come to a friendly wait-and-see impasse, and that, I thought, was the best we were going to do for a while.

But I still waited for Rob McCullough to say, "Marry me, Prentice. I love you," and with all our other problems, I should've let it go. After all, it wasn't a major issue at the moment, and the man had come all the way from England to spend time with me. But like an annoying moth, the omission flitted across my mind biting and gnawing and leaving little holes in my confidence.

Dinner, when it came, was fresh trout, flaky and delicious, and Rob and I ate it at a cozy table by the fire. Later, warm with wine, as we nuzzled on the sofa, I held his face in my hands and asked Rob McCullough just why he wanted me with him in England.

"What kind of question is that?" He tried to squirm away.

"Just answer it, Rob. Why me? You've never really said."

"I should think you'd know by now!" He was working into a huff.

"Maybe so, but I'd like to hear it . . . so why?"

"Well, damn it, Prentice, I like being with you and miss you when I'm not. I care for you! That's why."

"Care? You care?"

"Of course I do. What's wrong with you?" His voice had developed an edge.

"Nothing." I kissed him on the cheek and swallowed what might've become a great self-pitying cry. "I'm just tired, I guess. Feel like I've been scrubbed on a washboard and hung flappin' in the wind."

"I see," he said. And I could see that he did. "I'm sorry, Prentice."

I was sorry too.

"Damn it," I said to Dottie when I phoned her the next day. "Why did he have to have such blue eyes?"

"Aw . . . Prentice, I really hate this! Just give him a little time. Maybe things will work out."

I didn't think so. The night in the cabin had been strained, and if it hadn't been late and the two of us hadn't been drinking wine, we'd have driven back right away. Rob made a noble gesture and slept on the couch so I could have the bed. The man had flown all the way from England for a grand reunion that turned into a disaster, and I was sorry for that. But not so sorry I didn't sleep like a zombie, and when I woke the next morning he had the car packed and ready to go. The only good thing about the whole experience was, I was so miserable during the drive home, I forgot to worry about being followed.

"Where is Rob now?" Dottie asked.

"Had some business in Atlanta, and I think he plans to visit his mother in North Carolina before he flies back."

"Do you think you'll see him again?"

"I doubt it. At least not anytime soon." And probably not ever, I thought.

Rob had kissed me lightly on the lips before leaving me at Smokerise. "I guess the time's not right for either of us," he said. "But don't give up on me, Prentice. Please. Promise you'll stay in touch."

I would have promised anything just then because I knew if he hung around any longer I'd cry.

"Hey, listen, I'm here if you need me," Dottie said, her voice softer than usual. "I mean it. If you need a place to camp out for a while my rent's paid through the end of the month—and I make a mean lasagna!"

I felt a little better already.

I put on the kettle for tea and hunted in the freezer until I found that little hunk of date nut bread Augusta had made earlier. I missed Augusta, missed her funny mixed metaphors, her practical advice, and most of all the gentleness of her presence. But Mom and Ola needed her more. I was looking up the number to call them at Ellynwood when a police car pulled up in our driveway and Donald Weber got out. He seemed to be in a hurry.

I had the door open before he could knock.

"Good, I'm glad you're back," the deputy said, following me into the kitchen. "Kinda thought you might be gone a day or so longer."

"So did I," I said. I didn't elaborate. "Want some tea? Water's hot."

He shook his head. "Thanks, gotta get back. Came by here on the spur of the moment, hoping you might be here. See if you recognize this." He reached into his pocket and drew out a small plastic bag with some kind of trinket inside.

"Ralphine Totherow said Jasper gave this to their daughter to keep. Said she thought it was a charm for a bracelet."

He held the clear bag up to the light so I could see what was inside. "It doesn't belong to me," I told him. "I didn't even come close to earning one of these—in fact, I don't think I've ever seen one. It's a Phi Beta Kappa key."

"Right. I know. The honorary scholastic society. Thought maybe it might've belonged to you or your mom." Deputy Weber frowned. "Ralphine says she doesn't have a clue where Jasper got it and I was hoping you might know whose it was."

I reached out to touch the bag, then snatched back my hand as if I'd been stung. "Oh, God!" I said. "I'm afraid I do."

CHAPTER TWENTY-ONE

as my aunt Zorah seen this?" I asked Donald Weber.

"Why no, do you think it belongs to her?"

The fish from last night's supper flip-flopped in my stomach. I didn't feel so good. "I think it belonged to her husband. My aunt said Faris Haskell was buried with it."

I waited a second for this to sink in. "Ye gods and little fishes!" The deputy tossed the key, bag and all, on the table. "There are initials on the back, but it never occurred to me they might be his. Do you suppose Jasper took this off his body?" He didn't look too well either.

"Looks like somebody did. Aren't you going to see what the initials are?"

Reluctantly he picked up the bag and held it to the

light. "Kinda hard to make out, but it looks like *F.W.H.* Must be his, all right." He put the horrid thing back in his pocket.

"If you're going to see my aunt, give me a chance to speak with her first," I said, and he promised he would. After the way she'd been acting, I was afraid Aunt Zorah would need every doctor on her list when she saw Uncle Faris's long-buried "treasure."

For some reason that nobody remembers, the library in Liberty Bend closes at noon on Wednesdays, so I waited until my aunt had a chance to get home before I dropped by. I found her in the backyard on her hands and knees pulling weeds from her tulip bed. Aunt Zorah will do just about anything to avoid yard work and usually pays the boy down the street to do it, so this kind of took me by surprise. Besides that, she obviously still wore the clothes she'd gone to work in and had mud all down the front of her skirt.

"Let's go to lunch," I said.

"Good heavens, Prentice, you nearly scared me to death! I'm not hungry." She went on wrenching innocent plants from the ground.

"You're pulling up half your tulips, and you're supposed to leave that daffodil foliage," I pointed out, feeling faintly pleased that I knew something she didn't.

"Don't care. Just leave me alone."

I sat on her back steps. "Hey, things haven't been going so great in my life either. What's going on with yours?" I waited. "I'll tell you if you'll tell me."

My aunt stood and wiped her hands on her skirt.

"It's too god-awful to talk about. You wouldn't believe the mess."

"I might." I followed her inside, found something harmless in a can for our lunch, and told her about the Phi Beta Kappa key.

"Oh, what a tangled web we weave," she said, staring into her bowl of vegetable soup.

I covered her hand with mine. "I know Uncle Faris disappointed you, but that was a long time ago. Don't you think it's time to forgive him?"

I don't believe she even heard me. "If there's a bigger fool than Faris Haskell, it's me." And that was all she'd say.

The phone was ringing when I got home.

"How was your visit with Rob?" my mother wanted to know.

"We put things on hold," I said.

"Is that good or bad?"

"Depends on the way you look at it, I guess. Mom, I'm worried about Aunt Zorah." I told her about Uncle Faris's key and my aunt's strange behavior.

"Poor Zorah! Dear God, all this must be tearing her apart! Your dad said they tried every way in the world to keep her from marrying Faris Haskell but she wouldn't listen. Now just look at the trouble he's caused."

Just like Sonny Gaines, I thought, but I didn't say it. "How's everything at Ellynwood? I'm trying my best to get down there as soon as I can."

"That's why I'm calling. The weather here's been beautiful and I'd like to get Joey out more but we didn't have room for his stroller. Would you bring it when you come? And I'm running a little short on clothes— brought mostly winter things, and I think I left my good walking shoes under my bed; I could use a couple of pairs of shorts too."

"What about Ola?" I asked.

"I don't think she wears shorts." I thought I heard a little laugh here.

"I mean how is she? Holding up okay? You don't have any turrets there for her to jump off of, do you?"

"Prentice, what a thing to say! She's napping now, but she does seem sad, and she's on some kind of medication. I don't think she's well."

"You haven't seen any bearded strangers around, had any weird phone calls, have you?"

"No, thank heavens! So far, so good. What about you?" my mother asked.

"Lately I haven't had time to notice," I said. And that was the truth.

I also hadn't had time to check my phone messages. A part of me hoped there would be one from Rob saying he wanted to forget what had happened—or didn't happen—on our mountain trip and start all over again. The other part of me was relieved when there wasn't.

Dottie had phoned to say she'd had an encouraging response to some inquiries on our exciting new project and to keep my fingers crossed. The dentist's office called to remind my mother it was time to have her teeth cleaned, and some man I'd never heard of left a message to see if we'd be interested in leasing our property for a nursery and garden center.

I played the last message again. The man's name was Peter Whisonant. He and his partners owned a business in Cartersville, a town about thirty miles away, and were interested in expanding to our area, he said. He sounded gruff, businesslike, and to the point, and left a number for an exchange in Cartersville. I wrote down his name and number and filed it with a bunch of other stuff in the kitchen drawer that barely shut. This would be something I might refer to Mom's lawyer friend when he returned from his European travels.

Upstairs I found my mother's shoes under her bed as she'd suspected, selected some of her shorts and lighter clothing for the sweltering south Georgia climate, and set them aside with Joey's stroller. Bearded man or no bearded man, I was going to leave for Ellynwood in the morning unless something earthshaking occurred.

And what happened the next day might not have been earthshaking, but it created a heck of a quake in Liberty Bend.

I was finishing a hasty breakfast when Sheriff Bonner

called. "We need you to come down here for a few minutes if you can," he said without the usual polite preliminaries. And of course my first thought was of Aunt Zorah.

"What's wrong? Is it my aunt? Has she—?" I couldn't bring myself to finish.

"No, no. It's not that. We're holding someone for questioning in Jasper Totherow's death and possibly the death of the woman we found on your property. We'd like you to have a look at him, see if he looks familiar."

Was it the bearded man? But why would anyone in Sonny Gaines's family want to kill Jasper Totherow? As far as I knew, they didn't even know him.

I would just have to find out when I got there. I knew the police had questioned Ralphine but had found no reason to hold her. If they seriously suspected anyone else, I hadn't heard about it. I stuck my cereal bowl in the sink, grabbed my coffee mug, and hurried to the car, hoping that when I got to town we would know something at last. Was Jasper's murder connected with what had happened to Uncle Faris? Was that why Aunt Zorah was behaving so strangely?

By the time I reached the sheriff's office, I was gripping the steering wheel so tightly my fingers felt welded to it.

The suspect was being held in an adjoining building that housed the county jail, and remained in a small room for questioning. A policeman led me down a long corridor so that I could look through a window and see him.

He wasn't anything like what I expected. The man fidgeted in his seat, examined his hands, paced to the window, then back again where he sank heavily into the chair and drummed his fingers on the table. Except for the table and two chairs, the room was bare. The man was alone. I didn't know him.

"Anybody you recognize?" Sheriff Bonner wanted to know when I was led into his inner sanctum a few minutes later.

I shook my head. "I've never seen him."

"Are you sure? He has a beard."

"But he's not the man I saw. Not the one who came to our house. This man's older—much older, and fatter, and his beard's fuller, fuzzier. Also he wears glasses. The other man didn't."

The sheriff leaned back in his chair. "So you're never seen him?"

"Not that I know of. Why?"

"Because Suzie Wright said he looks like the guy she saw running into the woods on your property, the one wearing that purple cap."

I shrugged. "Could be, but I never saw him. Who is he?"

"Gives his name as Fabius Hawthorne." The sheriff smiled. "You probably know him better as Faris Haskell."

If I had been the fainting kind, I think I would've passed out cold right then, but the floor looked none too clean, and I was distracted by a most annoying noise that sounded like an old dog baying.

Turned out to be an old funeral director. "I'll swear to you I had nothing to do with that man's death!" Maynard Griggs hollered. "This is harassment—that's exactly what it is!"

I recognized the policeman as one of the detectives who had been at Smokerise recently. He looked a little like Peter Sellers, the actor who played Inspector Clouseau, and I halfway expected him to fall over a chair or something. Instead he led the elder Mr. Griggs into the sheriff's office and seated him gently. I didn't know whether to stay or go, so I stayed.

"We're not accusing you of killing anybody, Mr. Griggs." The sheriff spoke calmly. "We just need some information is all, and I understand you might be able to help us."

The old man's lip quivered. "I don't know anything about it. I've a right to a lawyer. And my son Harold—where is he, anyway?"

"Harold's on his way," the sheriff told him, "and here's the phone . . . or would you like us to call a lawyer for you?"

"I'll wait till Harold gets here." The old fellow looked up at me. "Oh, dear," he said. "This really is a quagmire."

Somebody brought water in a paper cup and Maynard Griggs drained it in a couple of gulps, then shook his head. "Oh, Lord, what will become of me? What's Ernestine going to say?"

"About what, Mr. Griggs?" the sheriff prodded.

"I should've known no good would come of all this,

and now that fellow's dead too. I told Faris it wouldn't work."

"What wouldn't work?" Sheriff Bonner asked.

"Why, killing him, of course! He wanted to, you know. Faris did. That Jasper Totherow. Faris was all for killing him so he wouldn't talk . . . but I couldn't. I just couldn't!"

The sheriff leaned across his desk and made a steeple of his fingers. "But you did know the woman we found in what was supposed to have been Faris Haskell's coffin, didn't you, Mr. Griggs?"

The man turned almost as white as the hair on his head. "I don't know what you mean."

"I think you do," the sheriff said. "And we have reason to believe you put her there."

CHAPTER TWENTY-TWO

You can't prove that!" The elder Griggs started to rise, then thought better of it and sat down again. "I can't believe it's come to this." He reached shakily for another cup of water. "And if Faris Haskell told you I had anything to do with killing Jasper Totherow, he's lying through his teeth!"

"But you did discuss it?" the sheriff said. "You and Mr. Haskell . . . Hawthorne . . . whoever. You talked about killing Jasper Totherow. Mind telling us why?"

"He was going to tell. Threatened to let everybody know Faris wasn't dead."

Sheriff Bonner frowned. "And I don't suppose you know anything about how Colette Champion got into that coffin?"

"Who?"

"I think you know who. We turned up a car rented to you from an agency over in Rome . . . seems it had some dents that hadn't been there before. Fellow said you told him you'd hit a dog."

"That's right, I did. Ran right in front of me. Unavoidable." Mr. Griggs crushed his paper cup into a microwad.

Sheriff Bonner just sat there and looked at him. He didn't speak.

"Look, I paid these people for the damages." Maynard Griggs tried to look away. "Is that what this is all about?"

The sheriff spoke softly. "That wasn't animal blood we found underneath your fender, Mr. Griggs. It was human blood. O negative. Same type as Colette Champion's."

"Blood? But how—I don't understand."

"Hard to get rid of bloodstains, Mr. Griggs. Ever read *Macbeth*? Some stains just won't go away." The sheriff looked at his hands. " 'Out, out damned spot!' " I was surprised he remembered the quote after what my mother had said.

Mr. Griggs examined his hands too. "It was an accident," he said. "I never meant to kill her."

Thornton Bonner drew in his breath. "Maybe we ought to start at the beginning—back when Faris Haskell 'died.' Tell me something . . . just what *was* buried in that coffin all these years?"

The older man sighed and his eyes were bleak as stagnant water. "Nothing. Just rocks. He wanted everyone to think he died when his car went off the road at Poindexter Point. I was coroner then and I filled out a death certificate and buried a coffin full of rocks."

"*You* were the one who dug up the grave!" I spoke without thinking and the others turned and looked at me.

"That was Jasper Totherow," Maynard Griggs mumbled.

"But the two of you hired him to do it," Detective "Clouseau" said, stroking his mustache. I resisted an impulse to smile. "Why?"

The old fellow blew his nose and looked behind him toward the door as if he might try to make a dash for it. "The two of us couldn't handle it alone. We told him the family was moving the grave to another cemetery," he said.

"So you and your friend paid Jasper to do the digging." The sheriff played with a pencil, wove it in and out his fingers. "Then later you meant to bury Colette Champion in that same place. What happened?"

"Hell, we dropped the darn thing getting it out of the ground, and you could hear those rocks shifting about." Mr. Griggs shook his head as if remembering. "Jasper couldn't tackle the coffin by himself so the two of us had to help him remove it. It was freezing cold, and dark as pitch; we couldn't half see. Had a devil of a time getting it out—and then that happened."

"Did he know who Faris was?" Sheriff Bonner wanted to know.

"Pretended he didn't, but he figured it out. Got more sense than we gave him credit for, I reckon."

"Let's get back to Colette Champion," the sheriff said. "How did she figure in all this?"

"I don't have to answer that." Mr. Griggs spoke louder, but there was a tremor in his voice.

"Her blood was underneath that car and her prints were inside it. I expect to find yours there as well." Sheriff Bonner paused. "Why did you kill her, Mr. Griggs?"

The older man shuddered. "I didn't mean to! It was an accident. You've got to believe me!"

I had heard rumors of the elder Griggs's infidelities, although looking at him today, it was hard to believe. Maynard Griggs had a wandering eye, according to Aunt Zorah, and I'd heard he'd had an affair with someone early in his marriage and paid her to have an abortion and leave town.

Apparently he had kept on paying. Things were tight back then and he was just getting started in his business. He couldn't go to his wife's family for hush money, Maynard Griggs explained. And at the same time, his wife Ernestine was expecting their first child.

And that was when my uncle Faris came into it, I learned. Faris Haskell gave his friend the money to pay off the woman and send her away. But it wasn't far enough.

"I knew Faris was up to something that wasn't right," Mr. Griggs admitted. "Too much money all of a sudden, but I was desperate. I didn't care where it came from!"

"Then later when Haskell needed your help to disappear, you buried an empty casket," the detective said. "And years later it seemed the perfect hiding place for the woman you'd just killed." He paced the length of the small room and back without even stepping into the wastebasket. "Colette Champion had no close relatives; few would notice her missing, and even if they did, who would think of looking in an old grave?"

The old man didn't say anything.

"So what stopped you?" the detective persisted. "Jasper?"

"No, we sent him on his way, but a car drove up just as we were about to—you know . . ."

"Put Colette's body in the casket?" Sheriff Bonner helped himself to the water, sipped it slowly.

Mr. Griggs nodded. "It was down there on that back road just below the cemetery. Kids park there sometimes. We couldn't take the chance."

"So you stored her in the shed, meaning to come back and take care of that business later?" The sheriff tossed his cup at the wastebasket and missed.

Maynard Griggs looked at me as if he recognized me for the first time. "I had no idea you'd come home, that anybody was around after your mother left. We thought the place was deserted."

"That still doesn't explain why you murdered Colette Champion." The Clouseau look-alike leaned against the wall, arms folded.

"I didn't *murder* her! I told you. It was an accident."

Colette Champion had been blackmailing him for

years, Maynard Griggs told us, until finally he'd had enough.

"So you decided to kill her. Is that why you went to that remote park and drove a rental car instead of your own?" Sheriff Bonner leaned back in his chair. It creaked.

"No! No, of course not! I drove a rental car because too many people might recognize mine, and I couldn't afford to be seen with her. I went there to call her bluff, that's all, to tell her she'd be getting no more money from me."

Maynard Griggs slumped forward, twisted his diamond-studded wedding band. "Look, is there any way we can keep this quiet—at least until after the election? This is a god-awful thing to happen right now while Harold's running for office!"

"A little late to think of that now," the sheriff reminded him.

"The woman wouldn't leave me alone! Just about drained me dry. Even threatened to tell Ernestine." Maynard Griggs shook his head slowly. "I didn't believe her. By God, she knew she'd never get another cent if she did that!"

He had picked up Colette Champion at the bus station in a rental car and the two drove to a small picnic area a few miles outside of town. "To talk," he insisted. "Merely to talk; I didn't want her making a scene in public."

They got out of the car and sat at one of the picnic tables, he continued. "When I told her there'd be no more money, she threw a fit. Screamed and struck at me, called me every name in the book.

"I was furious," Maynard Griggs said. "I knew if I hit her—and believe me, I wanted to—I might do serious harm. I just wanted to get away—drive off and leave her there until we could both cool off some." He looked at the three of us in turn. "I swear to you, I'm not a violent man. Anybody will tell you that, but that woman—well, she just about pushed me over the edge. I got in the car and started out of the park"—he closed his eyes—"but she came after me screaming, running, holding on to the driver's door. I couldn't shake her loose. The woman was crazy!"

Sheriff Bonner straightened suddenly. "So you ran over her?"

"She fell. I didn't mean to, didn't realize what had happened until I felt that sickening thump. By then it was too late. There was nothing I could do." He covered his face with his hands. "Oh, God, all I wanted was to get away from her!"

The detective filled another cup with water and held it out to him. He spoke softly. "So you contacted Faris Haskell to help you get rid of the body?"

"Right. I hadn't heard from Faris in years, but I knew where to find him. We paid Jasper to help us dig up the coffin, didn't think he'd ask questions." The old man sighed. "That's where we were wrong. When news got out about your finding Colette's body in the shed, Totherow put two and two together. The little weasel tried to blackmail us!"

"And did you pay him off?" the detective asked.

"Some, but he kept coming back for more. We knew he'd never be satisfied."

"And so you planned to kill him as well?" the officer continued.

"Look . . . maybe we did talk about it, but it never came to that. I'll swear it didn't!" Maynard Griggs was close to tears. His hand trembled as he mopped his face.

"Looks like you were pretty serious about it to me," the sheriff said, "since you'd already started digging a grave for the guy. That *was* meant for Jasper, wasn't it— that makeshift trench back of the Dobson place?"

"That's ridiculous! I had nothing to do with killing that man." Maynard Griggs folded his arms, reminding me of an aging Buddha, except he wasn't smiling.

"Then who did?" the sheriff asked. "Ralphine claims he went into hiding, says he was terrified of somebody. And *somebody* had to have killed him. Faris Haskell says it wasn't him."

"Maybe you'd better ask Zorah," the older man said. "Last time I saw that Totherow fellow, the two of them were going at it tooth and nail."

Get real! I was tempted to say. My aunt Zorah wouldn't get within hair-pulling distance of Jasper Totherow.

Sheriff Bonner smiled. "Come now, Mr. Griggs, surely you can do better than that."

"Joke if you like, but it's true. I heard them arguing—

shouting really. Zorah was furious about something, picked up a shovel. I saw her."

"And where was this?" The detective with the mustache barely looked up, as if he wasn't even interested, but I could tell he was.

"At the Dobson place—out there in the barn, and it was right around the time you say he was killed. Find that shovel and you'll see I'm telling the truth. Her prints must be all over it."

"Why didn't you say something earlier?" the sheriff asked. "And just what were you doing out there when all this was going on?"

"I was supposed to give him money. Wanted a hundred dollars more to keep quiet about Colette—and that was to be the end of it. I'd already told him that."

"And did you?" the detective asked.

"Did I what?" Mr. Griggs looked up under half-closed lids.

"Did you pay Jasper the hundred bucks?"

"Look, when I saw what was going on with those two, I didn't hang around. I was kinda hoping Zorah would scare the little bastard off, but I didn't think she'd actually kill him!

"Besides, I was in a hurry. My son wanted me to ride with him to Montgomery to pick up a body. Man who used to live here and wanted to be buried with his family. I didn't have the time or the inclination to worry about the likes of Jasper Totherow!"

"Seems an upright, law-abiding fellow like yourself

would've gone to the police about all this when Jasper turned up dead." The sheriff spoke with a straight face. I don't know how.

"What good would it have done? He was already dead, wasn't he? And certainly no great loss. For all I knew, it might've been Faris who killed him."

"Killed who?" The younger Griggs stood in the doorway looking more grim-faced than usual. "What's going on here?"

The sheriff told him.

"Dad, you don't have to answer their questions. I can't believe this!" Griggs the younger reached for the telephone. "I'll have the lot of you up on harassment charges. My father's not well. Been under a doctor's care for several weeks now." He fumbled through the phone book, then threw it down and rubbed his face with his hands. "Damn! I can't even find the blasted lawyer's number!"

"Let it go, son." Maynard patted Harold's arm. "The truth will out, and the sooner the better. This has gone on long enough. Frankly I'll be glad when it's over."

"Dad! Surely you aren't saying you had anything to do with what happened to Jasper Totherow?"

"Not Jasper, but it was my indiscretion that started it all. I'm sorry, son." And Maynard Griggs put his head in his hands and wept.

"Do I have news for you!" I told Mom when I phoned her later. Our telephone bill was going to be out of sight. "Maybe you'd better sit down first, mix a strong drink."

"Prentice, don't do this to me!"

"Okay, to start with, Uncle Faris isn't even dead." I told her about the rigged-up car "accident" and faked death certificate. "Seems Maynard Griggs had an affair with some woman around here and got her pregnant . . ."

"Colette Champion," my mother said.

"Uh—right."

"I remember Colette. No better than she should be, but then neither was Maynard. Everybody sort of suspected something was going on, and then she left town and that was that."

"Well, she had an abortion I guess," I told her. "Maynard says he paid her off big-time, but she kept coming back for more."

"What did Faris Haskell have to do with this?" Mom asked.

"Faris gave him the money to pay her. Money he'd embezzled, I guess, but Maynard wasn't in a position to be picky. Of course he had to pay him back in the long run by helping to fake Faris's death."

"This is almost too much to take in, but then it's like something Faris would do, and he and Maynard used to be thick as thieves—pardon the expression. But how did the woman end up in our barn?"

"Long story," I said, and told her.

I could hear my mother breathing in the silence that followed. "Mom, are you okay?"

"I'm all right, Prentice, but I'm not so sure about your aunt Zorah. Dear God, what will she do? Have they arrested anybody?"

"They've arrested Maynard Griggs for the murder of Colette Champion, and they're still holding Un—uh—Faris, but neither will admit to killing Jasper. You're not going to believe this, Mom, but Maynard Griggs is trying to blame it on Aunt Zorah!"

"Zorah! Prentice, that's not funny."

"Not meant to be." I told Mom about the shovel.

"Surely the police aren't taking him seriously. I always thought Maynard Griggs was more than a little peculiar. Whole family's nutty! They said his mama bathed with her clothes on.

"They haven't arrested Zorah, have they?" My mother sounded close to tears. "Prentice, this is a nightmare! I'd better come home."

"Not yet. What could you do? Let me worry about things on this end. If anything develops, I'll let you know."

"I'll feel better when you can join us down here."

"You know I'll come as soon as I can, but since things are in such a stew here, it's going to be a little later than we'd planned. If it's okay with you and Ola, Dottie said she'd be glad to drop off the things you need. She has a niece who lives at Hilton Head and she's been looking for an excuse to go and visit." I had spoken with Dottie earlier and she'd said she was more than ready for a break.

"Dottie Ives? Well, of course I'd love to see her. When can we look for her?"

"Sometime tomorrow. I'm leaving for her place in a little while and I'll stay with Dottie tonight in Atlanta, then drive back to Liberty Bend in the morning."

Frankly I was glad for an excuse to spend the night away from Smokerise. Even knowing it was Uncle Faris and company who dug up his own "grave" and left a corpse in our shed, we still weren't sure who killed Jasper Totherow, and I had an uneasy feeling Pershing Gaines and his gang were regrouping for an attack.

"Maybe Dottie will stay long enough for me to show off Joey," Mom said. "He's the sweetest baby, Prentice. I think he looks a lot like your dad, but I'd forgotten how demanding it was to look after one that age. By bedtime I'm worn out!"

"Doesn't Ola help?"

"Some. She gets up with him at night. I don't think she sleeps much anyway. The woman cleans house in the middle of the night, then claims she didn't do it."

"Really?"

"Can you believe it? I shouldn't complain; the place stays spotless, and once in a while she'll even bake something for the next day. Why, yesterday we had a loaf of dilly bread that was out of this world. Ola's a marvelous cook—of course she puts the pots and pans back in the wrong places."

"No kidding?" I smiled. "And she denies doing it?"

"Says she doesn't remember a thing about it. Claims it's an angel." My mother sighed. "I really do think the poor soul's slipping."

"I checked with your lawyer's office in Atlanta, Mom. Your friend Wally is due home sometime next week. Maybe we can work this out soon and Ola can get her own life back.

"By the way," I said, "a man called here yesterday and left a message, wants to lease the farm for a nursery. Thought we might ask your friend about that as well."

"What man?" Mom asked.

"Said his name was Whisonant. Peter Whisonant. Has a garden center in Cartersville. He left a number."

"Peter Whisonant . . . I've heard of his place. It's a huge operation. They have just about everything there. Hollis Prater gets all her day lilies from them. You remember Hollis? Used to be in my bridge club? Has about an acre of day lilies right behind her house."

"You think I should call him back?"

"If you think you'd be interested, and if he's really who he says he is," she added.

But how was I to know?

Sit down and think, a calming voice said. And so I did. I phoned for directory assistance and asked for the number of the nursery in Cartersville. It was the same one I'd written down the day before.

I was returning Mr. Whisonant's call, I told the clerk who answered, and would like to talk with him about the property near Liberty Bend. But talk was all I meant to do. Even after the trauma of the last few months, Smokerise, and the land surrounding it, was my home, just as it had been home to generations before me. I didn't know how I would manage to keep it up, but I wasn't ready to let it go. The house, the red soil, the huge old oaks, and the rolling hills were all a part of me, just as I was a part of them. The thought of this land belonging to someone else caused an ache so deep inside me it almost hurt to breathe. And I came close to calling the man back to tell him I'd changed my mind.

I was feeding the cat before leaving for Dottie's when he returned my call, and the unexpected ringing caused both of us to jump.

Their plan would include the construction of a large greenhouse and a couple of other buildings, Peter Whisonant told me. A major part of the acreage would be planted in trees and shrubs, and possibly an orchard later if things worked out.

"I don't know," I said. "Smokerise—this house—is our home. I was raised here. I'm not sure I like the idea of turning it over to strangers."

"I understand. And that's certainly negotiable," he said. "We don't plan to use the house itself, and you can determine what your boundaries are to be.

"I'd like you to talk with my nephew if you would. He's a horticulturist and one of the partners I spoke of and can show you on paper what we have in mind."

It sounded promising, yet I still wasn't sure I was

ready to commit to such an arrangement. I did agree to look at the blueprints with the man's horticulturist kin, who would soon be in touch, he promised.

When the phone rang a few minutes later, I thought it might be the nurseryman's nephew calling to set up a meeting, so I paused begrudgingly to answer it on my way out the door.

"I know you have the boy," a man's voice said, "and I won't stop until I find him. I'll be watching you every minute. Just remember that."

By the time I found the breath to reply, the man had hung up.

I couldn't get to Dottie's fast enough.

CHAPTER TWENTY-THREE

I should've known something else was about to happen. I guess we all expected it.

As soon as I got back from Atlanta the next morning, I found out Faris Haskell had been charged with the murder of Jasper Totherow. I learned it from Aunt Zorah who said she was on her way to see him.

I drove straight to her house instead of home, partly because I was putting off going to Smokerise alone, but I'd also made my aunt promise she wouldn't go to see Faris without me. She met me at the door, her brassy hair all tousled and lipstick askew, like she'd tried to put on makeup with a rubber stamp and missed.

"They've arrested that fool Faris," she told me without so much as a flicker of change in her expression. "They say he killed Jasper Totherow. Found his bloody thumbprint on the wall below the barn loft—blood type same as Jasper's, and he had scratches on his wrist that could've come from the dead man. Some policeman with a strong stomach and no sense of smell scraped residue from under Jasper's nails that might be human skin—maybe Faris's, although I don't know how they could tell it from all the dirt."

"Oh, dear," I said, and sighed. I didn't know if this was good or bad. It didn't feel good, and Aunt Zorah didn't look good either; in fact, she looked like somebody had told her the world would end tomorrow and it was five minutes till midnight. But at least they hadn't arrested *her*.

They had questioned her, she said. "And they went through my closet too—dresser drawers, everything—looking for I don't know what. The very nerve! I made them put every bit back how they found it." My aunt made a face. "Wanted to know if I'd whacked Jasper with a shovel."

"And did you?" I asked, hoping if she had, she'd have sense enough to lie about it.

"Can't say I didn't consider it," my aunt said. "Lowlife tried to blackmail me with Faris's Phi Beta Kappa key. Said he'd tell everybody what Faris did, that he was still alive. Wanted me to meet him there in the barn lot at Smokerise." Aunt Zorah moaned low in her throat. "Of course I already knew that by then."

I followed her into the kitchen where she stood for a minute looking as if she'd forgotten what she came for, then waited while she filled a glass with water and drank it.

240

"I've been such a fool, Prentice! Just couldn't stand the thought of everybody knowing, laughing . . ." She shook her head. "And what would it matter if they did?"

"So, what happened then?" I asked, although I wasn't really sure I wanted to know.

She shrugged. "I'm ashamed to admit I was going to be stupid enough to pay that piece of trash, but he didn't bring the key with him. Said he'd left it in a safe place. Idiot expected me to give him money for something he didn't even have!"

I shook my head as if in disbelief, although I wasn't one bit surprised. "And then . . . ?"

"Well, it just went all over me all of a sudden, and I picked up a shovel and made like I was going to cream the little weasel!" She laughed. "You should've seen that nitwit scramble up that ladder to the loft to get away—as if I might come after him!" My aunt snorted. "I'm not climbing into a hayloft after any man, especially that one!"

I waited for her to go on, but she didn't. "And that was all?"

"What did you expect, Prentice? Of course that's all! I realized what a fool I'd been and left the wretch up there. He must've fallen through that old rotten floor and landed on his head. They say pride goeth before a fall . . . seems it was my pride, but Jasper's fall."

She set her empty glass aside and slowly made her way through a dark book-lined hallway to the small sitting room.

"But somebody hit him from behind," I reminded her.

She tossed me a long-suffering glance. "Wasn't me."

"What happened to the shovel?"

"How should I know?"

"It might have your prints on it. You didn't—move it or anything?"

"Now why would I do that? Maybe whoever killed him disposed of it—if, as you seem to think, the shovel was their weapon of choice."

Don't go there, Prentice Dobson! I warned myself. *You've said too much already.*

"Have you spoken with Uncle Faris yet?" I asked as she gestured for me to sit in her ancient Morris chair with the fringed arm protectors. I sat carefully. I knew it had belonged to her father, maybe even her grandfather.

"Of course not," she said. "After all, I was the one who put him there." She shrugged. "Well, he put himself there, but I turned him in to the police."

"Why did you do that? When?"

"In Florida a few days ago. Faris took my silver. Had it in his suitcase. Can you believe he'd do that to his own wife? They caught him boarding a plane to Mexico."

I could believe Faris Haskell capable of just about anything. "You didn't go to a family reunion, did you?"

Aunt Zorah sat across from me. "No, I didn't."

"How did you find out? About Faris, I mean?"

"Didn't you notice that pile of rocks by his grave? They weren't there before. Had to come from some-where."

Of course I'd noticed them. I just hadn't thought much about it.

"And then Maynard Griggs started *reading*! Checking out books from the library. He's never been too bright, you know. If he had any sense, he wouldn't have married that uppity Ernestine. Why, Maynard hasn't read anything significant since Miss Mamie Pitts made us memorize *The Thanatopsis* in high school, and here he was taking home books by Dickens and Thoreau."

"I thought they were for his granddaughter," I said.

"Bah! She doesn't have any more sense than he does. And Ernestine never reads anything heavier than those magazines like that Martha Stewart puts out. I knew they were for somebody else. And he wouldn't meet my eyes either. Slipperier than a greased eel that one. Figured he was up to something. A little warning bell went off in my head—only it wasn't so little. Sounded more like Big Ben." My aunt straightened her glasses. "Never ignore a warning bell, Prentice."

"No, ma'am," I said. My own noggin vibrated from the tolling already. "But how'd you know how to find him?"

"Knew he had to be staying somewhere nearby, but not with Maynard. That wouldn't do. Not but one other place around here and that's the Liberty Leisure Inn."

"Oh, surely not!" I said. "Nobody stays there." Even the "in your pants after one dance" couples back in high school avoided that place. We called it the "crab lab" because of . . . well, just because.

"But that's just what Faris wanted. Even after all this time, he couldn't take a chance on being recognized, and nobody around here would be caught d—" Aunt Zorah cleared her throat. "Well, he could be sure no one he knew would be staying there. And sure enough I followed Maynard there one day, saw him dropping off some books; he never suspected a thing. I'll swear, if that man had bird brains, he'd fly backward!

"Anyway, after he left, I went in and looked at the register. Faris didn't sign his right name, of course, but I recognized his handwriting, and the address was the one in Florida. When the fool dropped out of sight a few days later, I knew where to find him."

"Do you think he killed Jasper?" I asked my aunt as we drove to the county jail.

She was quiet for a minute. "I think he has it in him to do it, and Jasper did have Faris's precious key. I found out later he gave it to his daughter to keep. How'd he come by it unless he stole it off of Faris? Damn fool thinks more of that key than he does himself, and if you don't want to make him mad, don't mess around with that Phi Beta Kappa key."

"He could've lost it," I suggested. "Maybe Jasper found it somewhere."

"Maybe," my aunt said. But I could see she didn't believe it.

Faris Haskell né Fabius Hawthorne wasn't at all happy to see us. We met in a small room with nothing but a table between us and he stood about as far away from that as he could get. "I don't have anything to say to you," he said to my aunt. He took a step backward, then another. Any farther and he'd back into a cement wall.

"I have plenty to say to you, Faris Haskell," Aunt Zorah said, "but I don't like to use words like that in front of Prentice."

The man looked around as if looking for a quick escape route, and for a minute I thought he was going to call the guard on the other side of the door. He had reason to be afraid. Aunt Zorah was using her forced calm voice. Not a good sign.

Faris spoke quietly. "I didn't kill that man, Zorah. Hadn't even seen him in over a week. I was in Florida when all that happened." He backed against the wall like he needed it to hold him up. He didn't sound convincing.

"Then how did he come to have your Phi Beta Kappa key?" my aunt asked. "I hope you have a good lawyer, Faris. You're going to need one."

I didn't think he was going to answer. He shook his head, crossed his arms, and sighed. He was an unattractive, shaggy man with a bulging middle, and the orange prison jumpsuit wasn't his color at all. I couldn't imagine what Aunt Zorah ever saw in him.

"We had a bit of a scuffle," he said. "But that's all it was. A scuffle. I bloodied his nose and I guess he scratched my arm. That must've been when I lost the key. It was somewhere in the barn lot; I tried and tried to find it, but it was already gone."

The man with the flashlight the night it snowed! The hat with purple ear flaps. Of course! Faris Haskell came back to look for his missing key. But Jasper Totherow got there first.

"He tried to blackmail you with it, didn't he?" I said.

"Hell no! Not about that. I never saw the man again after that. The fool threatened to go to the police after they found Colette Champion. Maynard paid him to keep quiet, but I knew that wouldn't be the end of it."

And then he tried to get money from Aunt Zorah.

"I've told them over and over I wasn't here when that man was killed! Why won't they believe me?"

"My goodness, I can't imagine! I guess you'll just have to prove it." My aunt pulled out a chair and sat in it. She didn't look at the man who had been her husband. "Maynard Griggs says the two of you meant to kill Jasper. Just how were you planning to do that, Faris?"

"Maynard's a fool!" he muttered.

"I won't argue with you there, but somebody dug a hole back there in the woods on the side of the hill big enough to hide a body. That where you were going to put him?"

"What do you want from me, Zorah? What do you want me to say? Yes, we did talk about killing Jasper Totherow, and yes, we did dig that trench to hide the body, but we both came to the conclusion it wasn't worth it."

That accounted for the ring around our bathtub, I thought. Neither Faris nor Maynard Griggs could afford to be seen covered in mud after digging that trench, and they'd enjoyed an early breakfast at Smokerise as well.

"Planning to kill somebody and actually doing it are two different things!" Faris Haskell paced as he talked, pausing only for audible huffing and puffing. Now he turned to Aunt Zorah with his face all red and purple, and if words could steam, we'd both be scalded. "I didn't kill that man, and I didn't take your damn silverware either!"

"Oh, my! Then how did it get in your baggage?" My aunt pretended shock.

I didn't have to pretend. The reality of what he was saying slapped me cold. Maybe Faris Haskell had killed Jasper Totherow and maybe he hadn't, but I knew he was telling the truth about the silver. Why would a man who had as much to lose as Faris Haskell risk trying to leave the country with stolen silverware? He might be a fool, but surely the man had more sense than that.

Faris had mean eyes, and his Coke-bottle glasses made them appear even bigger and meaner. Now he fixed them on me. "She put it there, you know. Your aunt put that silver in my luggage and she knows it."

"Now why would I do that?" Aunt Zorah said.

Maybe Uncle Faris hadn't been dead for all those

years the way we thought, but his eyes were, and now he fastened those cold orbs on my aunt. "Why indeed, Zorah? You tell me. Is this to be my punishment?" And he called for the guard to take him away.

"Did you?" I asked my aunt later when we pulled up in front of her house.

"Did I what?"

"Did you plant that silverware in his luggage?"

"Of course. It was the only way I could think of to keep him from leaving. You should've seen his face, Prentice, when I showed up on his doorstep in Florida. The silly man was all packed to fly out of the country. He knew they'd found that woman's body and that Maynard Griggs would eventually talk; their little ruse would soon become obvious. Faris has a record for what he did before he was so conveniently 'killed.' His company never did recover the money he stole. Faris has been living quite comfortably off his ill-gotten gains, and now he's an accessory after the fact in a murder case." Aunt Zorah drew her fringed shawl a little closer about her. "He also speaks fluent Spanish and was headed straight for Mexico."

"When you turned him in for taking the silver, did you tell the police who he really was?" I asked.

She shook her head. "No, but his fingerprints are a matter of record. It just took them a few days to match them up."

"Why do you care?" I asked. "What difference does it make after all this time? Couldn't you have just let him go?" Surely she still didn't want this creep back in her life.

"I suppose I could, and maybe I should've, but how did I know he didn't have something to do with that woman's death? When I think of the tears he caused, the shame—and now the humiliation, I'm not even one bit sorry!" And my aunt walked into her house and shut the door firmly behind her.

Maybe I should go after her, I thought. *Offer whatever comfort I could.* But how do you soothe an injury that deep? Besides, there are times when people prefer to be alone, and for my aunt, I felt sure this was one of them.

Ever since Augusta had left me to sojourn in the south end of the state, I'd felt as though an anvil hung over my head just waiting for the right moment to drop, and in the last couple of days that awareness had developed into a heavy dread.

It was odd that Aunt Zorah had mentioned a warning bell because during the drive back to Smokerise, the one in my head became deafening, like a hundred fire trucks clanging, and I knew something had gone wrong at Ellynwood. The closer I got to home, the stronger the feeling grew until it became oppressive, almost suffocating.

Then for a brief moment it lifted and Augusta was beside me in her golden gauzy clothing and sun-glow hair. "Come," she said. Then she touched my arm and was gone.

CHAPTER TWENTY-FOUR

ad I only imagined her there? I reached out a hand to the seat beside me—empty now, but the sweet scent of strawberries lingered still. Augusta was trying to tell me something, to warn me.

"I'm coming, Augusta! I'm coming." But would I be too late? A panorama of disaster scenes played across my mind. Ola Cress had disappeared with the baby . . . Joey was sick or hurt . . . Mom had suffered an accident . . . or Sonny's father had tracked them down and was . . . I didn't even want to think of it!

At Smokerise I raced down the driveway at breakneck speed intending to toss a few essentials into an overnight bag and leave immediately for Ellynwood. My heart seemed to have jumped into that space usually reserved for my brain and was pounding big-time—loud and fast, so it was just pure luck I avoided crashing into the car coming from the other direction. We both stopped in a squall of tires and scattering gravel on the narrow twisting road, our bumpers inches apart, and I didn't know whether to be relieved or annoyed when I recognized my cousin's familiar green sedan.

"Be-trice, I'm in a hurry right now. Don't have time to talk," I hollered, rolling down my window.

My cousin popped open her door and scurried around to lean bony arms on the side of my car. "I don't know what's going on here, Prentice, but some man called me trying to find you. Seemed to think it was real important. Sounded like a matter of life and death!"

"Called you? What man?"

"Wait a minute . . . I'm sure he told me his name, but it just went in one ear and out the other . . . Pug something . . . That sound right?"

I revved the engine and drummed my fingers on the steering wheel but Cousin Be-trice wasn't one to pick up on subtleties. "Never heard of him," I said. "Why did he call you?"

"Said when he couldn't reach you at home, he asked somebody down at the Kettle if they knew where to find you." My cousin drew herself up and threw out her chest—not that you'd notice. "Naturally they referred him to me," she said.

"Did he say what he wanted?" Peter Whisonant had mentioned setting up a meeting with his nephew to look over the property, but I wouldn't consider it urgent.

"Not really. I told him to call Zorah. She usually knows where you are." Be-trice pawed at the gravel with one foot and snorted. "Lord, that's some mess she's gotten herself into with that old fool Faris coming back like he did, and I hear she's even been questioned by the police! Reckon this man showing up has anything to do with that?"

"I don't see how it could. Look, I've really got to go." I gunned the engine again. I thought I knew who was trying to find me, and I didn't mean to stick around long enough to give him a chance.

"Something's wrong, isn't it? Oh, lordy, you aren't mixed up in all this gruesome business, are you? Prentice, are you in some kind of trouble?" My cousin hung on to the door of the car as if she had suction cups for hands.

I explained to her as kindly as possible that I didn't have anything to do with dead bodies and such, I wasn't planning to hang around long enough to get into trouble, and that I really was in a hurry to be on my way.

She squished her mouth into kind of a wad. "I don't know what all the big secret's about," she huffed, "and I can see you're not going to tell me. I just hope you know what you're doing, Prentice Dobson. I've a feeling you're getting in way over your head!"

I could see she was way past placating so I didn't really try. "Honest, Be-trice, I don't know a whole lot more than you do, but I'll let you know when I find out. Right now I have a long drive ahead of me and I want to get there before dark."

She promised to feed the cat.

The telephone was ringing when I reached the house. Dear God, don't let it be Sonny's creepy relative again! Or maybe there was something wrong at Ellynwood. I hurried to unlock the door and almost stumbled over Noodles in my dash to reach the phone.

"Are you all right?" my mother wanted to know. "They haven't arrested Zorah, have they? You sound out of breath."

"I was about to ask you the same thing," I said between gulps of air. Naturally I didn't tell her about Augusta's brief visit. "They seem to believe Faris killed Jasper, so it looks like Aunt Zorah's in the clear. Is anything wrong down there? How's Joey? You haven't had any problems have you?"

"No, no, Joey's fine. He and Ola have gone for a stroll. There are paths here on the grounds—just wait till you see this place, Prentice! It's good to see Ola get out of the house for a while, the fresh air will be good for her. She's been a bit mopish lately."

My mother was a great one for fresh air, especially if it was for somebody else. "I called to ask a favor," she said, and I could tell by her voice it wasn't a happy one. "Tomorrow would have been your father's birthday," she reminded me, "and I'd like some fresh flowers for his grave. The tulips should be blooming in that bed by the front steps—you know how your dad liked red—and you might mix in some forsythia, jonquils, whatever you can find in the yard. It's so much prettier than those stiff things you get from the flower shop. Do you mind?"

Of course I didn't mind, and I was upset with myself for forgetting the date. Mom had always made a freezer of homemade vanilla ice cream and a chocolate pound cake, Dad's favorites, to celebrate the occasion.

"I was just on my way upstairs to pack," I told her, glancing at the kitchen clock. I was surprised to find that it was barely past noon. "If I leave soon after lunch, I should reach Savannah before dark, and I'll stop by the cemetery on my way out."

"Then you're coming today? I'm glad! But I thought you were going to spend some time with Zorah. Are you certain she's all right?"

"No. She's bitter. Hurt. But spunky enough, I think. Mom, I've done all I can to help her right now." And more, I thought, but I wasn't ready to deal with that. "You're sure everything's okay down there? Ola didn't go far, did she?"

"Prentice honey, she hasn't been gone half an hour yet. My goodness, where would she go? We're miles from everything out here."

I knew, and that was what worried me. Augusta wouldn't summon me for nothing.

"You be careful driving, now, and don't worry about us. I'll have supper ready when you get here. How about a nice pork loin with some of those little new potatoes?" My mother sounded so cheerful I almost believed all was well and I was wasting my time charging to the rescue. After all, Augusta was sometimes over-cautious.

I checked the answering machine to find a message from Peter Whisonant telling me his nephew would be in the area for a few days, and would like to get to-gether this afternoon to discuss their proposal if it was convenient. It wasn't, and I phoned his business and told the woman who answered I'd have to get back to him later.

The tulips, I found, were in short supply, but I tucked in a few early iris, some sunny forsythia, and filled in with vivid pink quince for a colorful bouquet. Dad would approve, I thought. It took only a few minutes to pack for Ellynwood as I chose only comfortable, ca-sual clothing for playing with Joey and exploring the neglected estate. I tossed my luggage into the trunk and bumped my way along the furrowed back road to the family graveyard. Augusta's warning still rested like a stone in my stomach, but at least I was on my way.

It had rained a little during the night and the dirt road that circled the cemetery was pocked with pud-dles. I parked beneath the sycamore where Maggie and I used to sit and tell ghost tales, and as always when I thought of my sister, the familiar pang of sadness twisted in my throat. But now I had Joey to think of.

I'll take care of him, Maggie, I said to her innocuous

stone angel. *I'll love him, I promise.* And I knew I wouldn't even have to try. With large stones I anchored the billowing arrangement of spring flowers on my father's grave and lingered a few minutes to tell him we loved him and that he had a cute little namesake named Joey. Of course he probably knew that already, I thought. And I reminded myself to ask Augusta if they have homemade ice cream and chocolate pound cake in heaven.

I had almost reached the bottom of the hill where I'd left the car when something made me turn, and I saw him standing there. It was the man with the beard, the same one who had come to the house a few days earlier.

He was less than fifty yards away, but if I hurried I could reach the car in time. I bolted over the stone wall like an Olympic hurdler and immediately skidded in a patch of mud. My knees buckled, my arms flapped, and the rest of me performed a most ungraceful hula dance, but I managed to keep my balance.

I heard the man yell something that sounded like "wait," and looked up to see him standing in the same place. And he was *smiling*.

"Go away!" I shouted. "Leave me alone!" I slid (and I mean that literally) behind the wheel of the car and started the engine, giving it enough gas to soar over the treetops. It went the other way. I was stuck in the mud.

I did all the wrong things. The more frantically I pressed on the accelerator, the deeper I sank. Wheels spun futilely, flinging mud and stones in a dirty arc behind me. I swore, but Augusta wasn't around to censor me. If she had been, I might not be in this mess. When I looked again, the man had disappeared from where he'd been standing and I heard the alarming crunch of twigs and gravel. Oh, Lord, he must be right behind me! Quickly I locked my doors and tried to rock the car loose by switching from forward to reverse and back again. It didn't work. Mired in cemetery mud, I was digging my own grave.

"Please let me help. I'm not going to hurt you. Really." A voice spoke next to my ear, and my heart did a back flip to see him standing a few inches from my window.

Again he smiled. "I'm afraid you're only making it worse," he said.

"Don't you think I know that? Now will you please go away and leave me alone?"

He shrugged. "Okay, but I think you're going to need some pine branches under these tires for traction. I can get some if you like."

"Who are you? What do you want with me?" I was trapped. Helpless. He could break my window with a rock, bash in my head.

"Didn't my uncle call? He said he'd left a message."

"You mean Mr. Whisonant? You're his *nephew*?" I felt like a complete fool! The man was here on a perfectly innocent errand. "You're here about leasing our place for a nursery—you're the horticulturist!" I fumbled with the door lock and hesitantly offered a hand. I wouldn't blame him if he ignored it. "I'm sorry," I said. "I'm Prentice."

"I know. I'm Pug, and I honestly didn't mean to frighten you, but we really do need to talk." The man looked down at my half-buried tires. "I have a cardboard box in my car back there. We can put some of that under the pine branches—might help a little."

"Your car?"

"I drove up just as you were leaving and thought I'd try to catch you before you got away. Then when I saw you stop at the cemetery I parked out of sight so I wouldn't intrude. Car's just around the bend there; just give me a minute and I'll get it."

I waited while the man parked his car behind mine and watched him tear off pieces of corrugated cardboard to line the ruts made by my fruitless efforts to escape him. Together we layered boughs of pine until I had enough traction to get back on solid ground. I heard him give a victorious little shout when I roared free.

If I'd had a black veil I would've draped it over my face. Not only did I feel stupid over the way I'd behaved, but I was filthy to boot. My shoes were caked in mud and my hands sticky with pine rosin. Peter Whisonant's good-looking horticulturist nephew would probably go home and laugh all night and into next week.

On his first visit to Smokerise I couldn't see beyond the beard when I'd observed him from an upstairs window. Now I realized my visitor was handsome in a rugged, outdoorsy sort of way. But there was something else about him that puzzled me. Something familiar.

"I wish I had time to talk with you today," I said, wishing I could disappear as quickly as Augusta, "but I have to go out of town on some family business and I've a late start already."

He stood beside my car and leaned in the window; the tangy scent of fresh pine rose up around us. "Look, I haven't been entirely honest with you," he began. "I do want to go over plans for my uncle's project, but there's something else more urgent. I'm afraid your mother may be in trouble, and your sister's baby's in serious danger of being kidnapped. If you know where they are, I think you'd better warn them, and I wouldn't waste any time."

Oh, God. Realization came like a dousing of cold well water and I knew where I had seen this man before. He was the one who had followed Augusta and me when we left Ruby, the one I'd given the slip to in the restaurant.

CHAPTER TWENTY-FIVE

*Y*ou're one of them, aren't you?" I was surprised at the calmness in my voice.

He raised a dark brow. "One of whom?"

"The Gaineses. Sonny's family. I should've known! If you've done anything to hurt Joey or my mother—"

"Hey, wait a minute!" He held up a hand. "I'm on your side, believe it or not, and you'd better believe it because we're going to have to work as a team and we don't have a minute to lose."

"I don't trust you," I said. "I don't even know who you are."

He frowned and shook his head. "I'll tell you who I'm not. I'm not your enemy. I think we both want the same thing—the baby's safety. I care about Joey too."

"I doubt if you even come close to caring what happens to Joey," I said. "He happens to be my nephew."

"And mine. Sonny was my brother."

When he spoke his brother's name, his expression softened and I could see he was having a difficult time with his emotions. Well, that was his problem. If it hadn't been for Sonny Gaines, my sister would still be alive, and at that moment I hated him. Hated all of them. "If this is some kind of trick to lead you to Joey, you can forget it," I said. "I'll sit here till doomsday before I tell you one thing!"

"That's admirable of you, I'm sure, but meanwhile my father—who, I might add, is extremely volatile and emotionally unstable—has followed a friend of yours to wherever it is your mother is secluded and he plans to take that child!"

Now my warning bell was gonging big-time. This was what Augusta was trying to tell me! "How do you know this?" I asked. My insides felt like molten lava.

His words came quickly. "I know because he called me, told me what he'd done, what he planned to do. My father doesn't listen to reason, Prentice. If I don't know where he is, there's nothing I can do to stop him."

"He didn't say where he was?"

"No, only that he'd followed you to Atlanta where he thought he might find Joey. He didn't, but he saw you transferring a stroller and some other things to your friend's car, then waited around until she left the next morning. Stayed behind her all the way."

Dottie. And she never even suspected it. But I had.

I remembered the drive to Atlanta, the eerie feeling of being followed, but he must have stayed far enough behind so I never got a look at him.

"I tried to trace the call," Sonny's brother said, "but the old man's using a cell phone. He may be unbalanced, but he's not stupid."

"Your father is Pershing Gaines." The name sent a chill through me.

"Right, and so am I: Pershing Underwood Gaines. A bit intimidating. I go by 'Pug.'"

"Do you think he'd hurt them?" *Oh, please, say no!*

"Not if he were himself, and he'd never deliberately harm the baby, but my dad isn't himself—hasn't been since Sonny's death. And frankly, I've seen signs of mental deterioration before that, but nobody would believe me."

I had discontinued service with my mobile phone when I lost my job, and now I wished I hadn't. "Do you have a phone in your car? I hate to waste time going back to the house to call."

He did, of course. I reached across to unlock the door. "Get it and get in!" I said. I punched in the number at Ellynwood before we even turned out on the main road, hoping to hear my mother's voice on the other end, but there was no answer.

"Nobody's there," I said to Pug's expectant face. "But she might've gone to the store or something. She was planning a pork loin for supper." I swallowed, thinking of my mother humming as she scrubbed the small pink potatoes, marinated the meat. After the horror of the last few months, Joey had given her the precious gift of hope, and now this madman was out to destroy it. I drove even faster.

"Better hold off on the lead foot," my passenger advised. "We don't have time for traffic tickets."

"Maybe that wouldn't be such a bad idea," I said.

"What? Being stopped for speeding?"

"No, getting the police involved. Maybe we should call them, have somebody check on things out there. I'd feel a lot better if we did."

Pug reached for the phone. "So would I. What town are we dealing with?"

I didn't know for sure but I'd heard Mom say she bought groceries in a little place called Tanner's Crossing. But Tanner's Crossing, we learned, didn't have a police department. When we finally reached the county sheriff, we were told they couldn't do anything unless Pug's father had actually *done* something, but they would send a car out to check on things at Ellynwood.

I tried Mom's number again, then again a short time later. Still no answer. The fire in my stomach smoldered, and even though he may not be my enemy at the moment, I could have easily belched flames at Sonny Gaines's brother. In fact I could barbecue the entire family.

"So all that talk about leasing our land for a nursery was nothing but a smoke screen," I said.

"Not at all. Peter Whisonant's married to my aunt

Julia and he really is interested in expanding in your area. In fact, he's been looking around for over a year now for a place like yours." Pug Gaines smiled. "I just happened to be the one who found it."

"What do you mean?"

"Prentice, it may surprise you to know I've known where you lived for some time now. In fact, I even came to your house a few times, but no one was there. I knew as soon as I saw it that it was exactly what we'd been looking for, and Uncle Peter agreed. But except for chance, it has nothing to do with our looking for Joey."

"Then maybe you can explain why your father is running around terrorizing people when you admit he has serious problems?" I asked. "You must know his behavior's not normal. Why haven't you gotten some help?"

"As a matter of fact, he's been under a doctor's care. He was hospitalized for a while and when they did let him come home we had somebody there full-time. He slipped away while the nurse was in the shower—had another set of car keys we didn't know about. He's a crafty one, Dad is, and completely round the bend as far as Sonny is concerned."

I could sense Pug's eyes on me, but I kept mine on the road. "Believe me, Prentice," he said, "I had no idea what my father was up to until he called this morning. We were frantic—didn't even know where to find him."

"I'm surprised," I told him. "Your whole family has

such a talent for surveillance, you should change your name to Pinkerton."

"I suppose I should be insulted." Was he smiling? "You're referring to Aunt Julia, I suppose. She didn't mean to frighten you by meeting you at the mall. She thought you were expecting her."

I remembered the woman saying something about her nephew trying to get in touch with me to let me know she wanted to talk. "So *you're* the nephew," I said. "Your aunt gave me the impression she thought everything had been arranged, that you were supposed to have prepared me for her showing up like that." I swung around a creeping vehicle with an out-of-state license plate, pushed the speed up to seventy, and took my chances with the State Patrol. "Well, I wasn't," I said.

"Wasn't what?"

"Wasn't prepared. You know very well what I mean." I looked at the clock. It was after three and we were still over an hour away.

"Hey! That was hardly my fault. It's a little difficult to have a conversation with somebody who hangs up on me, avoids me like I'm foaming at the mouth." My passenger sighed. "We Gaineses really aren't a bad lot, Prentice. Honest, we're more or less a peaceful clan."

"Huh! Less is what I've heard!" I swerved to avoid a hubcap in the middle of the road.

"Who told you that?" Pug Gaines kept the roar in his voice to a minimum, but it was there just the same.

"If I tell you, promise you won't go after him with a lynch mob?"

He grunted. "I honestly don't know where you get these notions."

"The funeral director in Athens, Tennessee. I spoke with him a few weeks ago and he gave me the distinct impression your whole family was out for blood. Our blood." I glanced at him as I spoke. "That tended to make me a bit leery, if you know what I mean, especially since there was no rational explanation for it." I almost bit my tongue to keep from ranting further.

"I'm afraid our dad would be the reason for that," Pug said. "When Sonny was killed, he just went berserk; we couldn't do a thing with him. Aunt Julia— she's Dad's sister—and I finally got him calmed down, and my brother gave him a sedative. Willis is a general practitioner."

I nodded, trying to keep the relatives straight. "Just how many of you are there?"

"I have a younger sister in grad school and Willis, my older brother, is married and lives in Chattanooga, but I guess we seem like a crowd when we get together," he said with a laugh.

His voice sobered. "And then there was Sonny, the baby, and Dad's favorite. Always was—he made no bones about it. Sonny could do no wrong. Wild as a stallion and just as headstrong. I'm afraid Dad spoiled him rotten.

"That was his undoing," he added softly.

"Your father seemed to blame my sister for the accident," I said. "They said Sonny had been taking drugs, but I can't see where that was Maggie's fault. After all, he was the one who was driving."

Maggie had stayed away from drugs in high school, but I couldn't vouch for what she did after she left home. However, if my sister had anything like that in her system the day she was killed, it hadn't shown up in her autopsy report.

Pug Gaines touched me gently on the shoulder. "Now you see why I wanted to reach your mother and Joey as quickly as possible. There's no reasoning with my father where Sonny's concerned."

"How did your father know where to find me?" I asked.

He stretched his long legs and leaned forward, as if that would make us get there faster. "My dad has more eyes than a seed potato. I expect somebody told him, probably somebody back in Ruby. He has some old hunting buddies there."

I thought about the woman at The Toy Box Child Care Center who seemed a little more than eager about locating Joey. "Jackie Trimble," I said, glancing at my passenger.

"Ah, yes! Named after her old man. Jack Trimble and Dad went to school together. The guy has a lot of cousins . . . and they have cousins, and so on." He smiled. "Comes in handy, don't you think?"

"It certainly helped your aunt Julia track me to that mall. Poor Tisdale Humphreys! He had no idea he was harboring a spy in the man hanging his wallpaper."

Pug chuckled. "That was just a happy accident. I'm surprised you figured it out."

"Actually Ola Cress did. Besides her, Mr. Humphreys was the only one who knew where we planned to meet."

"I guess we do seem a sneaky bunch," Pug admitted, "and maybe we've handled this all wrong, but damn it, Prentice, this baby is important to us too. We were afraid we would lose him, that he might just disappear and we'd never know where to find him. We may have resorted to what seems like desperate measures, but you, of all people, should understand that."

I couldn't argue with him there.

We both grew silent as we got closer to Tanner's Crossing. Pastures became greener the farther south we drove, weeds straggled tall around fences, and the sun streamed in through the windows so brightly I had to turn on the air conditioner. After a while we left the main road for a straight and narrow lane where dark pine thickets pressed in on either side with their suffocating creosote smell.

"There oughtta be a covered bridge about a mile down the road here," Pug said, reading Mom's directions. "Turn left at the next road and it should be about a half mile on the right. There's a tabby wall, she says . . . that's that plaster made of crushed shells, isn't it? And a wrought-iron gate."

We thundered over the dark, narrow bridge and turned onto a sandy road lined with live oaks. Soon I saw the crumbling, vine-covered walls of Ellynwood and came to a stop in front of the gate. I don't know what I had been expecting, but it wasn't this. The place looked like Sleeping Beauty's garden after the grounds-keeper had taken a century-long snooze. Maybe it once had been landscaped, but now nature had draped it thick with vines, smothered it in dense green foliage.

"My God," Pug said. "Reminds me of the set of a Tarzan movie." He got out and swung open the creaking iron gate and it screeched shut behind us with a grating, metallic clang.

The road ahead seemed to trail into nowhere, yet somewhere at the end of it my mom and Joey waited. Or at least I prayed that they did.

CHAPTER TWENTY-SIX

If I'd been on foot, I think I would have tiptoed through the dark tunnel of foliage and held my breath until I reached the other side. The air was heavy with jasmine whose fragrant white blossoms trailed from tree to tree, and even though it was barely after four, the road lay steeped in twilight. I drove steadily, but not too fast, and thought of how appropriate it would be if our car had a figurehead like the bow of a ship to part the veil in front of us. The atmosphere was thick enough to swim in, and it wasn't all humidity. I was torn between my eagerness to get to the cottage and my dread at what we might find.

"Your father. He doesn't have a weapon, does he?" I said to the man beside me.

"I told you, he's a hunter." Pug looked straight ahead,

his hand on the door handle. "If he's here, you let me handle him," he said.

I didn't answer. If what Pug Gaines reported was true, his father had been at Ellynwood for a good part of the day. He had plenty of time to carry out his plans—and I whimpered to think of what his plans might be. But the people at the sheriff's department had promised to see if everything was all right and we hadn't yet heard back from them. Surely this must be a good sign.

When we finally did come out into the sunlight my spirits lifted. Azaleas that soon would be in bloom bordered an emerald lawn skirted by neat gravel paths. I heard the trickle of water and noticed a fountain in the center of what appeared to be a rose garden. Terraced steps led through a vine-covered wall to the bronze statue of a nymph perpetually pouring water. Storybook Land. But this was no fantasy, and if Pershing Gaines had his way, there would be no "happily ever after" for us.

I could hear Pug's breathing as he sat as rigid as stone beside me searching the landscape for any sign of the people we hoped to find.

The two-story stone house, flanked by enormous live oaks, was bigger than the cottage I expected and I wondered fleetingly what the house that burned must have been like. Mom's friend's family must have money to throw away to be able to afford the upkeep on a place like this.

I parked beneath one of the oaks and started for the door, but Pug held out a hand. "Let me," he said quietly, and I reluctantly stood aside and let him ring the doorbell, then waited while nobody came.

"I'm going in," I said, trying to push past him, but Pug Gaines held me back. "Wait," he whispered. "Just give me a chance to see if he's here. If I hear him, I'll try to signal you somehow." He had tucked the cell phone inside his jacket, and now passed it to me. "Here. You might need this." And with that he quietly opened the door and slipped inside.

I couldn't just stand there! Quietly I circled the outside of the house, walking on the soft green grass to muffle my steps, and in a small parking area in the back I found my mother's rental car. She had pulled it up close to the door of what looked to be the kitchen, probably to unload her groceries. I glanced in the window of the car, fearful of what I might find, but I only saw what appeared to be a discarded grocery list and Joey's stuffed rabbit on the front seat. His carrier was still in the back. Through the kitchen window I glimpsed Pug Gaines emerging from a room off the breakfast area and I tapped on the back door and signaled for him to let me in.

We found the back door unlocked as well. Pug shook his head. "Nobody's here. I've looked all over."

"That's Mom's car out back," I said, "and her keys are on the counter. They have to be here somewhere. Maybe they've gone for a walk."

I looked in the refrigerator where a bowl of fruit

salad, garnished with a sprig of mint, waited to be served. A tenderloin of pork marinated in something that smelled like ginger. My mother had gone to the store and made preparations for supper. A container of formula mix and a box of baby cereal waited on the counter. Three places were set at the table with a pot of hyacinths in the center. Their heavy fragrance perfumed the room, made me feel queasy. I opened the back door and stood on the steps where a robin twittered nearby. "Shut up!" I told him. I wanted my family and I wanted them *now*! Joey's nursery rhyme quilt and two of his bibs hung from a clothesline to the left of the door and a third had fallen to the ground. I brought them in and put them on a chair. But where in the world was the baby they belonged to?

"Wouldn't your dad have a car?" I asked Pug as we went through the house a second time. "I didn't notice it parked outside. How would he get here?"

"You saw how vast this place is, Prentice. I'm sure there's another entrance—probably several. He's too sly to park it right out in the open. If he's here, it's somewhere around here too."

I looked at the clock. It was almost five. I knew my mother, and I knew her habits. If she expected me for supper, she would be waiting for me with dinner in the oven when I arrived. "I think we should search the grounds," I said. "There's some kind of building out back that looks like it might've been a storehouse or something . . ."

Oh, God, what was I saying? What did I expect to find in there?

The small brick building sat about fifty yards from the house, and like much of the wall around the estate, it was almost hidden by vines. The one tiny window I could see was set high in the gable, and it, too, was obliterated by a proliferation of honeysuckle. I began to run as we approached the weatherworn wooden door that, I saw, had been fastened on the outside with a heavy nail bent through the latch.

"Is anybody in there?" Pug called out, and I heard a muffled thump as the old door shook.

"Mom! Is that you? Is Joey with you?" If I could, I would have poured myself through the crack as Pug removed the nail, then tugged open the heavy door. The tears I had been holding back came suddenly with a cry so deep it hurt. "Mama?" I sobbed, resorting to a term I hadn't used in years.

But it wasn't my mother who stumbled out of the dark, musty building. It was Ola Cress.

"You've got to find them before he does!" she said, sobbing. "Please, oh, please do something!" The woman was crying so I could hardly understand her, and she brushed her arms and shivered, although it wasn't cold. "Spiders!" she said, shuddering. "I hate spiders!" Ola continued to slap at her arms and looked back into the dank room behind her as if she suspected the creepy little varmints to be in close pursuit.

"Where's my mom? And Joey? What happened? Who did this?"

I took Ola's arm and tried to speak calmly. Although I really wanted to shake her, it wouldn't help the others for me to lose my cool. Pug disappeared inside the building to look around, but I could see with a glance that no one else was there.

"A man—at first we thought he was the gardener—but I'm sure it was that Pershing Gaines." Ola trembled as I led her back to the house. "He seemed to be weeding the same area of the flower bed over there for an awfully long time, and your mother got a little suspicious. He wasn't the man who has been here before she said, but I convinced her he was probably just a helper or something. I really thought we'd be safe here." Ola pointed to a hoe that had been thrown aside next to the garden wall. "See, that's what he was using."

"What has he done with my mother and Joey?" Back at the house I poured Ola a glass of water and made her sit down. Her breathing seemed ragged and it frightened me. "Do you have a prescription? Can I get you something?"

She gestured toward a bottle of pills on the windowsill over the sink and I hastily twisted off the top and shook one into her hand.

"I tried to warn your mother," Ola said after she gulped down a pill. "Yelled as loud as I could. I think she ran . . . I hope she did. Maybe they got away."

"But her car is still here," I said.

She nodded, frowning. "He said he did something to it—the distributor or something. Besides, she wouldn't have had time. He would've seen her, stopped her."

"But where could she go? And with a baby! Joey might cry and give them away."

"He'd just been fed, so he won't be hungry—and he's a good baby," Ola said, sitting a little straighter.

Pug came in and sat opposite us at the polished maple table, still set for supper. "Didn't the sheriff send somebody? We called earlier and they promised to check on things out here."

"About an hour ago, yes. In fact it was right before I went outside to see if Joey's quilt was dry. Of course we had no idea this would happen!" She took another sip of water. "If only they'd come a few minutes later!" Ola Cress frowned. "But how did you know to call them?"

Pug looked at me and I explained to the terrified woman as tactfully as I could that this was Pershing Gaines's son Pug, but that he was one of the "good guys."

I don't think she believed me. "He came at me from behind," she said. Water sloshed on the table as she set down her glass. "By the time I saw him it was too late to do anything but scream—and oh, God, I didn't know what he meant to do! Before I knew what was happening, he'd dragged me over to that awful old shed and locked me inside. I hollered and yelled and kicked on the door, but it didn't do any good . . . and then I heard you come and I screamed and kicked some more. I thought you'd never hear me!"

Ola's face turned white and her voice shook, so I made her lie on the living-room sofa and covered her

276

frail shoulders with a sweater. "I think you need a doctor," I said, remembering I still had Pug's mobile phone in my pocket. "And I'm calling the police."

The woman sprang up like a jack-in-the-box, throwing the sweater to the floor. "No! No, please don't! He said he'd kill her if we did that." She darted a nervous look at Pug. "That's the last thing he told me, and he meant it too. I know he did. Had a gun and swore he'd use it."

I looked at Pug. "So what do we do now?"

"We find them. I really don't think he'd hurt your mother, Prentice, but I want to be there when we find him. Maybe I can talk some sense into him." He turned to Ola. "Do you have any idea where she might've taken Joey?"

"None," she admitted, softly weeping. "This place is so big, full of all kinds of nooks and crannies, and it seems to go on forever. They could be anywhere."

"She would try to get to the road," Pug said. "And you can be sure the old man's watching that."

"He can't be everywhere. You said yourself there had to be more than one entrance," I reminded him.

"There is," Ola said, "but the gates are rusted shut. She'd have to climb over that high wall."

Knowing my mother, I thought she might chance it if she thought she'd succeed, but if I were in her place, I'd wait until it wasn't so light. I looked at my watch. It was just before six and would soon start turning darker. Unless this crazy man had already caught up with them, Mom had been out there in that jungle of undergrowth with Joey for over an hour. Soon the baby would become hungry again. We had to find them fast.

Pug held out his hand for my car keys. "I'm going to drive back and check the main entrance. Be sure and lock the doors behind me and don't do anything until I get back."

Don't do anything? My mother and baby nephew were fleeing from a madman and he tells me not to *do anything!* I went to the kitchen to make tea for Ola. Augusta Goodnight, I thought, you are one sorry guardian angel! We could surely use a little heavenly help about now.

I noticed the playing cards as I looked in the cabinet for mugs. They were on the kitchen counter next to Joey's formula and I didn't remember seeing them there before. Next to them was a narrow thin score pad for recording bridge scores. It said so on the front.

"Have you and Mom been playing cards?" I asked Ola, showing her what I'd found.

"Why no. I've never been any good at that, and with Joey we didn't have much extra time." She looked a little closer. "I think I've seen them around in a drawer somewhere though. Pretty, aren't they, with those strawberries on the front."

Strawberries. Of course. Now I detected a slight whiff of strawberry scent in the air. Why would Augusta set out a deck of bridge cards?

"Is there a bridge here on the estate?" I asked.

"Why yes, two or three I think."

"Can you tell me where to find them?"

Ola swung her feet to the floor. "I can show you if you'll let me go with you, but why?"

"Call it a hunch. I'll try to explain later, and I'd rather you wait here for Pug."

She took my hand in cool, dry fingers. "Please be careful, won't you? And bring my baby back to me. I couldn't stand it if anything happened to Joey!"

"I'll do my best," I promised. "Now, be sure to lock the door behind me and tell Pug where I've gone."

"Can we really trust him, Prentice?" Ola said, frowning. "After all, he is a Gaines."

"And so is Joey," I reminded her.

CHAPTER TWENTY-SEVEN

I hurried across the gravel drive, daring it to make any noise, and circled the sunken garden where the fountain splashed. Other than the trickle of water and an occasional birdsong, the grounds at Ellynwood were oppressively silent.

"Take a flashlight," Ola had directed. "There's one in that kitchen drawer by the door. It gets dark early with all these trees. And watch out for snakes. I always carry a stick."

Snakes! Oh, great! I clenched a long forked stick in one hand, the flashlight in the other. I'd almost rather meet up with Pershing Gaines and an arsenal of weapons. On the other side of the rose garden a narrow trail twisted off to the right, the pathway already deep in shadow. If I followed it for about a quarter of a mile, then took the left branch, it would bring me to a stone bridge, Ola said.

Each footstep seemed amplified. Why did the place have to be so blasted quiet? If Joey were to cry, or to make any of his cute baby sounds, Pershing Gaines would hear. He might be watching me now, lurking behind that huge pine tree, crouched beneath a spreading magnolia. Oh, how I would welcome noise! A rushing river, the drone of an airplane, a radio playing— anything but this tattletale silence.

The bridge, when I came to it, spanned a narrow stream, then the pathway divided again beyond it. I paused on the bridge just long enough to look down into the water on either side. Was I supposed to find some clue here? It couldn't be anything obvious that Pershing Gaines might follow.

"Okay, Augusta," I whispered, sighing, "what do I do now?" But Augusta didn't answer. I hoped it was because she was busy elsewhere.

Ola had said she thought my mother had mentioned another bridge farther on, but she herself had never gone that far. How was I supposed to know which way to go?

The scent of fresh pine greeted me on the other side of the bridge, and I saw that a small sapling had fallen over the trail to the left. Was this Augusta's way of telling me to take the right fork? I stooped to see what might have caused the tree to fall, but it appeared to be a clean break for no apparent reason, and it looked as if it had happened recently. The smell of resin was strong in the air. "Okay, Augusta," I said softly. "Right it is."

Spiderwebs brushed my face as I walked beneath the canopy of low hanging trees and I shuddered and tried not to think of whatever else might be in my path. What would I do if I were in my mother's place? If I had to snatch up the baby and run, where would I go to get away from this frightening man who seemed to have lost all reason?

If she went back along the road to the main gate, he would be sure to catch up with her. Would she try to find another way out, or wait and take a chance on evading him after dusk? Ola had thought perhaps Mom was carrying Joey in a slinglike snuggle against her chest, as she sometimes used one on short walks to lull him to sleep, and the baby's papooselike carrier wasn't hanging in its usual place. But Joey weighed at least eighteen pounds, and my mother wasn't used to carrying him long distances. Pershing Gaines wouldn't be hampered by the extra weight.

But Mom had at least two advantages. She knew the area better than he did, and she had Augusta on her side. I knew the angel was doing her best to lead me without giving away their hiding place to the man who pursued them. If I were trying to avoid him, I thought, I'd keep off the main paths and find someplace to stay out of sight for a while. But where?

The second bridge took me by surprise when I came upon the rustic structure around a bend in the path.

Wisteria twined around the log hand railings and the wooden floor didn't look too stable. I took one cautious step, and then another. The boards creaked but didn't give way. Behind me I heard the rustle of leaves and turned, expecting to see the bearded avenger standing there, and just about fainted with relief when a wren flew past me with a strand of Spanish moss for her nest.

As far as I knew I had used up my allotment of bridges, but I didn't know where else to go but forward. I had advanced only a few feet when I smelled the strawberries. Even in Savannah strawberries wouldn't be ripe in early March, and besides, there were no fields nearby. Yet there was no mistaking the sweet aroma. I must be getting close!

I walked faster—past a large clump of ferns, the dark skeleton of a long-dead tree draped with Spanish moss, and sniffed again. The scent grew fainter. Making an about-face I went back to the tree and stooped to look underneath. A grassy area bordered the creek bank, and beyond that in a tangle of underbrush and vines I could make out what looked like a stone wall. At one time very long ago, I thought, this was probably a working grist mill. And here the delightful smell of strawberries was almost overpowering. Surely my mom and Joey were close by.

"Thank heavens!" I said.

"You can say that again," Augusta whispered. "What took you so long?" She stepped aside and lifted curling tendrils of jasmine to expose a half-open door, and be-hind it sat my mother with a sleeping baby in her arms.

She smiled when she saw me and held a finger to her lips, and it was all I could do to keep from throwing my arms around the both of them and sobbing in relief.

The room was small and musty with a dirty stone floor, but I noticed glass in the two narrow windows, and there were a few pieces of furniture scattered about as if someone had lived here. I couldn't imagine who or why.

It was cold in the little room and I saw that my mother had wrapped Joey in her sweater. Over her silent protests, I draped my jacket around her shoulders. *Help is coming,* I mouthed, and she nodded, glancing anxiously behind me at the door. I just hoped it would come soon and that he would know where to find us.

Some of the furniture, I noticed, was child-size: a small wooden table with two rickety chairs, a cane-bottomed rocker with a hole in the seat. The building may have started out as a grist mill, but at some time during the last few years it had become a playhouse, and several colorful plastic milk crates had been stacked as shelves. I borrowed one to sit on and crouched down to wait.

Shadows crisscrossed the gray stone floor and it grew darker outside. My foot was asleep, I had a crick in my neck, and I heard the distinct rustle of what sounded like a convention of mice somewhere in the walls. Still

Joey slept, and his uncle Pug hadn't shown up. What on earth was keeping him?

When a figure finally appeared in the doorway I had to turn on the flashlight to see who it was.

"Thank God it's you!" I said as Pug stepped inside, stooping to keep from bumping his head on the low door frame. Ola, pale and shaky, tottered after him.

"Had to convince your friend here I wasn't going to pull a Benedict Arnold," Pug said with a grimace. "Can't say that I blame her, but we are running kinda short on time. And daylight. Maybe you've noticed."

I had. "Did you see him?" I asked, speaking, of course, of his father.

"Yes, but I don't think he saw me. At least I hope he didn't. And we found a back road that leads to this place. Grown up a little now, but I bulldozed a few saplings to get here and left the car as close as I could."

Joey had begun to stir and Pug went over and stooped beside him. "Oh, wow!" he said, beaming. "I hate to brag, but I think he looks like me."

"Joey's uncle Pug," I explained to my mother. "Sonny's big brother. Don't worry, he's here to help."

"All I want is to get you safely out of here," Pug said, noticing my mother's panicked intake of breath. "Dad's parked near the main entrance. Fortunately I saw his car before I drove all the way to the gate, so I parked off the road a little way and investigated on foot. He's not in his car, which means he's on the prowl, and God only knows where he is right now."

"God has nothing to do with it," spoke a thundering voice behind him. "And I believe I'll take my grandson now."

"Dad, don't!" Pug took a step toward him. "Stop this right now before it goes any further. You don't realize what you're doing."

"I realize my son is dead, and it's all because of that woman he married. She's the one who got him back on those drugs!" The man's dark eyes had lightning in them; grief, touched by madness, etched his long face. "That's Sonny's baby there. She took away my son, and now I'm taking hers."

I saw my mother's arms tighten around her grandson, saw the flare of anger in her eyes. Pershing Gaines would have to face her ire to get to Joey. The baby whimpered, probably sensing the conflict going on about him, and Mom kissed the top of his head and whispered softly to him.

I whirled toward the threatening man who was blocking the doorway, mentally unsheathing my claws. If he took one step toward my mother and Joey I'd tie that beard in a knot! "And just what makes you think my sister had anything to do with Sonny taking drugs? Maggie had no drugs in her system. She wasn't the one who drove in front of a train. Your precious Sonny did that; if it weren't for him, my sister would still be alive!"

The man would've lunged at me, I think, if Pug hadn't stepped between us. Taking my arm, he put me firmly behind him. "Prentice is right, Dad. It's time you faced the truth. The person to blame for Sonny's death is Sonny himself."

His father raised his arm as if he might strike Pug, then slowly let it drop. "What kind of son are you to take sides against your own kin? You know Sonny'd gotten off that stuff he was taking! If she didn't give it to him, who did? Why, he came by the house the night before he died, said he'd been drug free for several months and was going to try to get that wife of his to come back to him. Hell, he didn't even know he had a son—and neither did we until after the accident. Reckon she never meant to tell him. What kind of woman is that?"

"A cautious one," I said evenly. "One who was sick and tired of his drinking and abuse."

"We didn't know about Joey either," my mother said, obviously trying to calm him. "None of us did. We only found out by chance." I noticed that she avoided directing attention to Ola Cress who stood like a pale apparition in the background.

"If Jack Trimble's daughter back in Ruby hadn't learned who that baby's father was, I reckon I never would've known!" Pershing Gaines brought himself up straight and tall and his awful voice growled like a yard dog. "By the time I found out, that woman—that Cress woman—she'd taken that baby and gone off somewhere." Now he pointed a trembling finger at Ola Cress. "It's not right to take away a man's kin. That baby's a Gaines and we're taking him back. Now."

"No, Dad, we're not." Pug stepped behind my

mother and Joey, put his hands on her shoulders. "This is not the way to handle things . . ."

"Get out of my way!" his father commanded. "Can't you see these people are lying? And now you're lying for them." And Pershing Gaines drew a revolver from inside his jacket. "I didn't want to use this, but you're leaving me no other choice. That woman—that Maggie's as guilty as sin. She gave that stuff to Sonny, I know she did. She wanted him dead!" At the same time, Joey, frightened and hungry, began to cry.

"How dare you say a thing like that!" Ola stepped boldly out of the shadows to stand in front of my mother and Joey. "Maggie was breast-feeding. She would never have taken anything that might hurt her baby. She loved that child too much to go back to a man who might abuse them." Tears ran down her face and she looked as if a roar from this man would send her into a faint, but Ola's voice didn't waver. "Maggie Dobson didn't give Sonny those drugs. I did."

He looked as if he didn't believe her, and for a minute I didn't think he had heard her. I wasn't sure I had. Surely she was making this up.

"He came by my place looking for her, but Maggie was at work at The Toy Box and the baby was with her. We had all lived in fear of this day—that he'd find them, try to force them to go back." Ola looked at Mom and then at me. "She did love you, you know—wanted to come home, but she was ashamed. Ashamed of the choices she'd made. Maggie wanted to be free of her past mistakes before she came back into your lives."

Now Ola faced the fierce bearded man before her. "I know all about your *Sonny*, Pershing Gaines. Maggie told me. Your son created a living hell for that girl, and I wasn't going to let it happen to her sweet baby."

I thought of making a grab for the gun, but there were too many people close by. Now he waved it in front of him. "What are you saying?" he said.

"I'm saying I offered your son some refreshments—eggnog left over from the holidays. I told him Maggie was staying with me—he could see that anyway, no use trying to lie—but would be out of town for a couple of days and he'd have to come back later. He didn't mention Joey, I don't think he knew the child existed." Ola glanced at Pug, at me. "And I didn't mean for him to find out."

"Ola, what did you do?" I was surprised I had enough breath to speak.

"Fixed him a plate of fruitcake and a mug of that eggnog—added a good splash of brandy, and while he was in the bathroom I put in some of my medicine as well. Four or five of my heart pills . . . dissolved them real good."

"But that would be lethal, wouldn't it?" Pug's face was as gray as gloom.

Ola Cress didn't answer.

"By God, I'll kill you," Pershing Gaines said, and yet he didn't move, just stood there looking like somebody had yanked out his bones.

Now Ola turned to my mother and covered her face with her hands. "Virginia, Prentice, I'm so sorry. I never thought Sonny would find out where Maggie worked. Somebody must've told him . . . or he saw her car parked in front of the child care center. I just wanted him to go away . . ."

"You wanted him to die." Sonny's father shook his head. The hand with the revolver trembled.

"But not Maggie! Oh, God, if I could take her place I would. Forgive me . . . oh, please forgive me!"

Pershing Gaines's hand moved so fast I didn't have time to think, only to scream as the shot cracked loud as cannon fire in that small room, and Ola Cress gave a sharp cry, doubled over, and swayed to the floor.

CHAPTER TWENTY-EIGHT

Oh, my God, he's killed her!" Pug started toward the woman who lay curled at my mother's feet.

"Stop! Don't move!" His father fired again, and this time I saw the snake, a huge cottonmouth moccasin, coiled inches from where Mom sat holding Joey. The reptile flipped, writhed once, and was still.

Pershing Gaines turned without a word and walked out the door, and Mom clutched Joey, screaming now, and followed. Maybe Ola had only fainted. My knees trembled so I felt I might do the same as I knelt beside her and felt her pulse. It seemed much too fast, and her face looked blue in the shadows. "I think it's her heart," I said to Pug who stood beside me as if he hadn't yet decided where to go. Frantically I looked for signs of bleeding and found none. Both bullets, I assumed, had been meant for the snake.

"You've got to help me," I said. "We have to get her to the house. She needs a doctor."

I could understand why he might be reluctant to help someone who had poisoned his brother, but he nodded, scooped Ola in his arms, and carried her into the fading daylight. Pershing Gaines had disappeared, but Mom and I followed with Joey to where Pug had parked my car in a clearing not far away.

At the cottage Mom tried to get Ola to swallow one of her pills, but she either couldn't get it down or didn't want to make the effort. Pug phoned for an ambulance, but I didn't have much hope it would get there in time.

Ola lay on the living-room couch and reached out for Joey, now happily sucking down his liquid supper, and I held him close to her face. She closed her eyes and kissed him. "He won't remember me," she said, "but he gave me so much joy. I hope he can forgive me when he learns what I did."

I stroked her hand. What could I say? This woman had deliberately poisoned Sonny Gaines and caused him to drive in front of a train, taking my sister with him. Even if she lived, Ola would certainly go to prison. "I promise we'll love him as his mother did," I told her. "We won't let him forget you."

Ola Cress opened her eyes briefly and smiled. "She's here. I can go now."

"Who's here?" my mother asked.

"Why, the angel. Don't you see her? She's been here all along."

"Do you think Ola really saw an angel?" Mom asked as we drove back to Smokerise a few days later.

"I'm sure of it," I said, glancing behind me to see if Joey was still asleep in the backseat. Through Tisdale Humphreys we had finally gotten in touch with Ola's brother and made arrangements for her body to be shipped back to Tennessee. Pug had left with his father the day before, having convinced Pershing Gaines he needed to be under a doctor's care, this time with more closely supervised conditions.

"You know, she swore she saw her before—several times back at the cottage." Mom turned to me with a teary-eyed smile. "Said her name was Augusta."

I smiled back, couldn't trust myself to speak.

"Funny thing is," she continued, "for the first time in ages I felt peaceful there. Even with that worry hanging over us with Sonny's family and all, I felt protected at Ellynwood—at least until Pershing Gaines showed up."

"But . . . hey, he reduced the moccasin population!" I said.

"If it hadn't been for him, we wouldn't have been in that awful snaky place," my mother reminded me.

"How in the world did you know that old mill house was there?"

"Elaine said her children used to play out there with

their cousins, and I'd seen it when I was walking with Joey, but never thought about going in." Mom shuddered. "Prentice, it shivers me all the way to the bone to think that snake had probably been in there all along."

And so had the angel, I thought.

The baby woke and Mom reached back to reassure him. "About this Pug," she said, glancing at me. "Just what's all this about a nursery at Smokerise? Is he serious about that?"

"Seems to be. His uncle and some of his partners have been looking for a place, and Pug sort of lucked up on Smokerise when he was trying to get in touch with me. He asked around and somebody told him I might be interested in letting them lease it."

"And are you?"

"Maybe. Mom, I'd like to raise Joey." I waited for this to sink in.

"Where were you planning to do this?" she asked. I was surprised at the calmness in her voice.

"For now I thought I'd stay at Smokerise, at least until I see how things are going. I'd like to keep the house. Pug's uncle's more interested in leasing the land."

"And what about Pug? What's he interested in?"

"What do you mean?" I asked. I knew what she meant.

"Is he interested in raising Joey too? And what about his brother? And there's a sister too, I believe."

"His brother has three children already and the sister's still in grad school, and yes, I think Pug wants to be a part of Joey's life, but I think we can work it out legally to everybody's satisfaction. He seems to think so too."

My mother sighed. "Prentice, you must know I have no desire to live at Smokerise."

I started to answer, but she shushed me. "I want to be a part of Joey's life too, and I'll be there for you as much as I can, but my days in the country are over."

I laughed. "Mom, I know that."

"Living in Savannah has given me an idea of what I can do, what I'd like to do," she said, "but I do want to live closer, maybe get a little place outside Atlanta so it would be convenient for all of us." She touched my hand almost shyly. "I know you sometimes thought I favored your sister, honey, but that wasn't the case at all. It was just that . . . well, it seemed Maggie needed more attention."

I could see she was close to crying. "It's okay, Mom," I said. And meant it.

She smiled and sat straighter. "I don't ever want to be far from you."

"I don't think I'll be going away anytime soon," I assured her. "Pug tells me his uncle's interested in find-ing a public relations person, and Dottie's been lining up a few clients as well. Of course we have a lot more scurrying around to do, but I don't know why we couldn't launch our own PR firm."

"Then I suppose England's out?"

"England's on the other side of the big pond," I said, and I started to tell her about my experience with Rob when the mobile phone rang startling us both.

"Now who in the world could that be?" Mom asked. She had turned in her rental car in Savannah and we were using mine, but the phone belonged to her. "I don't remember giving anybody this number; did you?"

I groaned. "Afraid so," I admitted.

"Prentice! That you?" Cousin Be-trice asked. "Where are you now?"

She sounded even more breathless than usual. "About an hour away," I said. "Why?" I was afraid she was going to tell me the cat was stuck in a tree—or worse.

"It's Aunt Zorah. I swear I think she's really gone and flipped her lid this time. How fast can you get here, you reckon?"

"I don't know. What's she done?"

"Nothing yet, 'cept she won't eat and looks like an old cornstalk. Don Weber just called to tell me she's up there at Poindexter Point where Faris was supposed to have died in that wreck. He said she'd even called in the local press. God knows what she means to do!"

I almost ran off the road. "But why? She's not running from the police, is she?"

"The police! What makes you say that?" Be-trice warbled.

"Who?" Mom tugged at my sleeve. "What police?"

I waved her quiet. Now I would have to confess my suspicions about Aunt Zorah, admit what I had done.

"Be-trice, you said yourself they'd questioned her about Jasper," I reminded my cousin.

"Oh, him. Guess you didn't know. They've charged Maynard Griggs with killing Jasper. I knew it was him all along!"

"But I thought they were holding Faris . . . Shh! In a minute!" I whispered to my frantic mom.

"Couldn't come up with enough evidence," Be-trice told me. "Faris finally tracked down a couple of neighbors who had seen him in Florida on the day Jasper was killed.

"And then there was the button."

"What button?"

"The button off Maynard Griggs's shirt cuff. Jasper had it in his hand when he died."

So that was the secret evidence Don Weber wouldn't discuss! That must have been what they were looking for when they searched our house and Aunt Zorah's closet.

"It was some kind of fancy pearl button," Be-trice continued. "Not your ordinary kind. The old geezer may be stingy, but he doesn't skimp on himself; wears expensive duds." She laughed. "If he hadn't been too tightfisted to destroy the shirt, he might've gotten away with it. Maid found it while she was spring cleaning. Said it was stuffed way back on a closet shelf behind a big box of Christmas ornaments. Guess he didn't expect anybody to look there for a while."

"Seems Faris is off the hook for killing Jasper," I told Mom as we rushed to Poindexter Point. "Of course he's still an accessory to what happened to Maynard's lady friend." I explained about the shirt button and Faris Haskell's Florida alibi.

"But hadn't they already searched the Griggs place?" Mom asked. "Why didn't they find the shirt earlier?"

"You know what a huge house that is. It was hidden in a storage closet, and they must have been concentrating on his personal things."

Mom glanced back at Joey who was beginning to make waking noises. "Prentice, can't we go a little faster? We have to stop Zorah before she does something foolish! What on earth can she be thinking?"

I didn't answer. I only knew I was thinking the worst.

About fifty minutes later we pulled into the small wayside viewing area at Poindexter Point to find my aunt standing on the low stone wall overlooking the valley far below. Gathered about her were five or six curious onlookers who probably happened to be passing by, Stanley Causby, one-man staff of *The Liberty Bend Gazette*, and local radio announcer Bud Riley (who always put a *y* in the middle of *column*, and omitted the first *r* in *library*). Also on hand were Donald Weber and another policeman. And, of course, Cousin Be-trice.

"Oh, dear!" Mom threw open her door. "She's going to jump! No, Zorah! Don't do it! He's not worth it. Please! Oh, please don't jump!"

"My goodness, Virginia, I'm not going to jump," my

aunt said calmly. "I'm only here to take a step in the right direction. It's something I have to do . . . I know that now."

"What kind of step?" the deputy asked, edging forward.

"A positive step. I've been a fool too long. Today I mean to execute an act of justice long overdue." My aunt made a dramatic sweep of her hands that almost threw her off balance, and her spellbound audience gasped in unison.

My mother moved toward her through the crowd. "We'll work this out, Zorah. Come on now, do me a big favor and let's go home."

Aunt Zorah nodded and kinda halfway smiled. I think she was glad to see us. "All right, Virginia, but first I want to do a favor for myself." And she reached deep into her fringe-edged pocket and brought out Faris Haskell's Phi Beta Kappa key, then held it up for everyone to see and tossed it over the side of the mountain.

CHAPTER TWENTY-NINE

Wonder what will happen to Maynard Griggs,"
I said to Mom as we followed my aunt back
into town.

"He'll never see the light of day again after all he's
done, though I doubt if he'll make it to trial. Something the matter with his liver, I hear. Probably all that
formaldehyde."

"Can you believe it? Old Man Griggs—cold-blooded
murder!" I doubted if we'd be calling his son senator
anytime soon, although the unfortunate man had nothing to do with it.

"I remember when Maynard used to greet people
every Sunday at church." My mother shuddered. "Always held on to my hand a little too long when he
shook it. Made me want to go home and wash, but I
never thought he'd murder anyone!"

"He *says* Colette Champion's death was an accident, but he meant to kill Jasper Totherow," I said. "Waited until he saw Aunt Zorah leave after the two argued that day in the barn, then followed Jasper into the loft and hit him with the shovel."

"There were times when I felt like bashing Jasper myself," my mother admitted.

"Mom!" I pretended shock.

"Well, the little weasel deserved it—you know he did, although I wouldn't wish him dead. Ralphine said he was scared to death of somebody. Guess he found out the hard way he'd pushed Maynard Griggs too far."

"I'm just glad it wasn't Aunt Zorah!" I said.

"Zorah? Are you saying you suspected your own aunt of murder?"

I reminded her about the incident with the shovel. "She admitted she wanted to hit him, Mom."

"Who wouldn't? But what happened to the shovel? Did the police test it for prints?"

"No, and they wouldn't find any if they did." I looked straight ahead.

"And why not? Prentice, you didn't?"

"Oh, but I did. Went straight to Aunt Zorah's tool-shed, and there it was—right where that rat Maynard Griggs had planted it. Meant to incriminate her to throw the police off his own trial, only I didn't know that then."

"Did you really think Zorah put it there?" I could tell my mother was making an effort to keep her voice even.

"It was *Dad's shovel*! Remember that little crack in the handle? What was I supposed to think? I wiped the handle clean and hosed off the metal part. Last I saw, it was sticking out of a sack of manure in our shed."

"Prentice, you destroyed evidence. That was probably the murder weapon." Now Mom's voice really did crack.

"I know," I said. "But after what happened with Uncle Faris, it seemed Aunt Zorah deserved a break. I'm not proud of what I did."

I waited for Mom to speak. "I am," she said quietly.

"I guess we'll never know what makes Aunt Zorah tick," I said. "I can't imagine what made her do what she did today—and in front of all those people. You know how proud she is. She didn't have to humble herself like that."

"Says an angel told her to," Mom said.

"An angel?"

"That's what she told me. Said she came to her in a dream, and Zorah knew then what she had to do."

My mother smiled. "I wonder if it's the same one Ola saw."

I didn't doubt it for a minute.

Mom was going to spend a few days with Aunt Zorah to help soothe her fractured id, so I left the two of them in town and drove back to Smokerise with Joey. It was the first time I'd been responsible for the baby on my own, and I was a little nervous . . . well, okay, I was scared silly about it. What if he got sick? Wouldn't eat? What if he cried for Mom, for Ola—anybody but me?

Mom had fed and changed Joey at Aunt Zorah's and he'd dropped off to sleep in his car seat. Now I lifted him, all pink and warm against my shoulder, and carried him inside, dreading the cold, empty house. What on earth was I thinking? Was I really going to do this: Chance a new business venture with Dottie with few clients and very little capital? And I knew absolutely nothing about babies!

I hesitated on the bottom step, took a deep breath, and shifted the baby in my arms, feeling his soft hair brush my cheek. If I planned to begin my new life with Joey at Smokerise, I'd have to learn to deal with whatever came my way. And I might as well start tonight.

It was already dark outside but I was glad to see a light in the kitchen. At least the house wouldn't seem so gloomy.

I was surprised to find the back door unlocked, and for a moment fear held me paralyzed until I saw the fire dancing low on the hearth and knew who had put it there. Augusta, eyes half-closed in contentment, circled the kitchen, swaying in rhythm with the cat as a partner to a tune I recognized as the "Jersey Bounce."

I inhaled deeply. Something smelled wonderful. In all the excitement of my aunt's so-called press conference, I hadn't had time to eat and my stomach was unforgiving.

"Supper in twenty minutes," Augusta said with a feather-touch of her fingers to Joey's sleeping face. She wore her ginger-gold hair tied back with a vivid green ribbon and blew a kiss as she twirled past. Noodles nodded wide-eyed over her shoulder and kept time with her tail.

I snuggled Joey into his waiting crib upstairs and tucked the blanket around him. The puffy stuffed rabbit, an early Easter gift from Ola, grinned from the foot of his bed.

We were home.

There were two messages on my answering machine. The first was from Dottie who was excited over a definite "maybe" from a small construction company outside Atlanta. The second was from Rob. Four words: *I do, you know.* It wasn't enough.

Augusta had set the small drop-leaf table in the den with Mom's white damask bridge cloth and my great-grandmother Scott's dainty rose-patterned china. She served a vegetable casserole I knew I'd never see the likes of again, no matter how hard I tried, with crusty French bread, pears, and cheese. The wine was light and dry with a slight citrus flavor, and I'd never seen my mother's five-dollar garage sale stemware look as elegant.

Augusta touched her glass to mine. "To choices," she said.

"To choices," I echoed, lifting my glass in salute. But still I asked, "What choices?"

"Yours. Choices made and those yet unmade."

"You mean the *right* choices?" I asked, and Augusta seemed to study the gleam of firelight on her wineglass.

"Sometimes—many times—there aren't any right or wrong choices. It's how you live with the ones you make." She lifted her eyes to mine. "Your aunt made a choice today. You made one tonight."

It was a statement rather than a question.

"About Rob. Yes. I think I've known it all along."

"And would Joey's uncle have anything to do with it?" I saw amusement in her eyes.

I couldn't deny the attraction, and I sensed that Pug Gaines felt it too, but it was too soon. Much too soon.

"He cares about Joey," I said, "and I think he might care about me." It warmed me thinking of Pug's smile when he looked at the baby, the tenderness in his eyes, and I experienced a glow that had nothing to do with Augusta's presence.

"It seems the two of you have reached an agreement about the child. His future."

"He believes I should be the one to raise Joey. Pug's mother died several years ago, and his father—well, you saw his father."

"But there are other family members to consider," Augusta reminded me.

"A brother and younger sister, and there will have to be a family conference, of course, with both sides, but Pug seems to think they'll want to do what's best for Joey. Naturally I plan to take legal steps to adopt him as soon as things are settled."

"So it's definite then? You'll stay on here at Smoke-rise?"

I nodded. "There's no reason I can't work out of an office here, and with Pug and his uncle leasing the land for their nursery, he'll be able to be a part of Joey's life almost as much as I will."

"And a part of yours." Augusta sipped daintily from her wineglass and looked smug.

"I hope so," I said. There's no use lying to Augusta.

"Either way, Prentice Dobson, you're going to be all right." She reached across the small table and touched my cheek, and I knew what I'd suspected all evening. Augusta Goodnight wouldn't be here in the morning.

Part of me wanted to cry like a child, to beg her not to leave me, but I was Joey's mama now, or hoped to be, and I had a business to help run. I would be much too busy to cry.

Soon after, on a sunny April morning, I took Joey to that gentle walled hillside where his mother lay and found her resting place covered in a tangle of wildflow-ers as glorious as spring itself. The angel stone that marked her grave now wore an expression of someone who knew a pleasant secret, and I knew Augusta had been there. Just as she is there in the jump-up aroma of morning coffee, the smooth dark richness of chocolate, and all the music that makes my feet glad and my heart beat faster.

And when Queen Anne's lace nods in the meadow and honeysuckle fills the air with its sweetness, she will be there as well.